THE CAT LAUGHS

ALSO BY LOUISE CARSON

MAPLES MYSTERY SERIES

The Cat Among Us
The Cat Vanishes
The Cat Between
The Cat Possessed
A Clutter of Cats
The Cat Looked Back
The Cat Crosses a Line

NOVELS

Executor
The Last Unsuitable Man
In Which: Book One of The Chronicles of Deasil Widdy
Measured: Book Two of The Chronicles of Deasil Widdy
Third Circle: Book Three of The Chronicles of Deasil Widdy

NOVELLA

Mermaid Road

POETRY

A Clearing
Rope: A Tale Told in Prose and Verse
Dog Poems
The Truck Driver Treated for Shock

THE CAT LAUGHS

A MAPLES MYSTERY

Louise Carson

DOUG WHITEWAY, EDITOR

© 2025, Louise Carson

All rights reserved. No part of this book may be reproduced, for any reason, by any means, without the permission of the publisher.

Cover design by Doowah Design.
Cover icons: The Noun Project and Doowah Design.

This book was printed on Ancient Forest Friendly paper.
Printed and bound in Canada by Hignell Book Printing Inc.

Library and Archives Canada Cataloguing in Publication

Title: The cat laughs / Louise Carson
Names: Carson, Louise, 1957- author
| Whiteway, Doug, 1951- editor.
Description: Series statement: A Maples mystery ; 8
| "Doug Whiteway, editor".
Identifiers: Canadiana (print) 20250243806
| Canadiana (ebook) 20250245728
| ISBN 9781773241555 (softcover)
| ISBN 9781773241562 (EPUB)
Subjects: LCGFT: Detective and mystery fiction. | LCGFT: Novels.
Classification: LCC PS8605.A7775 C384 2025
| DDC C813/.6—dc23

We acknowledge the support of the Canada Council for the Arts, the Manitoba Arts Council, and the Manitoba Government for our publishing program.

Signature Editions
P.O. Box 206, RPO Corydon, Winnipeg, Manitoba, R3M 3S7
www.signature-editions.com

For Mum and Dad—always missed

CONTENTS

PART 1
MA
9

PART 2
DA
65

PART 3
PRUE
123

PART 4
MEOW
177

PART 5
PEETS
225

PART 1
MA

He would need help. And, obviously, one couldn't ask a one-year-old, however bright she might be (after all, she was his granddaughter), to wander around in the big old house. The house that was full of baby traps; two sets of stairs, the woodstove, the open fireplace.

It was nice she could see him though. He still wasn't used to being ignored by the living. Especially by his daughter. He shook himself free of dwelling on that sore point and watched as some of the smoky wisps of which he was now made trailed away.

He looked down at the small grey tabby cat. "No," he said. "It'll have to be you."

The cat, Trouble, as she was known in the cat world she inhabited, batted another small stick behind the living room curtain then followed the stick in to the small private area where the curtain met one of the room's corners. She was assembling quite a nice collection. She started to chew. The paper that wrapped each stick was pleasant, as far as paper went, but the cylinders themselves, while they had an interesting texture—harder than the plant stems she might find outside, softer than bone—tasted horrible. One bite and she felt the protective saliva that filled her mouth with foam whenever she ate something really awful begin. Too bad; that texture was really quite—

The ghost laughed. "And maybe one other."

Trouble squinted up to where the ghost hovered by the far side of the curtained window. It was male, unlike the majority of the house's spirits. Through a crack where the curtains met, she saw the gleam of a large star.

Trouble knew all about males—cats, that is. They roamed; it was just part of their makeup. They always had to crawl through the next hedge or cross the road. Unlike females, who were usually happy to find a comfy spot under a shrub or next to a wall and just sit. And watch.

Likewise, she supposed, with male ghosts. They'd be off visiting friends or enemies, prowling, while the female ghosts of this house would be sitting in rocking chairs in front of the cold ashes of the day's fire or gathered around the rarely used gigantic dining room table in the next room. Trouble's foam dripped. She wasn't bothered; it would stop when it would stop. She sneezed, spraying the curtain.

The ghost laughed again and moved. He wafted from the living room through to the dining room where, on this cold winter's night, cats slept on towels in cardboard boxes under the table, or on the upholstered seats of the chairs around it. Some of the family's other ghosts murmured as the ambulatory ghost passed.

Trouble paused by the woodstove to feel its warmth. The fire inside it still ticked and hummed. Several cats were curled up nearby. Then, reluctantly, she followed the ghost into the cooler air of the house's large foyer. He disappeared through the closed door of the mistress's special room.

Trouble sat down outside the door, uttering a tentative mew. Cats were not usually allowed in there, where the mistress vanished most days for large chunks of time. Not so much lately, it must be admitted, since the young miss had arrived.

Trouble stretched up and put two paws on the door. Slowly it opened an inch or two. It must have been left ajar by mistake. Trouble pushed through.

The man in the tent shivered. Minus degrees tonight. He could tell by the ice in the bowl next to his head. He'd have to thaw it tomorrow so they could drink. He lifted the plastic tarp that covered his nest of old comforters and blankets and counted the cats huddled close. One, *two, three, four, five, six. Everybody was here. The fire had gone out and he was too tired and cold to get up and restart it. Perhaps the temperature would rise tomorrow, and he'd be able to sleep then. He lowered the tarp, turned on his side and watched the vapour from his nose and mouth. In. Out. In. Out. Still alive. Still alive.*

1

"Happy Birthday to youuuuuuuuuuuu!"

The cheering and laughing, which accompanied the appearance of a white cake with two pink candles on top, made the recipient of all this attention look up from the pasta smeared on her high-chair tray. "Ba!" she said, pointing at the cake.

"Can she blow out the candles, do you think?" asked her half-brother David. "It's her first birthday cake, after all." He began puffing air in the direction of the cake.

Dot imitated him, smiling between puffs.

"Aim at the candles, Dot," David urged, showing her what he meant. Both candles (one for turning one year old and the other for good luck) went out and the rest of the family groaned. Dot, sensing something amiss and noticing that the pretty flickering lights were now black and smoking, wailed.

Her father pulled out a lighter and quickly relit them. "There you go, Dottie, candles back," he said kindly, his middle-aged face beaming.

Dot focused on the little lights and became calm. Everybody watched as the candles glowed and shrank. "We better blow them out soon," said her mother, "or we'll be eating candle wax with our cake. Okay, Dot, we're *all* going to blow out the candles." The family gathered around the infant and her cake. "One, two, three!" said Gerry.

"Blow, Dot, blow!" various people cried.

Dot blew and, like magic, the candles went out. Her brow furrowed in disappointment, and she considered crying again. But there was more cheering and clapping, and soon she was eating cake. She decided to be cheerful. She watched her parents talking to each other.

Gerry leaned over to Doug. "What's with the lighter? I thought you'd quit?"

He tried to look innocent. "What? Oh. You know. One or two a day. Just for fun." He took a bite of the vanilla sponge with strawberry jam filling and buttercream icing. "Great cake, by the way."

"Nice try, Best Dad," she said and kissed him. She was touched that all three of his sons, Dot's big half-brothers, and the eldest's girlfriend had made the effort to come to Dot's first birthday. This early in January they were still on vacation from school, but they all had part-time jobs. And social lives, she presumed.

Supper had been easy; everybody, including the birthday girl, loved pasta. Spaghetti and cake. Gerry groaned inwardly. Her pregnancy weight gain had been hard to shift. Ten pounds left and that was a lot when you were only five feet something, and a very little something at that.

Seven people were sitting in the living room of The Maples, around the rectangular dining table that comfortably seated six to eight. The table occupied roughly a third of the room—specifically, the back section facing the Lake of Two Mountains, which would have offered a wonderful view if it hadn't been after four o'clock on a January afternoon. As it was, the soft green curtains were closed against the dark and the cold.

The middle of the room consisted of a huge hearth where a fire blazed, fronted by a long brown leather sofa with two rocking chairs either side. A multi-coloured rag rug spiralled between the seating arrangement and the fire. Past all this, at the front of the house, a long wooden bench ran along the wall under a wide window with a view of the quiet country road's few passing cars. The Christmas tree shimmered twice—in the room and reflected in the glass. Gerry sighed, thinking of dismantling it, its dry needles dropping everywhere.

On the mantelpiece over the fireplace, his tail twitching, lay a large tuxedo cat. Below him, on the rug, various other felines reposed. And more were ranged on the sofa.

"Pre—*sents*! Pre—*sents*!" David began chanting, his older brothers, James and Geoff Jr., joining in. Dot banged her fists on her high-chair tray. Pasta and cake crumbs rose and fell. Julia, James's girlfriend, lifted a pretty gift bag onto the table. "This is a bunch of stuff from all of us," she explained, handing the bag to Doug, who passed it to Gerry.

Gerry, seated next to Dot, reached into the bag and pulled out a lump roughly wrapped in tissue paper. She wiped Dot's fingers and tray and gave her the package.

Dot, no doubt with Christmas unwrapping still fresh in her mind, yanked at the paper. A kitten-sized soft toy cat tumbled to the floor. A small live cat, black with white legs, dashed to the toy.

"No, Jay," said Gerry, bending over to retrieve the gift. "Not this time." She gave the toy to Dot, who put one of its paws in her mouth. "Though I'm sure you'll be sharing it soon enough." She reached into the bag again. A larger parcel was revealed.

Julia said, "Dot can open it, but they're more for you."

Dot scrabbled at the paper. Bits flew onto the floor where Jay pounced on them. A skinny white cat with a black mustache perked up his ears at the rustling noises and joined Jay.

Gerry lifted the stack of bibs away from Dot. Dot wailed so Gerry handed her one of them. Into Dot's mouth it went. Gerry admired the remaining ones and thanked the gift-givers. "We go through more than three a day, so we can never have enough. Great." She rolled up a piece of tissue into a ball and tossed it at the white cat. "Here you go, Ronald."

More cats were rousing themselves. The next to arrive were three grey and black-striped brothers. Dot dropped the bib on the floor where the cats delicately sniffed it. Dot babbled at the cats. They looked up at her. They might have been asking: *What else you got?* She flung them a spoon.

"Okay," Gerry said resignedly. "What else is in here, Dot?" She held the bag sideways so Dot could peer in. The three grey cats, Winnie, Frank and Joe, looked at the spoon. Not much of a toy seemed to be the general consensus. One, Frank, tentatively put out a paw and pulled the spoon toward him. He gave it a lick. Ice cream!

"Ba," said Dot.

"That one?" her mother asked and pulled out a rectangular wooden pencil box. She handed it to her daughter. Dot bit into a corner of it and made a face. Everyone laughed. She shook it and it rattled.

"Show her how the lid works, Ger," said Doug.

Gerry slowly slid the lid to one end. Dot's eyes opened wide. "Ga!" she said triumphantly, seeing the crayons inside. Gerry quickly retrieved a piece of pink construction paper from the bag and dumped some of the crayons out of the box onto Dot's tray. Dot, already familiar with crayons, and knowing better than to put them in her mouth, worked her way through the colours, grabbing then dropping each onto the floor for the amusement of the cats massed around her chair.

"It may be a bit soon for these unless she's being supervised," admitted Gerry. "She sees them more as something to throw around than to scribble with."

"Coffee? Tea, anyone?" offered Doug. Gerry yawned.

"Should we think about going?" asked James, taking the hint. "It's after seven. When does she go to sleep?"

"Gerry or Dot?" quipped Doug.

"Good questions," Gerry replied with a tired smile. "Dot? When she wants to. So, no, you don't have to leave already. Have some more cake. I'd love a cup of tea, Doug. And great presents, guys. Thanks a lot." She yawned again. "She's teething so some nights are worse than others. Last night was tough. And that's why everything goes into her mouth. Biting down helps the teeth cut through the gums. And relieves some of the pain."

"Oh, poor Dot," David said sympathetically.

Dot chose this moment to throw a violently pink crayon at the nearest curtain. It fell in front of *another* grey-striped cat, a petite female. She languidly batted at the crayon, sending it back toward the high chair.

"Thank you, Monkey," Gerry said, bending to retrieve the crayon. "You're being helpful."

The cat—sister to the three brothers, though she usually preferred the company of other cats—gazed blandly at her mistress, then looked past her to a spot near the ceiling.

"I don't think I know that one," Julia began doubtfully, "but I really only know a few of them by name."

"Tubble! Tubble!" Dot babbled. She too looked up to where the cat was staring.

"That's a new word," Doug said amusedly. "What's tubble, Dot?"

Dot grabbed a fistful of crayons and showered them on the cats. Monkey backed away.

Gerry raised her eyebrows and smiled wearily. "As in— nothing but?" Doug laughed. Gerry addressed Julia. "Monkey is one of the cats even I don't notice much." She yawned again. "Oh, sorry, guys."

James rose. "Okay. We're going. Who wants to warm up the car?"

The silence was broken by Geoff, the middle of Doug's three sons. "Well, seeing as how you're already up—"

James kissed his little sister with difficulty, as she was hanging over the side of her chair, watching the shifting panorama of cats, crayons and crumpled wrapping paper. She noticed him and held up her arms. "Ba!"

"Can I?" he asked Gerry.

"Oh, sure." She unbuckled Dot and James plucked her out of the high chair. He swung her high over his head. Dot chortled.

"James!" Gerry admonished. "She just ate!" He sheepishly stopped the game.

"Yeah, bro," teased David. "You want to wear spaghetti and birthday cake?" He took Dot from his brother. "Don't you have a car to start?"

James kissed Gerry, and Dot again, and he and Julia left. Doug removed Dot from David's arms. "Thanks for coming, everybody. And the gifts were great. Weren't they Gerry?"

But Gerry was yawning again.

She had lost something but couldn't remember what. She stumbled from room to room, looking everywhere. The strange thing was, she was alone. No cats. No Doug. No Dot. Just her, alone in the creaky old house.

She arrived at the door to her studio. It was partially open. She knew the lost object was in there. She pushed on the door—

"Waaaah! Wah, wah, wah. Waaaah!"

"I'll go," mumbled Doug.

"'S all right. I'm awake." Gerry shrugged on her robe and slippers. The cats that had been sleeping on the bed made up their minds. Some—Seymour (one-eyed black short-hair) and Lightning (tailless tortoiseshell)—stayed where they were, snuggled by Doug's feet. The other two—Bob and Jay—followed Gerry as she shuffled to the room next to hers.

Dot stood in her crib, her hands clutching the rail. She lifted her tear-stained face to Gerry. "Maa, maa," crooned Dot. When

Gerry picked her up, Dot tried to nurse, nuzzling and patting Gerry's chest.

"No, no, sweetie. Remember? We don't do that anymore." Gerry's voice sounded sad. She quickly switched tones, asking cheerfully, "Are you hungry, love? Want bottle?"

Bob groomed himself on Dot's yellow banana-shaped rug. Jay sniffed the perimeter of the room. Both paused when they heard Gerry's voice switch from soothing to questioning.

Dot nodded. "Ba!"

All processed down the wide staircase, Jay first, Bob providing the rearguard. Gerry walked through the dining and living rooms, eyeing all the drowsy cats. "Hey, you guys, where were you all in my dream? Oh my God! What's that?" She stared at a dark patch on the floor near the kitchen door. She snapped on a light, put Dot in her high chair and investigated on her hands and knees. Jay and Bob assisted, carefully smelling the object.

Gerry was used to cat messes, but this was extreme, even for one of them. Many different colours mingled with slime. She was horrified. Then she laughed. "Hoo boy, that must have felt gross coming back up." She turned to her daughter who was craning her neck trying to see. "Somebody's been eating your nice new crayons, Dottie. Let Mommy clean it away and then you can get down."

The two cats, satisfied the mess had nothing to do with *them*, resumed their chosen activities: Bob on the hearthrug to complete his toilette while Jay explored this room's corners.

Cleanup accomplished and milk warming on the stove, Gerry released Dot who immediately crawled to investigate the now dry patch on the floor. Looking around, Dot yanked on the curtain and pulled up, standing unsteadily. "Oh, Dot!" exclaimed Gerry, detaching her child from the fabric. "Good for you for standing up. Not so good for using the curtain. Oh. What's this?" She lifted the bottom of the curtain and found a cache of crayons on the floor. "Did you put those there? No, you couldn't have; you went to bed when the family left. Must have been the crayon-eating cat. Whoever *that* was." Gerry scooped up the crayons and put them on the mantel.

Bob paused in his work and looked up at his favourite perch doubtfully. He must have decided to allow the trespass, because he switched from licking one foot to the other, splaying his toes.

Gerry picked up Dot, gave her the bottle, and, feeling a bit cold, moved slowly from room to room as the baby fed.

In the dining room, she paused by the still warm woodstove. One cat, a large marmalade tabby, hopped out of her snug bed in a cardboard box and rubbed against Gerry's legs. "You know, eh, Mother?" Gerry said softly. The cat, famous for her motherly ways and patience with the small, weak or ailing, purred. She followed Gerry as she walked into the foyer. Bob and Jay caught up with them there. All three cats looked up at Gerry as if to say, *now what? Back to bed?*

Gerry looked down at Dot. The baby was almost finished her bottle, and her eyes were getting that half-closed satisfied look that came with feeding. Gerry felt a rush of tenderness. As she swayed slowly from side to side, soothing Dot, she looked around the foyer and frowned. "Oh, rats," she said quietly. The studio door was slightly ajar. Someone must have gone in then out and closed the door too gently. She walked over and pushed.

At first, she didn't see the cat, a grey-and-black oval on the antique sofa. It lifted its head, yawned, then stretched, its claws snagging on green velvet. "No, no, no, Monkey," Gerry said calmly, flicking on a light. "This is *not* the way to endear yourself to me." She looked down at the carpet. "And yuck." She'd stepped in the mess there. The cat jumped off the sofa, gave a tentative lick to one paw, paused, and looked up and over Gerry's shoulder.

Gerry, accustomed to this kind of feline behaviour and suspecting it was an ancient tactic once used to distract prey before a pounce—now repurposed by house cats to deflect human censure—sighed, removed her soiled slipper, and chided her pet. "You silly cat. You and I better hope Prudence has a remedy for crayon wax ground into a valuable old rug."

Monkey, looking as if she didn't know to *what* Gerry could possibly be referring, ran from the room.

2

Prudence Catford loaded the tiny spoon with just enough warm cereal and advanced it toward the open mouth.

"*Good* girl, Dot," she praised when the mouthful was accepted. She wiped mush from Dot's chin. "Now, *keep* it *in* your mouth. And *swal—*low."

Obediently, Dot performed the required motions. She grinned at her feeder, a plain, middle-aged woman, before thrusting a small fist into her mouth. "Oh, I *know* they hurt, dear, and you shall have your soother as soon as you eat up all your cereal."

Another spoonful advanced and Dot removed the fist to receive nourishment. Gerry, who'd been standing in the hall, eavesdropping, entered the room. "Hello, everybody. Prudence, how do you *do* that? I'd be covered in spit-out mush by now."

Prudence smiled a little, but remained focused on Dot. Out of the corner of her mouth, she said, "I don't *ask* her; I *tell* her."

Gerry sighed and went to the kitchen to pour herself her first cup of coffee, wading through an expanse of cats—all nineteen of them—finishing their breakfasts. Holding the mug, bowl-shaped and warm in her hands, and staring out at the winter scene in her carport—snow piled high at one end, surrounding trees limned in white—she sighed with contentment. For today was one of the three wonderful, fabulous, marvellous days every week when she felt somewhat like her old pre-Dot self. The days Prudence came to babysit.

Prudence would arrive early. Doug, having risen with Dot whenever Dot woke, and having fed the cats, would hand her over to Prudence, and Gerry would *sleep in!* Well, until eight or eight-thirty anyway, which these days counted as sleeping in. Especially after a night like the previous one when she'd spent at least an hour feeding and resettling Dot before trying to fall back to sleep herself.

"And how long do I have you for today?" she called from the kitchen.

"Well, I can stay till after lunch. Then Bertie will be ready for a break from the café. Fridays are pretty busy. Say—I leave here at a quarter to two?"

"Great," said a dismayed Gerry, who always hoped Prudence would say, until four or five or six. She looked at the kitchen clock. Eight-thirty already! She went and stood next to Dot, giving her a kiss on the top of her head. It didn't *look* as though there was any cereal there. "See you girls later."

Dot pounded the high-chair tray with the flat of her hand, sending a light splatter of mush in all directions. Gerry smiled as she left the room. So, Prudence didn't have Dot as under control as it seemed. She thought—a quick shower and then to work. Lovely, lovely work!

Two hours later, Gerry lifted her head from her task and set down her pencil. As the creator of the comic strip *Mug the Bug*, she was responsible for six strips a week. While she'd been on maternity leave, the newspapers had recycled her oldest work, but the last few months she'd been back to grinding out fresh ones every week. She'd gotten faster. She'd had to. Today, for example, she'd gotten two ideas and roughed them out. Later, she'd produce the finished product and maybe even have time to work on her passion project, her second children's book—*The Candy King of Bubbly-Sauceton*, laid aside when Dot had been born. Right now, though, all she wanted was a second cup of coffee and maybe a piece of toast.

Carefully, she opened the studio door and listened. Thank God! She could hear Dot's babble coming from upstairs. She dashed to the kitchen, made her snack, and dashed back to her studio, zigzagging to avoid any cats in her way. "Ha-ha!" she announced to the empty room. "I made it!"

Then she remembered the mess on the rug from the night before and looked. "How does she do it?" she wondered aloud. For the mess was gone and, she assumed, must have been cleaned up by the redoubtable Prudence before Gerry had even awoken. All that remained was a patch of carpet slightly paler than the surrounding area. Gerry gobbled her toast (with strawberry-rhubarb jam she'd made two summers ago—there had been no time for jam-making last summer, not with a crying, continually feeding infant to tend) and returned to work. It was just past noon when she again stopped. Lunchtime! And she would remember to thank Prue for cleaning the rug, not really part of her remit any longer.

Back at Dot's feeding station, the work was ongoing. Prudence was offering little amounts of various foods and Dot was pushing most of them out of her mouth and smearing them on her tray. Interested cats remained in the vicinity; they never knew when something good might be dropped or fall onto the floor.

"Hello, you two!" Gerry said brightly. "Any progress?" She passed into the kitchen to fix her own lunch.

"She still doesn't like the meat," Prudence replied. "But if I mix a little with the carrots, some of it goes down."

"Did you eat yet?" Gerry called.

"I thought I'd eat with you. After I get this one to sleep."

"Well, if anyone can make Dot nap, it's you. I'll just put the kettle on."

"Ba, ba, ba. Ba, ba, ba. Ba, ba, ba, ba, ba, ba, ba!" was Dot's way of signalling she'd had enough. That, and pushing Prudence's hand holding the spoon away.

"My sandwich is heating. I'll clean her up," offered Gerry.

"I don't mind," said Prudence, already wiping down Dot and surroundings with a couple of wet rags. She lifted the baby from her chair and smiled. "I really don't."

"Bye, Dottie," said her fond mother. "Have a good one."

Cats moved in to minutely inspect the recently vacated feeding area. As she waited for Prudence's return, Gerry put her elbows on the table, supported her head on one hand, stared out the window and relaxed.

Across the frozen lake stretched a dark band of pine, framed in the near distance by the bare trees in her own backyard—a view she never tired of, no matter the season.

The days Prudence could spare her for child-minding had become oases of calm in an increasingly fatiguing life. Gerry hoped Dot couldn't sense her mother's ambivalence with her new role. Or, perhaps, the child was aware of how distracted Gerry was. By her work—or not-work, as it were. She sighed ruefully.

She squeezed as much productivity as she could into these half- or three-quarter days Prue took from managing (with her husband Bertie) the thriving café they'd purchased the previous year. And it was nice that Prudence genuinely loved Gerry and Dot and wanted to be around them. The fee she charged for the babysitting was ridiculously low.

Gerry had had to hire a cleaning service to "do" The Maples once a week. They seemed a nice couple, in their late thirties or early forties, but they were not there to socialize, as Prue had been, when—pre-Dot—she'd arrived twice a week to restore order from the chaos Gerry and the cats created. And that was as it should be, as the cleaners did two houses each day and had no time to waste. On the mornings the Markovs—Sergei and Natalya—were working, Gerry just tried to keep out of their way, amusing Dot, taking her outside for fresh air, or shopping. She knew she was lucky to be able to afford them.

And, of course, on weekends and evenings, Doug was sometimes available for the cranky baby handover. Having helped raise three sons to adulthood, he had some experience. But Doug was a general handyman and odd-jobber and had to work all hours. He'd also started working for the Hudsons, general contractors who handled much of Lovering's snow removal, and that meant getting up at ungodly hours during heavy snowfalls.

Gerry made a pot of tea. "Tea, Earl Grey, hot," she ordered the teapot, mimicking the hero of one of her favourite TV shows from childhood, still glimpsed in reruns. She took her warm sandwich from the oven and sat down just as Prudence rejoined her. "The usual?"

Prudence nodded and smiled. "You, too, I see." She took a parcel from her purse. "Some books for Dot, for her birthday. You can open them with her later."

"Oh, thank you, Prudence. Fun!"

They munched contentedly—Gerry on a croissant with ham, melted Swiss cheese, mustard, and mayo; Prudence on her usual peanut butter and sweet pickle sandwich on brown bread, accompanied this time by a small bag of dill-flavored potato chips. The chips varied; the sandwich never did. There had been a brief period recently, when, feeling unsettled in her personal life, Prudence had flirted with egg salad and tuna as fillings, even, unbeknownst to Gerry who had been travelling at the time, eating lunch by herself in a restaurant. Now she was comfortably married (late in life it must be admitted—she in her late fifties, he early sixties), she'd returned to the excellent lunch her mother had made for her the first and every subsequent day she'd been at school.

Some of the cats, finished supervising Dot's lunch, left the room; others—Max, Jinx and Cocoon—repaired to the sofa and bedded down. Gerry looked at them fondly as she ate. Two of them were getting elderly; well, Cocoon, a fluffy grey and white, would be sixteen this year so, not getting, but getting more; and Max, equally fluffy but orange and white, would be eleven. Jinx, a petite, somewhat fluffy grey with a white bib, was still less than ten, which counted in her favour. They were part of a friend group (the fluffies, thought Gerry) that usually included Monkey (who was not fluffy), which reminded her: "Thanks for cleaning my rug, Prudence. But how did you even know it was dirty? And how did you get the stain out?" She poured the tea.

Prudence took one of the Snoopy mugs—two of Gerry's Christmas gifts from Doug—featuring the insouciant canine dancing in a field of daisies while Woodstock fluttered nearby. "Doug mentioned it. He was warning me to watch out if I went in there. He needed a pencil or something off your desk and didn't have time to clean it himself. And just the usual way: hot soapy water, a brush and plenty of paper towels. These old rugs are pretty resilient."

"Well, thank you. It's not in your job description anymore so I appreciate it. You have moved on from being the extraordinary housekeeper to the extraordinary nanny. How is the small person, anyway?"

"Conked out at around one, so you have until maybe two thirty or three."

"Oh, please God, let it be three!" Gerry prayed dramatically. "More tea?"

"Sure. And I brought a few cranberry-lemon scones from the café." She held out a white paper bag. "Want one?"

Gerry groaned. "Oh, I shouldn't."

"Nonsense," her friend replied. "It's perfectly normal for women to gain a bit of weight as they age and—"

"*You* didn't," Gerry pointed out, taking a scone.

"Well. I never had a baby," Prudence said matter-of-factly. "And you just did."

Gerry, who knew Prudence would have liked to have had children, felt sad. "Sorry, Prue," she mumbled.

Prudence didn't miss a beat. "And, as I was going to say before I was interrupted, winter is the worst time to try to limit your food. Your body's trying to keep warm, for heaven's sake." She drank some tea. "Is the cat okay?"

"Huh?"

"The cat. The cat that threw up crayons on the Persian carpet."

"Oh. Monkey. She's fine. Well, she was fine last night when I evicted her from the velvet sofa in the studio. Maybe I should—"

At that moment, Monkey entered the room, walking to its exact centre, pausing to sit and lick a shoulder, then strolling to the corner where her crayon stash had been. Finding nothing behind the curtain, she sat near Gerry's chair and regarded the women.

"She's a funny one," said Prudence.

"Yes, she is." Gerry dropped a hand down for the cat to sniff. "You okay, Monks?"

Perhaps offended by the impromptu nickname, the cat ignored the hand and sauntered over to the sofa, hopped up, joining her friend group, circled, kneaded an old afghan blanket that lay there and went to sleep. Max, who'd been sleeping on the afghan, sat up and stretched, before resettling nose to tail with her.

"Evidently, she's fine," Prudence said dryly. She seemed to decide it was time for a more interesting exchange of information, and asked, "Have you heard about the latest burglary?"

"Which one? There have been so many. I know about the hardware store, the bakery, and the seniors' residence. Has there been another?"

For the sleepy little town of Lovering (population five thousand and a bit) had been plagued with a string of thefts in the run-up to Christmas. And what made it all so odd was the very specific nature of each theft. At the hardware store only some tarps and a staple gun were taken; at the bakery, an industrial-sized mixing bowl; and from the seniors' residence, a few old rugs from the common area. The rugs' theft had made people think that the thief—or thieves—must have had access to transportation, at least on that occasion. The smaller items could have been carried by hand. So, it was possible the thief didn't even live in Lovering.

Between Christmas and New Year's there'd been a lull. Prudence replied to Gerry's question. "There *has* been another. At the Legion."

Gerry's thoughts flew to Doug, who sometimes worked at the Legion, grooming the curling rink ice, tending bar, shovelling the steps and paths so the mostly aged members could safely come and go. "What was taken this time? The kitchen sink?"

"No," Prudence said grimly. "Something more basic—the cash box from bingo night. He, or they, broke in the back door and helped themselves. Nobody would see them in the middle of the night. There are only the train tracks and one of the town's equipment yards back there."

"How much is likely to be in the box?"

"I have no idea. Probably not much. It doesn't cost a lot to play."

"Huh, a smash and grab, like the other robberies."

"It wasn't smash and grab at the seniors' residence. Someone buzzed him in; and it must have taken a few trips to get those rugs out. He'd have to have propped the door open."

"Unless it was a gang," Gerry speculated. "Then, in and out."

Prudence glanced at her watch and stood. "Well, I've got to get going."

"Oh. Too bad. *We* were just getting going."

"How do you mean?"

"Figuring stuff out. You know—investi– er, problem solving."

"You mean *crime* solving. And I wasn't aware that that was what we were doing." Prudence smiled down at Gerry. "What are you up to this weekend?"

"Getting ready for Dot's kids birthday party on Sunday. And we thought we'd drag her around on her sled. Maybe go up into the woods for a bit."

"Nice," said Prudence. "I'll see you Tuesday then."

"See you Tuesday. Thank you for the books."

Back in the studio, Gerry replaced her cartoons with her work-in-progress, *The Candy King of Bubbly-Sauceton*.

> William's hand shot out to stop the marble from rolling off Mrs. Brooks's store counter. "Mrs. Brooks, I have an idea." And he proceeded to share it with her.
>
> Minutes later, he walked out of the store minus his special marble, but holding a bag of hard candies. Prince Charles advanced, droopy tail wagging, and eagerly sniffed the bag, expecting a sweet treat.
>
> William held the bag over his head. "No, Charles, they're not for us."
>
> The dog's expression changed to one of deep sadness. Unlike William, his enjoyment of candy was not limited to chocolate.
>
> The two walked back home where Prince Charles flumped onto his side in the gravel and dirt behind the pub. William busied himself in the barn, found what he wanted, and dragged the objects into the barn door's wide opening as curious barn cats watched. One largish empty wooden crate. One smallish one. And a piece of plywood about one by two feet across. All were very dusty.
>
> Tigs, who'd sidled over and sat himself on the larger box, sneezed and jumped off as William awkwardly brushed away the dust with a long-handled broom. "Sorry, Tigs."

The cat sneezed again then jumped back onto the now cleaner surface. "What's he doing?" he called to Charles.

The prince didn't move a muscle except to growl. "*Not* eating that bag of candy." Then, as William went into The Furtive Beagle's back door, he lifted his head and whined, "He said it isn't for us."

"*That's* weird," said Tigs, now sniffing the plywood leaning against the smaller box.

William came back out of the pub with a metal tray and some felt markers. He put the plywood onto—

"Waaaaaah!"

"Rats!" Gerry came back to reality with a crash. Literally. There was a thud from upstairs, a faint tinkle, and then the wailing stopped. Gerry jumped up, out of the studio into the foyer and up the stairs, yelling, "Dot! Dot!"

When she came into Dot's room, she only had eyes for her daughter, expecting to see her on the floor next to her crib. But Dot was sitting in the crib, smiling and looking up at her mother. "Ba," she said.

"Ba?" said Gerry, picking her up. "What—?" Then she saw: a framed black and white family photograph had come off its hook and fallen behind the room's bureau. And, sitting on the bureau, was Monkey, her green eyes slowly blinking at Gerry.

After Gerry got a broom and dustpan, after she put Dot back in her crib with a bottle while she cleaned up the mess, and after they were all, including the cat, in the living room having a snack, only then did she wonder: how had Monkey shifted such a heavy object?

She looked at the now slightly creased photo, still in its frame and with the brown paper backing intact, and held it up for Dot to see. "There's my daddy, Dot. His name was Gerry too. And that's his sister Mary and little sister Maggie. And behind them are their parents, my grandparents." With a pang, she remembered that Dot would never have the comfort of grandparents, Doug's and her parents being gone.

Dot pointed at the picture and, rather predictably, said, "Ba!"

"Oh, ba, ba, ba!" said Gerry teasingly and leaned forward to kiss her. She made a mental note to buy a new frame. "Want to open a present, Dot? From Prue?"

Around Dot's chair, cats crept toward a dropped cookie.

3

Doug and Gerry had fun Saturday towing Dot—bundled up in her snowsuit and blankets—in her wooden sled. It was a miniature version of the old horse-drawn sleighs sometimes seen in Lovering around Christmas, hired by the merchants or the council to ferry people from one end of town to the other. But instead of wheels, Dot's sled had wooden runners, and it had been miserable to pull—until Gerry had the brilliant idea of coating them with cross-country ski wax.

By the time they made it up the lane beside Cathy Stribling's B&B, Fieldcrest, crossed the field in front of the cottage whose owners left every winter, and passed over the train tracks, Dot was fast asleep. Gerry and Doug took the opportunity to share a bit of chocolate (packed by Gerry) and a few kisses (initiated by Doug).

After their break, Gerry slipped a hand inside Dot's snowsuit to feel her fingers and toes. "Snug as a bug," she said, "as my dad used to say." Dot, roused by invasive cold air, woke briefly, complained, then slept again. "We'll pay for this tonight, you know," Gerry said dolefully, "when she can't sleep."

"I know. But it's pretty great right now."

They looked around. The old forest lay silent under the snow, made up mostly of deciduous trees with a few hemlocks. Many were giant maples. A winding path led up the hill, and near where they were standing, an old sugar shack waited to be refurbished.

Gerry had happy memories of visiting the spot once or twice during childhood vacations with her parents.

"Do you think we could tap a few trees this year?" she asked hopefully. "I mean, as long as Mary gives us permission." The land had belonged to Gerry's Uncle Geoff; with his death, it had come to his wife Mary.

He nodded. "That's easy enough to do. But I can't guarantee I'll find the time to replace the sap boiler. We'll have to carry any sap we collect, or use the sleigh, back to the house and boil it there."

"That'd be great!" she enthused. "Tap a few more trees each year, and get a new tank, and it'll be up and running again!"

He smiled. "Could work. Want to turn back?"

She nodded and they took turns dragging their sleeping daughter home.

On Sunday, they got up early to prepare for Dot's children's birthday party. Only four children and their mothers were expected—women Gerry had met in a prenatal yoga class. Though they were all older than her, they'd bonded. She planned to keep the party in the living room next to the kitchen, so that was the only space they cleaned and tidied. The cleaners came on Mondays, so the room was pretty dusty and full of pet hair, as Doug found out as he swept.

Gerry made a fire and erected the heavy screen Doug had built to keep babies away from the hearth. She apologized to the nearby cats as she set up the screen. "I know; I'm sorry, guys. No lying close to the fire today, I'm afraid."

Harley and Kitty-Cat, two enormous black and white short-haired brothers, stalked majestically from the room. Gerry always imagined she could hear booming noises coming from their heavy footfalls. Lightning and Seymour, who usually kept each other company, were more amenable; they shifted from the comfy rug to the nearby sofa.

Gerry reached out to stroke Bob where he lay stretched out on the mantelpiece. "All right, Bobby?" she said in the special voice she reserved for him, her favourite. He blinked sleepily. As Top Cat, his mission was to supervise the cattery, and, when necessary, defend it. Gerry stroked under his chin and he fired up his purr. Life was good.

"Eek!" Gerry snatched away her hand, startling Bob awake. He opened his eyes and sat up as she ran over to the table where Dot was trying to pull herself up using the paper tablecloth Gerry had purchased for the party. Of course, every time Dot managed to raise herself halfway up, the paper tore and she sat back down.

"No, no, Dottie. Nice paper. Here."

Gerry popped her daughter into her walker—a frame made of two attached circles, the lower wider to prevent tipping. A fabric seat hung from the upper circle and eight little double wheels made Dot mobile. Dot, her feet going fast, propelled herself toward her father, driving through the pile of dust, crumbs and cat hair he'd carefully collected in the centre of the room.

Doug sighed, swept up what he could, and watched Dot careening around. He remarked to Gerry, who was repairing the tablecloth with tape, "Well, if it's any consolation, it'll be much messier in here after the party than it is now. Multiply Dot times four."

Gerry smiled at him. "I know. I remember when cleaning before a party mattered. Now we might as well leave it to after. Makes me wish we had a dog. You know: to lick up all the crumbs." She looked around at the cats. "Just kidding! Just kidding!"

"What?" asked Gerry, leaning close to Heather's ear.

"I *said*—" Heather, a pleasant-looking woman with medium-length brown hair, paused to look at the corner of the room where all the screaming was coming from. "I said, how's Dot's feeding going?"

The toy bear—retrieved by an adult from the baby who had taken it and then quickly lost interest—was returned to its rightful owner, and peace was restored to the birthday party. Comparatively speaking. There was still quite a buzz, as five women, five babies, one man and the hardier of the cats mingled. The feasting and present-giving over, the table had been abandoned and most babies were on the floor, playing or crawling or toddling around. Gerry and Heather were on the sofa in front of the fire; Christine was seated in one of the rocking chairs nearby.

Gerry replied into the lull, "Pretty good, I guess. I mean, she eats. That's all that matters, right?"

Heather nodded. "I agree."

Christine—who they knew either purchased or made her own organic baby food for little Jane—smiled. "We'll agree to disagree about that." With her black hair, cut longer on one side than the other, and her face tastefully made up, she was the most sophisticated-looking of the group.

Gerry and Heather made conciliatory noises then Gerry changed the subject. "Anybody know anything new about the robberies?"

They murmured their negatives. Hilary, her son Noah tearfully clutching his teddy bear, approached the sofa group and sat down and grinned. "No. But a pair of oven mitts went missing just this morning at my house." She extracted a scrunchie from her pocket and attempted to tame her exuberant Afro.

"Oven mitts?" said Gerry.

Hilary nodded and enumerated on the fingers of one hand. "Oven mitts are just the latest. An apron—not one I like very much, but still—a pair of clip-on earrings, and—what was it?—oh yeah, a scarf."

The others looked at her blankly. "It must be one of your other kids, playing jokes," suggested Heather, who had one child older than her son Peter.

"They swear not," said Hilary. "I threatened them with severe punishment if they lied; none of them owned up. Pretty judicious of me, I thought." She grinned. Hilary was a lawyer.

"Huh," mused Gerry. "I wonder—"

"Wonder what?" asked Doug from across the room, where he'd been chatting with Cyndi—plump, blonde, loud and cheerful—who'd just left the room with her daughter Sydney, holding the child away from her body in a clear signal that a cleanup and change were needed. He picked up Dot and joined the others, setting Dot down on the rug before leaning over the fireguard to stoke the fire.

Gerry replied. "Hilary had quite a lot of ordinary things go missing in her house. Do you think the thief is starting to target houses?"

Hilary snorted. "How'd he get in? We have security."

"So do we," said Heather.

"We do too," added Christine.

"Nah," said Doug. "Hilary, it must be your kids."

Hilary shrugged. "They say they're innocent. And I believe them. Speaking of which, anyone hear from Monica?"

Monica had been the other member of their pregnancy yoga class, had had her baby, but because of her husband's death (in unpleasant circumstances) shortly after the birth, had decided to move away. Some of the little group of women gathered at Gerry's house thought they knew the truth of Monica's husband's death. They weren't sure if anyone else did.

"Got a Christmas card," Heather said quietly. Where Cyndi was boisterous and Hilary could be argumentative, Heather, a psychologist and some-time social worker, was unflappably calm.

The others murmured similar responses.

Heather continued, "So I phoned her. She seems okay."

There was a silence broken by the crackling of the fire and the quiet babbling of the children. Cyndi entered the room, carrying baby Sydney and the usual small odoriferous bag.

Doug jumped up. "I'll take that," he offered. "We need more wood anyway."

Christine's Jane began whimpering so Christine began to nurse her. Christine, who was on her third baby, believed they should nurse until *they* decided to wean. And as she didn't have to work, this suited her and Jane just fine.

Gerry watched and felt a pang of longing, then remembered how exhausting breastfeeding had left her. She relaxed, looked at Dot and smiled. "Good birthday party, Dot?"

Dot, busy sorting some new wooden blocks into an order known only to herself, barely looked up.

On Monday morning, after the cleaners arrived and Dot had been fed, Gerry bundled her into her snowsuit, strapped her into the red and white Austin Mini, and drove the five minutes to Lovering's small business district.

First, the groceries, she thought, because they can stay in the cold car while I do the other errands. "Come on, Dot." She unbuckled the baby, carried her inside, then plunked her in the child seat of the shopping cart.

At this early hour, the store presented a sleepy, empty quality, yet every person they met as they dawdled from aisle to aisle had a smile or a greeting, sometimes both, especially for Dot.

Until they reached the cash. There, they were met with indifference by the middle-aged women Gerry privately called "The Lifers." No greeting, not even to Dot. As Gerry began to unload her items, her cashier walked away.

Gerry paused, watching as the woman kept walking. Confused, Gerry looked behind her, where the other cashier was staring into space. Keeping one hand on Dot, who was getting fractious from being confined, she used the other to return her groceries to the cart and approached the second register. She began to unload again.

Now the first cashier returned to her post with a newspaper she began idly flipping through. Gerry's new cashier languidly rang up her items. The first cashier commented on something in the paper and Gerry's cashier replied. Both continued to ignore their customer. Gritting her teeth, Gerry got on with it, paid and then, as she passed the reading cashier on her way out, leaned in, flashed her sharkiest smile, and urged the woman to "Have a nice day!"

Unloading her groceries into the Mini's ridiculously tiny trunk, she muttered to Dot, "You have a *bad* mama, Dot. A *bad* mama. Onwards to the next store!"

She carried Dot to the liquor store (which was next door to the grocery store) for some wine. "Oof! You're getting heavy, love," she remarked as she paid, heaving Dot higher up her hip, and hoping the bloated liquor store employee didn't think she meant him. She drove to the pharmacy for diapers on sale and other necessities, then to the Great British Emporium for milk chocolate–coated oat crunchies, biscuits without which she'd lately found she could not live. She drove to the drop-off box for the charity rummage sale and made a deposit of old clothing. After checking her car clock, she drove to her final destination.

"Want to go see Bea?" she asked Dot as she released her from her car seat. Dot, who'd been nodding off, made a fretful noise. "I know, sweetie," Gerry soothed. "I'll give you a bottle in a couple of minutes."

"It's Gerry and the Dotster!" the woman in the wheelchair remarked happily as she opened her door. Dot began to cry. "Oh, no, is it something I said?" Bea continued, "Come in! Come in!"

"She's just fed up going in and out of the car," Gerry replied. "And probably she's thirsty. Could you heat this up for me?" She fumbled for Dot's bottle in the diaper bag.

Bea took it and wheeled away into the kitchen. "Coffee?"

"You know me well," Gerry replied, unzipping Dot's snowsuit and letting her crawl away after Bea. Gerry followed. "How was your trip?"

Lucky Bea. With husband Cece—and despite her MS—she had just returned from a two-week trip to Spain and Portugal. "Fabulous! We ate so much fish, I might be turning into one!" Looking down at Dot, who was pulling herself up using Bea's legs, she crossed her eyes, puckered her lips, and sucked in her cheeks. Dot laughed.

Gerry laughed too, retrieved Dot's bottle from the microwave, and offered it to her. Dot ignored it, entranced by Bea's expression. Bea relaxed her face. "Do I look like a fish, Dot? Do I?" She made the face again. Dot laughed again, then turned and took a few steps toward her mother. And a few more...

"That's new!" Bea exclaimed.

Gerry scooped Dot up and began to feed her. "Yeah, the last few weeks."

Bea put some little cinnamon doughnuts on the table. Gerry offered Dot a tiny crumb of one. Dot made a face.

"Animal crackers coming right up," Bea said and brought the cookies and their coffees to the table. Contentedly, they munched their snacks.

Gerry felt a cat caress one of her shins. "Oh, hello, Cee," she said fondly.

The little black cat with four white legs was a littermate of Gerry's cat, Jay, one of five Gerry had hand-reared when her cat Mother had rescued and brought the weeks-old kittens to The Maples two years previously. Her full name was Cecelia, but only Bea called her that. Cee purred and jumped up into Bea's lap and from there onto the table. Dot threw her a cookie. Cee sniffed then rejected it. Dot threw another. Gerry removed the cookies. Dot began to cry. Gerry sighed. "Time to go, maybe," she said resignedly.

"But you just got here," Bea protested.

"I know, but that's just how it is."

Bea, who was childless, wisely refrained from further comment. "Well, drop in anytime," she said cheerfully. "Always glad to see you two girls." She added, as Gerry wrapped Dot, "You should get a babysitter and come over for supper one night. You and Doug."

Gerry smiled. "Great idea. I'll see what I can do." But as she strapped Dot into her car seat, she thought grimly: how can I explain that all I want to do most evenings is sleep? Just sleep. Seeing Dot's eyes beginning to close on the short drive home, she tried to keep her awake by calling her name. I'm ruthless, she thought, as tears came into her eyes.

When they got home, the Markovs had gone, and shocked cats, who never got used to the noise of vacuum cleaners, were reappearing. As usual, when she saw her house lovely and clean, Gerry cheered up. "Hello, cats. Was it very bad? Never mind. Hungry for lunch, Dot? You just had a bottle and lots of cookies, so maybe not."

She put Dot in the baby walker and let her zoom off after putting a baby gate in the living room doorway. Stepping over the gate, Gerry rushed to her studio, grabbed sketch pad and pencils, and rushed back to her daughter.

Most of the cats were able to easily negotiate the baby gate, leaping over it, but on her return, Gerry lifted a waiting Cocoon over the barrier. "All right, sweetie?" she asked the aged feline and cuddled her. Cocoon struggled in her arms. When Gerry put her down, Cocoon dashed into the kitchen to eat. "Cat-crane unappreciated," Gerry mumbled. She sat at the table and amused herself drawing real cranes lifting cats, which gave her an idea for *Mug the Bug*. She'd never drawn Mug as a construction worker.

Dot went by, going rather fast. She stopped at the back wall near the table where Gerry was working. "Ba ba," she said.

Gerry looked sideways, vaguely registering her daughter. "Ba ba," she echoed.

"Ba!" said Dot and began rocking in her chair. Gerry looked down.

Dot was parked next to the curtain. The curtain was eddying in the warm air exiting a vent. Gerry put out a hand to enjoy the heat from the oil furnace, which kicked in whenever the woodstove wasn't on. A tail appeared on the floor, poking out from beneath the curtain. Gerry lifted the curtain. There was Monkey, lying with one of Dot's blocks between her front paws, gnawing on it. Little bits of wood were stuck to her muzzle, paws, and on the floor. Gerry picked up the cat. "What is *wrong* with you?" It went limp on her lap.

"Ba," said Dot, pointing at the block, one of several in the curtained corner. The chewed block displayed, or had, in blue, the letter 'G'.

"And *this* one has been eating the oddest things. And hiding them. Over there." Gerry pointed first at Monkey, nonchalantly grooming in the doorway to the kitchen, and then at the curtained corner of the living room.

Prudence, who'd seen a lot of varied cat behaviours in her many years as housekeeper and now nanny at The Maples, barely acknowledged Gerry's remarks. All her attention was on a cranky Dot, determined to refuse her breakfast of mush and banana. "Mm," said Prudence.

Gerry continued. "And then she threw up. The cat, I mean. All over the rug in the den. Just when Doug and I were settling down to watch some TV last night. A block. Pieces of a wooden block." Gerry stretched an arm out on the table and laid her head on it. "Have you heard a word I've said, Prue?"

"Cat, block, rug, vomit. And this one? Why's Dot so out of sorts?"

"She wouldn't nap yesterday, then she fell asleep around five, so I worked until Doug got in, then she woke up and entertained us in front of the TV until almost midnight, conked out for three hours and woke crying. It was Doug's turn to feed and walk with her, but I'm still exhausted."

"So I see," Prudence said drily. She refrained from commenting that surely if they wanted the child to sleep, letting her watch TV with them till all hours getting hyper-stimulated was not the way to go about it.

Monkey looked at the women and child, then with great dignity walked to the hearthrug. Doug had made a fire before he'd gone to work at the Legion. Something about washing and waxing the floors of the hall, he'd said to a sleepy Gerry. The three cats who made up Monkey's friend group—Cocoon, Max and Jinx—were already on the rug, basking. Monkey sat next to a dozing Cocoon and began licking the elderly cat's head.

Another friend group was ranged on the sofa: Blackie, Whitey, Mouse and Runt. Blackie and Whitey were sister and brother, and where Blackie was a pure black longhair, Whitey was more a light beige, though as fluffy as his sister. Mouse was a grey and white shorthair, and the last member of the group, Runt, a small grey tiger.

Gerry called them The Honour Guard. According to Prudence, when she had discovered Gerry's Aunt Maggie—her employer, cousin, and best friend—dead in her bed years ago, these four cats (along with a fifth, Marigold, who had since passed) had been lying beside her, keeping her company. To this day, they still preferred to sleep in what was now the spare room at the back of the house.

Looking at the eight cats, Gerry groaned. "What now?" asked Prudence, who'd given up on Dot's breakfast and was wiping her down.

"All these cats, five of them fluffy. I haven't groomed them since before Christmas."

"Go get the brush and comb. Perhaps Dot would be amused to watch me try to groom her pets. And you can either go back to sleep or work."

Gerry sat up. "You don't mind?"

"Of course not. We have to do something and it may as well be fooling around with the cats."

"It's a deal," said Gerry and rushed out of the room.

Perhaps it would be kind to draw a veil over the ensuing scene, or scenes, as the indefatigable Prudence, seizing first one then another moggie, tried to persuade them that grooming was *not* about play, as the younger ones seemed to indicate by first biting then attacking the brush, nor was it meant as an assault on their person, as some of the longhairs interpreted her actions with the long-toothed comb.

She pursued them from room to room, Dot enthusiastically following in her walker. Cats leapt out of Dot's way. Some hid.

Though Prudence had long been associated with the many cats that came and went from The Maples over the years, her previous duties had been to feed them, to clean out their litter boxes, and to remove their hair and dander from the home.

So, with no cat of her own, she had no real experience of tending to their persons. (She *had* fostered a cat for a sick friend a year ago, but only for a few months, and he a shorthair.) She left lion taming to the lion tamers: Maggie Coneybear, deceased collector of cats, and now, Maggie's niece Gerry.

After an unexpected contretemps with the eldest cat, Cocoon—when a metal comb snagged on a mat of fur and resulted in a scratch on Prudence's wrist—she remembered the leather gauntlets she had occasionally seen Gerry wear while wrangling cats.

Leaving Dot safe in her walker, Prudence went to the little porch off the kitchen where cat-related supplies were kept. As she rooted in the box there, she was surprised to feel a tap on her shoulder. And even more surprised when she turned.

4

Meanwhile, in her studio, away from all the cat-related carrying on, Gerry reread the last few paragraphs she'd previously written of *The Candy King of Bubbly-Sauceton*. "Oh, yeah, he's got the stuff to make his store," she muttered.

> William came out of the pub with a tray and some felt markers. He put the plywood onto the smaller crate, knelt, and began printing in large letters: C A N D Y. He frowned, drew a vertical line through the Y then frowned again before making the line fatter till the Y had become I. He added E S. Below, he put: 2 cents.

Gerry smiled and stared out the window over her desk. It faced the street and her cousin Andrew's house where he lived with his wife Markie. She was thinking about her father, Gerald Coneybear.

When he was a little boy, there was a store in a red brick, two-storey building that sold candy, ice cream, and cigarettes just a short walk or bike ride from The Maples. The owners lived upstairs. Although the business also included a couple of gas pumps, young Gerald paid no attention to that.

Mrs. Light, short and plump, presided over the shop; her husband, tall and thin, pumped the gas. And it was in their establishment that, Gerry's father had liked to joke, he'd been inspired to create his first business.

Gerald had commandeered the square of asphalt beside his home, The Maples—right outside the kitchen door—and set up shop near the edge of Main Road, selling candies he'd bought for a penny a pop at a two-cent price: a hundred percent markup. He lost interest after a few days, but it had been fun while it lasted.

Gerry decided William, the boy in her story, would drag his boxes and sign around to the front of his parents' pub—The Furtive Beagle—and try to attract the attention of the pub's clients. She drew the scene from William's point of view, as he sat on the smaller crate with Prince Charles by his side. So, most of his customers were portrayed from the waist down—a pair of scuffed, old shoes; baggy, wrinkled nylons; the edge of a skirt with the slip showing; an outstretched beringed hand offering a few coins. Instead of including text for all of this, she drew a panorama of the winding main street of Bubbly-Sauceton and the front of The Furtive Beagle, with William, Charles and the boxes small objects in the middle distance. The customers followed in a series of little individual vignettes.

> Business was good. Pub regulars were kind enough to buy a few candies to slip into their pockets. And word spread among the neighbourhood children who came to shop from William just for the fun of it.
>
> All would have been well if it hadn't been for Kevin the Corgi.

Gerry snickered. She'd wanted to write and sketch this dog character since she'd been walking a quiet stretch of Main Road and heard a man calling, "Kevin! Kevin!" A corgi had appeared and run onto the road. Checking that no traffic was coming, Gerry had crossed the road, collared the friendly beast and called, "He's here!" Kevin had been handed over to his owner and Gerry had walked away, smiling, saying to herself, "Kevin the Corgi! Really?"

Her pencil was dull, but rather than breaking the flow by sharpening it, she automatically reached for another one. The tray where she kept writing implements was empty. *Huh?* Doug might raid her studio if he needed the odd pencil or pen, but not to this extent. "Weird," she said to herself, opening a drawer and extracting a box of pens and one of pencils. She filled the tray and was beginning to sketch Kevin, deciding what sort of facial expression he would have—sly, perhaps—when she happened to look at the clock.

"Rats!" Eleven in the morning and sometimes Prudence left at noon. Reluctantly, she put Kevin aside and gave her cartoon strip *Mug the Bug* some attention. One idea, she pleaded with her reluctant brain. Just give me one idea. The snowplow drove by, sending up a white plume.

"Okay," she muttered, and Mug was off, first loitering unawares at the side of the road, then, caught up on the plow itself, riding by, shouting and waving to the surprised people he passed.

She threw down her pencil in disgust and crumpled up the paper. "Way to go, Gerry. Show kids that snowplows can be fun, not dangerous."

She thought for moment, then started again, having Mug, even though he was now standing well back from the edge of the road, get buried in the tsunami of cold wet slush the plow threw at him. He tunnelled, meeting a mouse doing the same thing; a very hungry-looking mouse. Panic, scrabble, then up popped Mug a few feet away from the mouse. "Do mice eat bugs? Anyway, it needs work," she sighed and laid the strip aside.

She emerged from her studio and shivered in the cold hallway. That reminded her—she headed into the dining room where the faint sounds of kids' TV drifted through the den's closed door. "Hello, everybody," she said quietly to the cats in the dining room. "You'll be glad to know, I'm going to make a fire in the woodstove."

Bob, who'd been lying on the huge table (it could seat fourteen), yawned, stretched and came over to the edge nearest where Gerry was crouching. She reached up to pet him. He was her favourite because, when she'd arrived at The Maples—was it only three years ago!—he'd been the first of Aunt Maggie's cats to be openly affectionate with her. And he had a purr that wouldn't quit. He activated it now and Gerry switched to stroking under his chin. "Sadly, Bob, I need both hands to make the fire." She turned her back on him.

Now Jay turned up to rub back and forth against Gerry's haunches. Her second favourite of the cats, if truth be told. When you've known someone since they were small and helpless, Gerry ruminated, that's a special kind of love. She spared a hand for Jay then stacked her newspaper twists, twigs, and chopped kindling before striking a match. The fire's crackle and smell never failed to satisfy.

She added more kindling then sat cross-legged on the rug and watched the fire take a good hold. The sound of the TV show ended and behind her she heard the den's door open then close. "I'm down here," she called and raised a hand above the table's edge.

"She's asleep in her playpen," Prudence said quietly.

Gerry added a few logs to her fire, adjusted the stove's screen and door and rose. "Why don't we have lunch in here so we can hear when she wakes up? It'll be warm soon."

Prudence nodded. They got their lunches and sat at the corner of the table closest to the stove. "So, how did the grooming go?" Gerry asked.

"Harder than it looks. I see why you put it off."

Gerry noted the bandage on Prudence's wrist, smiled and pointed. "Not serious, I hope. Who did that?"

"Cocoon. She had a bad mat on her belly, but I got it off." Prudence offered Gerry her bag of bacon hickory chips, as was their tradition. "Er." She paused.

"Mm?" Gerry took a chip (well, maybe two or three) and crunched.

"It's happening again," Prudence said flatly.

"What?"

"I'm getting a feeling—"

Gerry stopped eating. "Go on."

"Someone—some thing tapped me on the shoulder!" Prudence blurted out. "When I was in the side porch."

"Tapped you? Like what happened in the woodshed?" (Gerry was referring to an incident, years earlier, which had involved Prudence, Gerry, Bob, and a skeleton found under the woodshed floor.)

Prudence nodded. "But it can't be *him*? Can it?"

"I shouldn't think so," Gerry mused. "So…someone new. I mean old. I mean—oh, you know what I mean."

Prudence nodded again. "*You* haven't noticed anything odd, have you?"

"You know me," Gerry said cheerfully. "The one most insensitive to ghosts. I mean, the room could be full of them and I'd never notice." She frowned. "Wait." She got up and left the room, returning with the photo from Dot's room. She laid it in front of Prudence. "This—fell, or was pushed, har har, from the wall last week. I thought it was the cat, but—"

"Which cat?" Prudence asked sharply. She lifted it by the frame to look more closely.

"Monkey."

"Monkey, hm? Her again." Prudence raised her gaze to Gerry's face. "Don't you remember? When one of the cats starts acting strangely, or 'things' start to fall—in *this* house, it all means something's going on."

"Is it? Like what?"

Prudence's lips pursed before she spoke. "It means someone is trying to make contact."

"But this is great!" Gerry said excitedly.

"Is it? Is it?" Prudence sounded grim. Though sensitive to ghostly communications, she was not a fan of them. (After years of attending seances, to "talk" with, first, her father, then her mother, the death of her ex-husband had cured her of wanting to contact the dead. He'd be the last person she'd wish to hear from.)

Prudence had to go right after lunch—she had an interview with a prospective baker-trainee for the café—but offered to return the next morning.

Gerry prepared Dot's bottle, then gently woke her. They sat on the couch in the den, surrounded by Dot's toys. As the baby fed, Gerry mused on times past and present.

Take the room they were sitting in, for example, a mid-sized square, off the dining room. When Gerry had moved in, it had contained some of Maggie's extensive collection of porcelain figurines, which she'd bequeathed to her nephew Andrew. Much to Gerry's relief—she'd thought the big-eyed children, winsome ladies and animal representations hideous, especially en masse. Once the room was emptied, she'd used it to display her art. Then, pregnant, and faced with Doug moving in with her, she'd decided the house needed another sitting area, one with a larger TV than the little old one that had been Aunt Maggie's in the living room. It had become briefly Doug's den, where he could watch sports and snooze on the couch, and was now their family room where they tried to contain most of Dot's toys.

Her mind returned to Prudence's tapped shoulder on the kitchen porch, and to the family photo. She wondered who the enquiring spirit might belong to. Someone in the photo? Her grandparents seemed unlikely, but she really knew very little about them. So, not impossible. And her Aunt Mary was still alive. That left either her father or Aunt Maggie.

Of course, the spirit could be someone else trying to communicate *about* someone in the photo. Or the photo and

Prudence's experience could be unrelated. But if Prudence had a feeling…and what about the cat?

Dot finished her bottle. Gerry asked her, "Want to go outside, Dottie? It's not too cold. Let's do that." She made a phone call, loaded up the woodstove and dressed herself and Dot warmly. On the side porch, where their boots were kept, Gerry paused and waited. Nothing. No spirit wanted to reach her. She sighed and turned her attention to her daughter.

After dragging Dot around the backyard for a bit, letting her lick snow from her mitten, and holding her up to the living room window to see Bob and Jay on the windowsill—both cats pawing at the glass and pacing as if they wanted to come outside too—Gerry had exhausted the delights of winter for a small someone who couldn't quite walk yet.

She put Dot back in the sled and walked around to the front of the property. Andrew's and Markie's house looked all right. They were on vacation in the southern United States where Markie had lived for many years, and Cathy, Markie's sister, was checking the building for them.

Gerry walked a short distance along Main Road before crossing to the other side. A long lane marked "PRIVATE" skirted a field on the right, where the Coneybear family burial vault stood, while Cathy's expansive lawn stretched out to the left. Gerry walked slowly up the lane, telling Dot about its points of interest.

"That's where some of our family are buried, Dot. From long ago. A mama and her babies. Oo, look at the pretty red bird that just landed on it. Oh, there's another one. And red berries in the shrubs. Some black berries. These big orange ones used to be roses. I don't know why they're called hips—rose hips.

"Remember a few days ago we walked all the way to the end of the lane? With Daddy? Today we're going to turn here and go see Cathy and Prince Charles. Remember Prince Charles, Dot?

The doggie with the big droopy ears?" Gerry wondered if Cathy would mind she'd stolen Prince Charles's name, personality and appearance for the dog in *The Candy King of Bubbly-Sauceton*. She frowned. *Am I being unkind in my description of Charles? I'd better go back and check.*

Whether Dot remembered any of what Gerry was describing to her was moot, for, having just ingested a bottle of milk and played outside in the cold for half an hour, her eyelids were closing as her mother prattled on.

"Oh, no!" said Gerry, pulling up to the veranda by Cathy's front door. "You're asleep again? My nights are doomed!" Dramatically and only half-comically, she threw her arms out to the side and addressed the majestic oaks in the vast front yard. "Doomed! Doomed to broken sleep again, I tell you! Forever!"

The door behind her opened. "Whatever are you doing, Gerry!?" Cathy Stribling, the short, plump doyenne of Fieldcrest Bed and Breakfast exclaimed. "Poor Dottie is going to freeze to death!"

Gerry laughed. "*She's* alright. Warm and cozy, aren't you, Dot?" She released Dot from the sled and climbed the stairs.

"Give her to me," ordered Cathy, taking the baby with greedy hands. *Another loving, childless woman,* thought Gerry. With a pang, she resolved to count her blessings and try not to complain about Dot's sleep patterns so much. In the warmth of the entrance hall, they disrobed quickly.

"A-roo-roo-roo-roo!" bugled Prince Charles, a weird blend of basset, beagle and *something* with curly hair, low-slung and mournful-looking. Hearing this salutation, Dot fully woke and struggled to be put down. Cathy let her go. Charles, sensing attack was imminent, lumbered away toward the living room, his toenails clacking on the old hardwood floors, Dot, also on all fours, in swift pursuit.

"You go and watch them; I'll get the tea."

Gerry followed Dot and found Charles on one side of the coffee table while Dot had pulled up on to the opposite side. The two were conversing: Dot using her favourite syllable—ba; Charles whining through his nose and alternately panting heavily.

"Here we are," Cathy announced triumphantly, entering with a tray and setting it down between her beloved dog and Dot—the child of her brother-in-law's cousin, as their relationship could best be described.

Gerry, seated on the sofa, said what one usually says on such occasions. "Well, this is very nice." And, more specifically when having tea at Cathy's, "I'll just move these nice biscuits a little further away from Charles's mouth, shall I?" Charles's beady eyes followed the plate. "Dot just had a bottle for lunch, so she's probably ready for one, though." She handed Dot a rabbit-shaped sugar cookie.

Charles's eyes narrowed and he stopped whining. His teeth almost came together around his hanging tongue. Gerry's fear for Dot's life was negated when Cathy took a squirrel-shaped cookie, broke it into morsels, and fed Charles bit by bit. Now his focus was all on her.

Gerry watched Dot reduce her cookie to mush and crumbs and winced. "Sorry about the mess, Cathy," she muttered, as she tried to gather the remnants into a napkin.

Cathy waved a hand dismissively. "Not to worry. Charles will go over everything after you leave. He's better than a dustbuster."

"I can believe it," Gerry said with a smile, eying Charles's face closely for future reference when drawing him. "He's greedy, like me." And she took another cookie for herself.

5

"So, how did the interview go yesterday?" Gerry asked Prudence, who was encouraging Dot to try a little pea purée. Dot's mouth closed on the purée, her nostrils flared, and the green slush was pushed back out. Before Prudence could wipe it from Dot's chin, Dot had smeared it off and was inspecting the mess—no doubt trying to figure out why it tasted so odd.

Prudence sighed.

Watching from the sidelines, Gerry felt comfortably uninvolved. After all, she went through this at every meal when Prudence wasn't around. "You know—the wannabe baker?" she added.

Prudence wiped Dot's hand and returned to feeding her some nice sweet mashed banana. Dot showed her approval by rocking violently forward and back in her chair. "She was fine. I had her bake some muffins from one of my recipes and they came out good. She's self-taught." Prudence looked up from her task and smiled. "Like me. Now I need to look for another waitress. What did you do?"

"We went outside and played; then over to Cathy's for tea."

"Nice. What did she make?"

"Animal-shaped sugar cookies. And, weirdly, she said she's been losing stuff around her house. Little things, mostly ornaments. A brass tray from one bedroom, a vase from another."

"Why is that weird? Doesn't she think it's her guests?"

"At first, she did. But then a little bowl went missing from *her* room, which she locks whenever guests are present; that's where she keeps her petty cash. And *it*, the cash, wasn't taken."

"Huh. That is odd."

"Yeah. And—Hilary! My friend Hilary had some stuff missing from around her house. Kitchen things and some earrings. So there are big thefts from public places and little ones from people's homes."

Prudence frowned. "I don't see that the two types of theft are necessarily connected. In Hilary's case, the thief or trickster is probably one of her kids."

"I've been missing things, too, Prue. Those crayons that were behind the curtain in here. And yesterday, a whole tray of pencils!"

"Yes, but those were probably just taken by a cat."

"Monkey? Yeah, maybe. We know she took the crayons, not the pencils, although maybe she took those too. She just likes to see things roll, I guess. After she's taste-tested them. Wait a minute." She left the room for a couple of minutes and returned clutching a handful of pencils. "Behind the sofa in the studio! All mixed in with the dust bunnies!" She held one out. "Teeth marks!"

Prudence pursed her mouth. "There shouldn't be any dust bunnies."

"Oh, there will never be another cleaner like you, Prue. I've made my peace with that; you should too."

Prudence smiled smugly. "Thank you. I will. You think the cat hid them there?"

"Who else?"

"Time for a nap," Prue said, indicating the now visibly drooping Dot.

"Coffee or tea?"

"Coffee, I think."

"You don't get enough at the café?" Gerry teased, as Prudence carried the sleepy child from the room.

Gerry made her lunch and a pot of Belgian chocolate-flavoured coffee and brought it all to the coffee table in front of the open fire. Assorted cats were ranged nearby, looking inscrutable. She built up the fire and flopped on the sofa with a sigh as Prudence joined her. They ate.

They were savouring their coffee with small Bakewell tarts Prudence had produced, when Gerry asked, "So when does your new baker start?"

"She's there today," Prudence said with some satisfaction. "Bertie's supervising her. So for once, I don't have to rush off."

Gerry pumped her fist in the air. "Yes! Er, I mean, good. No, really, Prue, I'm desperate for ideas for *Mug the Bug*. I'm just tired of him. I want to finish *The Candy King of Bubbly-Sauceton* and then I have an idea for another book…"

Prudence considered. "Well, can you afford to quit the comic strip? I mean, do you have to do it for the rest of your life?"

"No to your first question—cartooning is regular money. The first book earned nothing much, maybe a thousand. And you know this place is expensive to run—*and* maintaining the cats. No. I can't quit comics."

"Can you retire Mug, then? But come up with a new idea to replace him and sell the idea to the papers before you retire him?"

"Retire Mug. I never thought—well, of course, *some* day, I guess. No. Good suggestion, Prue. You've made me think. Thanks."

Excitedly, Gerry returned to the studio to struggle some more with Mug. She managed one strip before giving up. In the old pre-Dot days, she'd sometimes managed two or three a day, but that was becoming more and more a rare occurrence. She spent the rest of her time trying to see if she could adapt her still vague ideas for a third book into a comic strip instead. She was startled when Prudence tapped at the door.

"Teatime, Gerry, then I must go."

"Gosh, that went fast. Okay. I'm coming."

They drank their tea in the den, so Dot could crawl around amidst her scattered toys. Gerry, who'd observed that Prudence had done the dishes and scooped the cats' litter boxes clean while Dot had slept, congratulated herself on scoring such a babysitter. "Do you feel like talking about yesterday's tap on your shoulder, Prue?"

"I know you do," Prudence said resignedly, "so we may as well. There's nothing more to tell. He tapped—I think it's a he—and I jumped."

"And you didn't get any feeling? Happy? Sad? Anything?"

Prudence shook her head. Monkey sauntered into the room. Dot threw a soft toy at her.

Monkey paused, then padded over to the sofa where the women were sitting. She jumped up between them, climbed onto the back of the sofa, and settled among the potted African violets on the windowsill.

The women turned to look up at her. "If you ask me," Prudence began, "we should look at the people in the family photo this one had a hand in dislodging."

Monkey closed her eyes superciliously, as if to say "*Moi*?"

Gerry got up and retrieved the photo. Harley and Kitty-Cat followed her into the den, as well as Monkey's friend group, Max, Cocoon and Jinx. Wisely, the latter three hopped up onto the relative safety of the sofa. Only the two behemoths—the black-and-white splotched "cow-cats"—stalked around the room's perimeter before nestling inside a white wooden cradle. Once Dot's, now used to store dolls, their hefty forms filled the cradle. Their large, round heads surveyed the scene.

"I *did* look at it—it didn't help. And we don't really *need* it, do we? I mean, we know all the people." Gerry passed it to Prudence, adding, "I keep meaning to get another frame for it."

"I may have one the same size at home. Hm. Nothing written on the back. Obviously taken in the back yard." The Lake of Two

Mountains was a flat grey backdrop for the group posing on the lawn of The Maples.

"My grandparents and their three kids, circa—?"

"*My* aunt and uncle and my cousins," Prudence said quietly, "and I'd say your father looks about sixteen, which would make Mary ten or eleven and Maggie six. So, about 1954."

"I wish I'd known my grandparents," Gerry said wistfully. "Do you remember them?"

"Of course. I was twenty when Matthew died and Aunt Ellie died two years later. My parents and I would visit them here, more in the winter, when my parents weren't so busy on the farm. At Christmas, of course. And when I was a kid, I'd come to play with Maggie when someone could drive me; they thought it was too far to bicycle."

Gerry thought of Maggie and Prudence, playing at The Maples, with Mary and Gerald somewhere in the background. "I somehow can't picture Mary playing with you and Maggie."

"She rarely did, scornful of us 'babies' as she used to call us. And when she did, it usually ended in unpleasantness. One time she threw one of Maggie's cats, Mr. Puff, into the lake, and when Maggie waded in to get him, crying, pushed her over so she got all wet too."

Gerry laughed lightly. "I can so see it."

Prudence smiled, then the smile faded. "How is Mary? I haven't seen her around."

Mary, Gerry's aunt, had been dealing with breast cancer for the past year and had taken the loss of a breast—and the subsequent chemo-induced hair loss—very personally. Gerry had tried to be there for her, but with Mary's diagnosis coming shortly after Dot's birth, she hadn't had much time to give.

"Oh," she replied, "we got together over Christmas at her house, with the boys. She even let Doug come, grudgingly."

Doug had been married to Margaret, Mary's daughter, with whom he'd had James, Geoff Jr. and David. Long divorced, Margaret was no longer in the picture—for other reasons. Gerry heard from the boys—who occasionally visited her at the residence where she lived—that she seemed okay. At least, as okay as someone could be who was capable of both premeditating and suddenly initiating extreme violence against her closest relatives.

Gerry added, "Mary says, as, she's the boys' grandmother and Dot is their half-sister, she 'may as well' be Dot's grandmother too." She made air quotes with her fingers around "may as well."

Prudence laughed. "'May as well.' Sounds like Mary. Is her hair growing back?"

"I guess not very much, because she was wearing a nice blonde wig. But she seemed better, more energetic."

"Good. And her doctor-boyfriend? Was he there?"

"Ed the endocrinologist? Yup. I don't know how she does it, but her men are always so nice." She paused as they remembered Mary's husband, Geoff Petherbridge, dead for a few years now, one of the best men Gerry had ever known.

Gerry took a deep breath. "Anyway, where were we?" She looked at the photograph again. "So, if the person, ghost, who, em, made themselves known to you—the shoulder-tapper—is male, and is to do with this picture, it's either my grandfather, your Uncle Matthew, or my dad, your cousin, Gerald."

Prudence nodded. "*If* the two are linked in any way, and that's a big if." Her brow wrinkled. "But why would either of them try to contact me? At this time. I mean, what's changed?"

As one, the two turned to look at Dot, now pulling up on the doll's cradle and gently thumping with a small fist the long-suffering cats inside. Harley and Kitty-Cat's ears flattened but they refrained from responding to the pummelling with violence.

"Oh," said Prudence with a note of surprise in her voice.

"Oh," Gerry said, weakly. "Oh. Dot, stop hitting the cats."

On the windowsill behind them, Monkey began to purr.

After supper—frozen fish and chips for the adults, baby food and a very tiny bit of fish, rejected, for Dot—and while Dot and Doug relaxed in the den, Gerry wandered back into her studio. She didn't mean to be long, so she left the door open.

Her work was as she'd left it, the pages of *Candy King* laid out in order, a file of Mug cartoons nearby. She took another file, containing a miscellany of sketches of her cats caught in acts of mischief, to the room's sofa and sat down.

It *might* work. But the new concept would need a connecting thread to bring the daily strips together. Or did it? It would be more grounded in the real world than *Mug the Bug*, certainly, and would appeal to more people. Maybe. People who liked cats. She was full of doubts.

She returned the drawings to her desk and retrieved an old family photograph album from one of the room's shelves. Someone had printed dates on the books' spines; she selected 1952–1956. She'd show Doug and Dot pictures of her father's family when he was young.

She didn't notice the slim grey tiger who had slipped into the room as she left and hidden itself under her desk.

The little family spent a happy half-hour or so looking at pictures. Dot got whiny, so Gerry judged her to be tired and they put her to bed.

"Fingers crossed," said Doug, as they returned downstairs to the den. "Now for some sex and violence!" Gerry raised her eyebrows. "TV!" he protested. "I'm going to watch some crime shows."

She laughed. "Okay, but there's a special on PBS I want to see at nine." They both knew he'd be asleep on the couch long before then. "I'll just put this back," she said, picking up the album.

She passed through the dining room and into the hall. "Rats. Left the door open. Oh well, it's only been an—"

She paused in the doorway, her jaw dropping.

The culprit was not in evidence.

"My own fault," she grumbled as she picked up and sorted her scattered and crumpled papers from the floor. "I can call this vignette 'When Cats File,'" she added and laughed.

Back in the den, she snuggled up to Doug. "Do you think it would be okay if I took a day off on Friday?"

He turned to look down at her. "Ah, the guilt of the freelancer. I know it well. Of course you can take a day off. What do you want to do?"

She sat up. "I know—Prudence will be here, so I'll take the train into Montreal and maybe go to the museum. I haven't done that since—"

He finished her sentence for her. "Since before Dot was born."

"I'm stale, Doug. I was full of beans when I came back to work after maternity leave, but now, I just don't know. I feel blah."

"It *is* January, you know. Two or three more months of winter. It gets to everybody."

"Yeah." She flopped to one side, resting her head on the sofa arm. She wasn't ready to confide that she was thinking of giving up her main source of income, which they needed to maintain their household. "Yeah, you're probably right. January. Sheesh. Who needs it?"

As her eyes closed, he covered her with a throw. As if they could sense a prone body from afar, Seymour, Lightning and Jay padded into the room and arranged themselves on or next to Gerry. She smiled and drifted away.

She walked into the living room of her family home in Toronto. Her father was sitting in his old worn recliner watching a football game. With one hand he pulled up his sweater and pinched an inch of belly. The other hand rose, holding a needle.

"Daddy, what are you doing?" Her young voice wobbled with fear.

Her mother appeared from the kitchen, holding a dishcloth. "Gerry, don't bother your father. He's taking his medicine."

And now ten-year-old Gerry was pushing off from the ground, rising just above the treetops, then floating gently along, looking down at her neighbourhood. But it all appeared blurry. The trees were green blobs without distinct leaves; the paved streets were parallel lines that ended at the edge of the page—

She woke with a snort. The TV had been muted, and Doug, his head drooping, was asleep. She felt her cats pressed close. I was in one of my childhood drawings, she thought sleepily. I haven't had that flying dream for years. "Wake up, Doug. Time for bed."

As she did the last chore, cleaning out the seven litter boxes lined up in the downstairs bathroom, she remembered the dream before the flying one.

Except, it hadn't happened like that at all—her finding out that her father was diabetic. He and her mother had kept it from her. And even after her mother had died, when Gerry was fourteen, he'd not confided in her. Such a private man. She'd been astonished to learn the truth only after his death, when diabetes had been noted as a possible contributor in the sudden heart attack that killed him at sixty-two. Otherwise, he'd been in good health.

As she sprinkled a little baking soda in each box and topped them up with fresh litter, she recalled she'd gone to check on her father when he hadn't returned several of her phone calls and found him in his recliner.

She'd never told Doug—when he remarked on her choosing a sofa without recliner features for the den—that this was why she preferred footstools. The image of her father's slippered feet propped in the air, his body slack and lifeless, was one she knew she'd carry with her to her grave.

PART 2
DA

Of course, he ruminated, the truth was that ghosts went around touching people, living people, all the time; it was just that so few of the living were sensitive enough to notice.

And he'd always liked his cousin, Prue; how her visits to play with his youngest sister Maggie, ten years his junior, had evened the playing field for Maggie versus her older sister Mary. Two against one, in that context, had been quite fair.

He frowned as he surveyed his daughter's workspace. Why did she waste her time with cartoons and children's books? Mug the Bug! Cake-jumping cats! A candy king—wait.

He leaned over half a dozen spread-out pages. A little boy sat on a wooden crate behind a larger crate. He read "CANDIES" printed on a piece of plywood that was propped against the larger crate. He grinned. At the boy's side sat a funny-looking dog, its nose lifted as though it was about to howl.

The dog didn't look like Prince, who'd been a tricolour collie mix. If he'd been a living man, he supposed, instead of what he was now, his throat might have felt a lump form, his eyes might have begun to water.

Had he ever told Gerry about the worst day of his childhood? How, while pedalling his bike to the Lights' candy shop, with Prince galloping along behind him, a car had passed them at a curve in the road, met an oncoming vehicle, and had to swerve—hitting Prince and almost hitting Gerald. How he'd knelt at the side of the road, in the long grass, and watched his best friend twitch and die. How the driver of the car, full of apologies, had lifted Prince and Gerald's bicycle into his car trunk and driven them the short distance home. How Gerald had buried Prince behind the house at the side of the lawn where the wild roses and raspberries grew.

He sighed and lifted his gaze away from his daughter's papers. Did what he was trying to do—influencing his daughter's life choices—matter? Should he even bother? And maybe the other thing—communicating to his cousin about their shared past—was also best left alone.

He looked down at the small accomplice waiting to do mischief and smiled. "Better get busy," he said, and left her to it.

The man woke to the tickle of a paw in his ear and to the feeling of dread that had descended on him sometime in his twelfth year and not yet lifted. Not in forty years. He groaned. "Mandy, I know that's you." He opened his eyes and found himself nose-to-nose with his black cat. She mewed.

With shaking fingers, he rolled over and extricated a cigarette from its crumpled package and lit it. His breath, already visible in the cold tent whether he was smoking or not, hovered over him. A tent, he thought. My home. Structure. Abode. More like an architectural abortion. Some part of its frame—metal poles scrounged from people's garbage, tree branches—was visible as he gazed up.

A hissing and snarling came from somewhere near his feet. He raised his head to see the two males, Growler and George, fighting. "Okay! Enough!" He threw a paperback book near them and they scattered.

His head hurt. And his fingers, his neck. So, what else was new? Mandy mewed again. She was hungry. He could resist the other cats, but not her. "Okay, honey, I'm coming."

He crawled out of his warm nest and immediately donned the parka he'd discarded sometime in the night. Funny, how even in a flimsy structure like this, at some point the body warmed itself in sleep. He opened the shallow plastic container where he kept the cats' kibble and placed it on the floor.

Mandy, Growler and George, along with the other three females, Chirp, Cheeky and Buzz, rushed the container. He finished *his cigarette and reached for another. Two left. He swore. That meant a trip to the store at the other end of Lovering. Cat food, cigs, something for him to eat. He wondered what day it was—or what date. If it was the end of the month, it might be worth checking to see if his money was there. Not a cheque in a mailbox he didn't possess, but at the bank. He laughed bitterly, picturing a mailbox at the end of the path into the woods. Check the mail—that was a good one.*

If he was going to town, he wouldn't make a fire and thaw some water for the cats and for his instant coffee. He'd go to the diner first for a coffee and to warm up, and the cats would just have to find some water on their own. "Good thing you guys are feral, eh? Like me. Eh?" He smiled and stroked Mandy, who'd finished eating and was busy grooming.

He found the money, extricating it from the tin it had come in, and stuffed it in an inner jacket pocket. As he left the tent, he swayed and almost fell.

6

Gerry bit into her warm *pain au chocolat* and took a swig of cappuccino. She closed her eyes to savour the commingled tastes and listened to the noise of the railway station concourse. Unintelligible public announcements, the rumble of enormous idling engines, the distant beep beep beep of baggage carts backing up. She opened her eyes and watched commuters scurrying by the café terrace where she sat. The shadows of pigeons flying above the clear glass roof fluttered across the floor.

She'd grown up in a city—Toronto—and felt none of the anxiety she'd been told afflicted some country people when entering such a metropolis. Granted, she didn't know Montreal very well—though she had memories of visiting this very terminus with her parents—but she was gradually learning how to find her way around alone.

She was daydreaming, planning her possible activities, when a voice at her elbow jerked her out of her pleasant reverie. "What is a country?" it asked.

A tall woman with long grey-brown hair was standing the other side of the rope-and-post barrier by which the café claimed the extent of its territory. She held out a small paper. "What is a country?"

Gerry stuttered. "Ah, ah, do you mean Canada?"

The woman said pleasantly, "Any country you like."

"Er—"

"A bowl of flies in water."

Taken aback, Gerry said, "Flies?"

The woman nodded. "In water."

"I see," Gerry responded, thinking, this is just part of city life—the loonies. She looked the woman over. Slim, neatly dressed, albeit in sweatpants, a somewhat bedraggled long, faded rose-pink, puffy winter coat and men's heavy black winter boots. She seemed clean, and there was no accompanying shopping cart of rubbish.

Encouraged, the woman continued. "And what is your mouth?"

"*My* mouth? I guess—my mouth is my mouth?"

The woman shook her head. "My mouth is slaughter."

Gerry wasn't enjoying the encounter any more. She looked around for someone to rescue her.

The woman handed her the paper she was holding. "It's called 'Dictator, interviewed.' It's a micro poem."

Feeling surreal, Gerry unfolded the paper and read what was typed there:

Dictator, interviewed

What is a country?
A bowl of flies in water.

And what is your mouth?
My mouth is slaughter.

"Oh." Gerry took a breath. "You write poetry."

"Yes," the woman said patiently. "I'm a poet and this is a guerilla poetry performance. Would you like to hear another poem?"

Wondering if there would be gorillas in the next one, Gerry gulped and said, "Sure." She looked at the woman. "And would you like a coffee?"

The woman looked at Gerry, carefully assessing the young redhead. "All right," she said. "You don't look like a crazy." Gerry's eyes twinkled as the woman stepped over the barrier and sat down. "Yvonne," she said after shedding her coat to reveal a grey fleece top to match her pants. "And I can't afford this place's prices."

Gerry rose. "I'm Gerry. And it's on me, of course. Would you like a snack with your coffee?"

Yvonne looked at Gerry's plate. "I wouldn't mind one of those. Please. And a large regular."

Well, well, thought Gerry as she waited in line at the counter, I did not think I'd be spending the time before the museum opens entertaining a poet.

When she returned to the table, another folded piece of paper had appeared at her place. "Thank you," Yvonne said humbly and began to eat. Gerry unfolded the paper and read:

She bakes a cake

no shoes, ponytail a little bit loose
empty wine bottle on the stairs

she bakes a cake

brown sugar sandcastle upside down
it wears a crown of cinnamon

"Oh," Gerry said with pleasure, "I like this one."

"Yeah," Yvonne said gloomily. "They usually do. Don't like the political ones as much."

"Flies?" Gerry asked gravely.

Yvonne nodded. "Flies."

"You're the second poet I know."

"Yeah? Who's the first?"

"Blaise Parminter. He's my neighbour."

"That old guy? I'm surprised he's still around. Must be in his nineties."

"You know Blaise? He *is* in his nineties and still living in his house. With some help." Gerry surveyed Yvonne's slightly lined face. She looked about sixty or so. "How do you know Blaise?"

"I don't *know* him. But I've read his books. Years ago."

"Well," said Gerry, wondering how this encounter would end.

"Well," said Yvonne, rising. "I'm guessing you have somewhere to be. Nice meeting you. And thanks for breakfast." She walked purposefully away.

Gerry sat and mused for a moment then slipped the two poems into her backpack. She must remember to show them to Blaise. She retrieved one of the poems and unfolded it. Printed at the bottom of the page, she read: *Yvonne Punt*.

Gerry walked around the art installation slowly. She was doubtful this *was* art. Four chairs and a square table, wood and metal, of the type she might expect to see stacked in any church hall or community centre, had been painted bright red and set up, as if for a game of cards. I don't get it, she thought, and moved on.

The next piece occupied about half of a large room. On one wall, about twenty feet high and fifteen wide, moss and bark had been mounted and tropical plants inserted. As far as Gerry could see, the plants seemed real. A big palm tree lay on its side, perpendicular to the wall, looking as if it had been torn up by its roots. She supposed the artist was referencing the destruction of natural habitats by man? Or was it about climate change? Or both. Finding it uninspiring, she looked around her.

The remaining three walls of the room displayed about twenty photographs, hugely blown up, which showed flood damage in various locations across the globe. Gerry heaved a sigh. *Not* the refreshment for her creative juices she was craving.

She wandered around the museum feeling let down. Where was the beauty? Then she cracked a grin. Should that be capital 'B'—Beauty? Feeling better at poking a hole in her own pretensions, she went back to the museum lobby to wait for her friend.

She saw a taxi parked out front and glimpsed a head wearing a mink beret in the back seat. "Can I just go out and get my friend? And then get back in again?" she asked the museum greeter by the door.

"Of course, Madame, as long as you have your ticket." He politely opened the door for her.

She ran down the steps. The rear passenger door was open and someone in a full-length mink coat was waiting. The taxi driver removed a mobility scooter from the trunk. Gerry arrived in time to assist Marion Stewart from the car to the vehicle, catching a pungent whiff of perfume and mothballs as she did.

"Kiss, kiss, and all that," Marion said, "but let's get out of this cold." She engaged the machine's motor and headed slowly for the ramp, Gerry following. The greeter pressed the "open" button before they reached the door and directed them to the elevator.

"Don't you have to pay?" Gerry hissed in Marion's ear.

"Free for the disabled. *And* their caregivers, so next time wait to view the art till *after* we have lunch and you'll get in for nothing." Marion, who did not have to worry about money, cackled. "Now," she asked, her finger poised near the elevator floor buttons, "up or down?"

Up would mean dining in the museum's fancy restaurant with cloth tablecloths and napkins, heavy cutlery and wine. Down would take them to the basement cafeteria with its noisy families seated in comfortable booths.

Vastly preferring the latter choice, Gerry gamely said, "Oh, up, of course."

Marion glowered. "You're humouring me, aren't you?" Nevertheless, she pressed up. "You're looking well," she commented, surveying Gerry from head to toe. "Mothering must suit you."

Gerry just smiled, not wanting to go into all the conflicting emotions motherhood continued to evoke in her. Not in an elevator, anyway. They arrived and were ushered into the restaurant's hushed interior and to a window table. Outside, one of Montreal's most elegant streets was visible—lined with small art galleries, bistros, and a church directly across from where they sat. Marion kept her hat and coat on; Gerry draped her jacket off the back of her chair. The room was meagrely inhabited by elegant waiters and equally elegant diners, mostly older people.

"Well," Gerry said brightly, "this is nice."

Marion, her attention given to the menu, mumbled a response. Gerry looked at her menu. Very expensive and somewhat boring. What wouldn't she give for a nice juicy hamburger with a side of—

"I'm having the sirloin. What about you?"

Gerry looked at the price and inwardly winced. She hoped inwardly. Of course, Marion had unerringly chosen the most expensive item. "Okay. I'll have that too."

Marion beckoned to the closest waiter. "Two sirloins, please, and I'll have a glass of the cabernet sauvignon. You?" Gerry shook her head, knowing she'd just feel sleepy drinking with lunch. "Now," said Marion, taking a sip of water, "tell me all your Lovering news."

So Gerry told her. About how wonderful a nanny for Dot Prudence was. (Marion nodded and interjected, "Well, she *would* be." Marion had a lot of time for Prudence, who had married one of Marion's oldest and best friends, Bertie Smith. They'd all met when Bertie and Marion had helped Gerry over the matter of a lost, and valuable, painting.) About how energetic and funny Dot was. About how happy she was with Doug living with her at The Maples. About the cats; Monkey's antics stealing and hiding pencils and pens and other objects. (She didn't mention all the vomiting.)

At this point, Marion commented, "And yet?" Their meals arrived and conversation ceased. Marion, like Gerry, was a serious eater.

When the last bit of sauce had been scraped off the plate and the last drop of Marion's wine drained, their table expertly cleared and their dessert orders taken, Marion repeated herself. "And yet, you're filled with a vague dissatisfaction. Am I right?"

Gerry nodded. "I feel like something's missing, but I don't know what. My work doesn't satisfy me anymore; that's the exact word—satisfy. I feel like I'm short-changing Dot by needing to get away from her. And really, I am spoiled. I have a big house, people who love me." She paused.

"You're not spoiled, just fortunate. You've worked for your artistic success, haven't you? What does Prudence say?"

"She says I should think about changing my work. I don't have to do the same thing my whole life."

Marion nodded. "Yes. Maybe a change. Ah—dessert!" She regarded her wedge of blueberry cheesecake greedily. Gerry had opted for a walnut and date cake with caramel sauce. Both women swooned after their first tastes. Marion said, "You've got to admit, this was better than a tuna sandwich and rice pudding with a cherry on top."

Gerry smiled. "You are so right. Now, let's go find some beautiful art to look at."

They worked their way from Impressionism, which Marion was, as she said, "a sucker for," to examples of mid-twentieth-century Abstract Expressionism, which was where Gerry's special interest lay. They paused to admire one of Paul-Émile Borduas's smaller works. The painting—one of the artist's late examples of Tachism (from the French word for stain or splash)—had been part of Gerry's inheritance from Aunt Maggie. It was sold to the museum a few years earlier, after first vanishing from an art auction and later being recovered by Marion and Bertie. But that's another story.

THE CAT LAUGHS

As they were looking and talking quietly, a brash voice screeched from behind them. "Marion! Is that you? Darling, I love the coat! *Too* retro!"

Marion craned her neck. "Oh, hello, Francine." From the lack of enthusiasm in her voice, Gerry inferred this was *not* a friend. She turned to see an elderly woman, probably in her eighties like Marion, short hair dyed black, thin-faced, her skin tanned and wrinkled, wearing what could only be described as a robe— green, embroidered—dropping as it did from shoulder to floor, the whole accented with rings, necklaces, bracelets and earrings.

"*Who's* your little friend?"

Gerry, who wanted to snarl, "Who're you calling little?" instead replied with her name.

"Well, Gerry Coneybear, are you Marion's *keeper*?"

Marion clucked her tongue, rolled her eyes and sighed. "Francine, *if* you'd been paying attention at the last board meeting instead of flirting with Dr. Legasse, you'd have noticed I don't *have* a keeper. Gerry's a friend. An artist."

"Well, at our ages," Francine forced a laugh, "things can change fast. An artist, eh? Have I heard of you?"

"No," Gerry replied modestly. "I doubt it. Not unless you read the comics in the paper."

This revelation left Francine speechless. Marion piped up. "As I said, she's an artist. And she used to own this Borduas. See?" She pointed at the painting.

Francine leaned in for a closer look, murmuring, "Wonderful, wonderful." She straightened. "Well, I'm just going to pop in to Conservation. Want to come?"

Gerry looked quizzically at Marion, who asked, "Want to?" When Gerry nodded, they set off, Francine gossiping about museum employees and volunteers along the way.

They arrived at Conservation and entered a large, high-ceilinged room where several people were working, bent over wide tables or peering closely at paintings on easels. The atmosphere was hushed, and even Francine, when she spoke, did so quietly. "It's such fine work; I don't want to disturb their concentration." One of the workers noticed them, smiled, got up and spoke with Francine.

"Francine is the board of directors' member in charge of liaising with Conservation," Marion informed Gerry as they moved away to look at a medium-sized painting that was upright leaning against a wall. It obviously awaited the specialists' attention, looking rather the worse for wear, especially its once-gorgeous gold frame. Gerry read from a piece of paper on which had been typed: Bust-length portrait of Napoleon in ceremonial robes.

The conservator and Francine walked over to Marion and Gerry. The conservator smiled. "Good afternoon, Mrs. Stewart. How nice to see you."

"Hello, Susan," Marion replied, and introduced Gerry.

Susan turned to her. "I understand you're an artist. Any interest in conservation?"

Gerry tried to remember anything from her Fine Arts education. "Um, not a lot. I was in the commercial arts stream."

"Well, if you ever want to try your hand at it, let me know. We're desperate." She indicated the portrait of Napoleon. "Got a show coming up in a few months, which this is supposed to be in, but I'd like to get it cleaned up before then."

"I'm kind of busy with other projects right now," Gerry replied, "but I'll keep it in mind."

"Here's my card, anyway. Nice to meet you."

After escorting Marion to a taxi, and running to catch her train home to Lovering, all Gerry could see as she stared out the window was the pale oval face of the Emperor Napoleon in his battered gilt frame.

7

"And it would be temporary—for three months and part-time. And they'd pay me, but not much, as I'd be an intern, learning on the job."

Doug took his eyes off Dot, with whom he was negotiating supper, to look at Gerry. "But I thought you were exhausted from doing too much, sweetie. And now you want to do more?"

Dot grabbed the forgotten, outstretched spoon, mangling its contents with her fingers. She licked them and decided: maybe mashed potatoes were pretty good after all. She hung her arm over the side of the high chair and shook her hand. Small blobs landed on the floor where Ronald and Jay were crouched, waiting. Of all the cats, they and the three brothers, Winnie, Frank and Joe, were the most enthusiastic about human food.

Gerry handed Doug the ever-present wet washcloth. "I know. You're right. I *am* exhausted. But I think it's by my routine, too, as well as Dottie. A change, you know—" She brightened as a thought came. "I bet I could jot down ideas for *Mug* during the train rides. An hour each way."

Doug wiped Dot's fingers and offered more potato. Dot opened her mouth obediently and looked up at her father. He cooed, "Who's a good girl, using a spoon? Who is it? Is it Dot? Is it?" He played peekaboo, hiding then revealing his eyes. Dot gurgled and copied him, rewarding him with an open-mouthed mush-decorated grin. He turned to Gerry. "She looks so much like you, doesn't she?"

Gerry, regarding the gruesome but adorable object in front of her, said, "Well, when she was born, she *did* look like an old, wrinkled potato. Then she looked just like my dad for a few days; she had his square jaw and even his determined look in her eyes. Then she just got fat. Now? I don't know."

She observed the baby's playful eyes and red-gold curls and wondered if those were what made Doug imagine a resemblance. "I really don't think she looks like anyone but herself. So, do you agree with me going in to the city one day a week? It would be one of the days Prudence is here, of course—I like Fridays—so it wouldn't interfere with *your* work." It occurred to her that Doug never seemed to feel he had to justify *his* work hours to her. She pushed the thought down. He worked as hard as she did, certainly—physically much harder.

He smiled at her. "You know you're free to do whatever you want, Gerry. I just want you to be happy."

With that response, he completely disarmed her. She leaned in for a kiss. Dot, fingers once again coated with potato, lovingly patted her mother's head.

As Doug removed mashed potato from the hair of his beloved, he said, "I love you when you're wearing supper."

Gerry laughed and went into the kitchen for an impromptu shampoo, applying dish soap over the sink. As she patted the side of her head with a dish towel, she mentioned, "I gave a hitchhiker a ride this morning, on my way to the station. That tall, thin guy that you see on the road all the time. What's his name?"

Doug frowned. "You mean Ian? Ian Murchison? Bit older than me?"

"Yeah, but I'd say, a lot older. He's such a regular hitcher, I figured I'd be safe. He's not dangerous, is he?" She came over and sat at the table, where Jay jumped up and began sniffing Gerry's now damp hair. "No, Jay, stop! The potato is gone." Apparently, it was not, as Gerry felt Jay's rough little tongue rasping against her scalp. She removed the cat from the table.

"N-no," Doug replied slowly. "I think he's just very shy. I bet he didn't say anything, did he?" Gerry shook her head. "Maybe he has a mental problem, but I never heard he was violent. The other way around. He was picked on when he was a kid, I heard. A loner."

"Where does he live?" Gerry got up again to put on the kettle. She returned with an apple pie. "Want some?" They were busy with the pie for a few minutes. Dot watched them eat with interest, then banged her empty spoon on her tray.

"Okay, Dot." Doug scraped some pie filling onto his plate, mashed it with his fork and offered a spoonful.

"It's full of sugar!" protested Gerry, who'd just had a long earnest discussion about the dangers of sugar for baby teeth with the other mothers at her weekly playgroup.

"So? She had birthday cake, remember?"

"That was a special occasion," mumbled Gerry, giving in. After all, who was she to condemn the eating of sweets, one of *her* life's greatest pleasures? "Just clean her teeth before she goes to bed," she warned.

Needless to say, the pie was a hit with Dot.

Doug asked, "What did you just ask me?"

Gerry brought the tea. "I asked you where Ian lives?"

"Oh, yeah. Uh, in the woods behind Station Road. Kind of opposite Prudence's house, well in from the street."

For once Gerry was speechless. Her eyebrows went up, remembering the street people she'd observed that day in Montreal. "He's homeless? In Lovering?"

"Yeah. It's a sad story. He never left home. His parents died, and he stayed in the house with his cats."

Gerry's eyes opened wider. "He's got cats? Does he still have cats? Out in the woods? In winter?"

Doug shrugged. "Well, that's the story. Anyway, he never did anything to his parents' house, so eventually the roof leaked and water got in. Part of the roof fell down, so he just moved to a different part of the building for a while. Then the town got involved. He didn't pay his taxes, and the house was unsafe to live in, so they evicted him and demolished it. After that he built a shelter on the property and stayed there for a few more years. But the town removed the shelter and sold the land for back taxes. I guess social services tried to house him, but he really can't deal with other people so he moved into the woods. End of story."

"How many years has he been living out there?" She shuddered, imagining the cold.

"Enough," Doug said grimly. "When he ventures into town, people buy him meals, give him money. He must get some kind of disability pension or welfare or something, 'cause I've seen him at the bank."

"A disability pension! But that's nothing!"

Doug nodded. "I know. But he's not paying rent or heating or anything like that. It's enough for cat food and smokes, I guess."

"He did *reek* of cigarettes in the car." She remembered her other unusual encounter that day. "I met another, ah, 'different' person in town. A gorilla poet—whatever that is—came up to me at the railway café this morning and, just, like, read at me."

"Oh, cool. Guerilla poetry. Like graffiti."

"Wait, I thought she said 'gorilla.' Oh, *guerilla*, as in, a sneak attack. Yeah, that *is* cool."

"Did she want money?"

"Dunno. I bought her breakfast."

Doug smiled at her. "You are so nice, you know?"

She leaned in front of Dot to kiss him. "I know."

Dot, aggravated that the steady flow of sweet apple had ceased, reached a sticky hand out again.

8

"It's really neat. The frame is covered in at least ten layers, they say, though I can't see them. Added on over the years. Paint, lacquers, gesso, something called bole, which is a kind of clay—or is it glue?—and several coats of gilding."

Gerry rose from the rug in front of Blaise Parminter's fireplace and retrieved Dot, who'd found some dust bunnies under a table and was putting them into her mouth. "Here, Dot, nibble on this." She handed her a cookie. "So, having all this stuff, this gunk, on the wood means the details of the fine carving are obscured. It's really fancy—bees, bay leaves, different flowers, and this fabulous carving of an eagle on the top."

A month had passed, and Gerry and Dot were having morning tea with Blaise Parminter, her elderly next-door neighbour. He was sitting in a green high-backed wing chair with his cats: the female, petite, black and white Ariel, curled on his lap fast asleep; and Graymalkin, the male, steely grey, resting on one of the chair's arms keeping an eye on Dot. "So what have they got you doing, Gerry?"

Gerry was careful to also keep an eye on Dot and the cats. Ariel, though seemingly gentle, was something of an unknown quantity to her, originally a feral cat brought home to Blaise by Graymalkin one cold winter night. Graymalkin and Gerry had a history. He was one of the cats she'd inherited from her aunt, but Gerry later gave him to Blaise—whom Graymalkin preferred over her. He'd made that evident from the first. In her house, he'd been known as Stupid, because one never knew when he might lash out at humans and other cats. He and Bob had a special mutual hate that had led to some pretty dramatic scenes, including wounds.

"So far, I have spent four Fridays scraping and sanding a tiny bit at a time. It sounds dull, but it's actually interesting and relaxing at the same time."

"I'm glad you're enjoying it. And there's always the fascinating history around the object to consider. Tell me about that."

"When Napoleon was emperor of France, he had lots of these paintings made to send to the places where his power was represented. It was his way of reminding everyone who was the boss—or at least, that's how it's been explained to me."

"And lending them a bit of reflected authority with their underlings, don't forget," said Blaise. "Chain of command. Like us having the Queen's portrait up in city hall."

"I never thought of that," said Gerry. Dot, having finished her cookie, crawled over to her mother and patted her chest. Gerry got out a bottle and cuddled her as she fed.

A silence fell on the room. Graymalkin let his eyes close and Dot fell asleep on Gerry's lap. When Gerry looked up, she saw Blaise too had nodded off. She stared at the electric fire. Though fake, it did give off a nice heat. She took a deep breath, leaned back against the sofa, and felt herself relax.

It had been interesting adjusting to the Friday commute to the museum and back. She had found it possible to sketch ideas for *Mug the Bug* on the train; perhaps less so on the ride home when, tired, she was content to stare out the window.

She worked quietly on the frame while the other two conservators worked nearby—Susan, the chief conservator, and Susan Two, her assistant. This might have been confusing, but Susan One was so obviously a Susan, and Susan Two, so obviously a Sue (Sue Two in Gerry's mind, or should that be Sue, Too?—she couldn't decide), that it worked out fine for those around them. Of course, on the phone, it was another story, and then last names became necessary.

The two women were both self-described art nerds and, far from looking down on Gerry for being a cartoonist, were in awe of the fact that she could make a living actually doing art! Yet they loved their jobs, lingering among mostly old objects, gently restoring them to some part of their past glory.

Blaise slowly lifted his head and spoke. "I guess the next thing will be your birthday."

She nodded. "Couple of weeks. Last year's is a blur—I don't *think* we did anything. No, I remember. We went to the Parsley for lunch." The Parsley was the Parsley Inn, the nearest restaurant to their houses, just down Main Road less than a mile. "It was still the lull before the storm."

Gerry was referring to Dot having been one of those babies who spend the first few weeks of their lives mostly sleeping or feeding, and after that, well, *colic* is a vague term for what Gerry and Doug had gone through for the next three months. Crying all night sounds like an exaggeration but that is exactly what Dot had done. "I bet I had a hamburger—theirs are so good. Maybe we'll do that again; it might be fun—what am I saying? Dot in a high chair, dropping or smearing food everywhere. No go."

Blaise smiled. "We were all like that once. So, a nice party or meal at home then. What day of the week is it?"

"A Sunday, I think," Gerry said absently. "Blaise, I met someone downtown about a month ago who seemed to know you or know of you. A poet named—Veronica? Virginia? I remember her last name: Punt. Yvonne Punt! She read a couple of poems at me and I bought her breakfast. Do you know her?"

"Yvonne Punt," he murmured thoughtfully. "No, I can't say I know the name. Interesting though, that she knew mine. Of course, I used to go to poetry readings in Montreal quite a lot when I was younger." Dot stirred in her sleep and sighed. Blaise beamed. "She really is a lovely child, Gerry. You are so fortunate."

Gerry looked at Dot. "I know, Blaise, I know."

Back home, Gerry fed Dot while eating her own sandwich. She wondered what they might have for supper, thought about her shopping list, and debated whether she could put off her errands for another day. Then she remembered she was hosting Dot's weekly playgroup the next morning. She sighed—she'd have to shop today. She sighed again, knowing that meant Dot would likely take a series of short, unsatisfying naps in the car—just enough to recharge her and make an early bedtime unlikely.

"Stay awake, Dottie, stay awake," she pleaded as she backed the car out of the driveway. She popped in a CD and began loudly singing along to "The Cat Came Back." Checking to see if Dot's eyes were closing in her rear-view mirror, she saw the slender figure of Ian Murchison trudging along. She stopped the car, put on its hazard lights, and began slowly backing up.

She rolled down her window. "Hey, Ian, want a lift?" He nodded and shambled over. Gerry lowered the volume of the music and raised the heater to maximum. "Hi! I'm Gerry. I gave you a lift a while back, remember?"

"Hi," he mumbled.

"Not too cold today."

"Mm."

"And a nice sun."

"Mm."

"That's my daughter Dot in the back there."

Ian turned to look at Dot. "Hello, Dot."

"Da-da," said Dot.

Ian turned back to face frontwards.

For some reason Gerry felt embarrassed. "She's just babbling. She doesn't really mean—"

"I know," he said calmly. She could see his hands, ungloved, were clenched.

She waited a beat. "So, how are you today?" She could feel how fake-hearty her voice sounded. When he said nothing, she recklessly plunged ahead. "I mean, my, er, partner Doug, Doug Shapland—do you know Doug?" He nodded. "Yeah. So Doug told me that you live outside all year round?"

"Mm," he said, as if it didn't really matter.

"With some cats?"

"Mm."

"I have cats. I have nineteen cats!" This interested him enough that he turned his head to look at her. "Yup. My aunt left them to me when she died. There were twenty but one died. How many do you have?"

"Six."

"Six. Wow. That's quite a lot." There was a pause. "Uh, is there nowhere you could stay? At least in winter? With a relative, maybe?"

He shifted nervously in his seat.

"Sorry. I shouldn't be so inquisitive." She laughed nervously. "My friends tell me so."

From the back, Dot piped up. "Da da da da, da da da. Da da da da, da da da."

"Not enough," he mumbled, his voice trailing off.

"What?"

"Not enough money," he said loudly and with force through clenched teeth, then added more quietly, "Should be enough. I don't know."

"You get a payment? Every month?" He nodded. "So you could also qualify for subsidized housing, no?"

He licked his lips. "I can't—" Dot droned on behind them. He turned to look at Gerry. "I can't stand people," he blurted out. "Most people. You can let me out here."

Gerry pulled in to the curb in front of the bank. As he got out of the car, she said, "If you ever need anything, we live at The Maples, near where I picked you up. Me and Doug and Dot." He nodded then walked up the bank's stairs.

"I hope that wasn't a mistake," Gerry said to herself quietly as she drove the short distance to the grocery store. "I sure hope that wasn't a mistake."

9

She was used to the routine by now. Where she had once worried—just after Dot's birth—about hosting a group of mothers and their babies, many of them more experienced and some already on their third child, she now took it for granted that she was one of them too, even if she was still on her first.

With Dot in her walker, Gerry swept and tidied, prepared snacks for the mothers, and brought toys from the TV room into the living room. When the doorbell rang, her spirits lifted—quality time to spend with the people who perhaps best understood her life/work balance conundrum.

The women helped themselves to coffee and treats—a selection of Prudence's café's best—and relaxed. Their children fooled around with each other, sitting on the floor, one perhaps politely offering a toy or cracker, others crawling or toddling around the room.

Some of Gerry's cats had made themselves scarce, but those that stayed chose high perches—windowsills, the back of the sofa; Bob was up on the mantelpiece—far enough away to avoid exploring hands, which were not always sure just how sensitive a cat's eyes or whiskers or tail might be.

The talk came around to missing objects. Gerry's pencils and Dot's crayons had been easy enough to find; Hilary's bits had turned up—at the bottom of a pile of luggage in her basement. Now Heather had started to notice some of her jewellery was absent. She mused, "But it's funny, only the pieces my husband's given me over the years are gone. Some cheap, some valuable. What do you make of that?"

"*We* don't know," snorted Hilary. "*You're* the psychologist."

Heather smiled, a little.

"At least the things seem to reappear," said Gerry. "Now that I think of it, my friend Cathy had some of her little ornamental containers disappear. A box, a vase, a bowl. From her and the guests' bedrooms."

"Our great-grandmothers might have blamed the fairies," Heather said.

Christine took a swig from her water bottle (she was on a lemon cleanse) and said, "Well, we've been missing food. Whole packages of dried fruit or nuts, wheat-free crackers."

Cyndi laughed and took another custard tart. "Mice! You've got mice! Gluten-intolerant mice!" She took a large bite of the tart and looked teasingly at Christine.

Christine watched her plump friend with slitted eyes. "Wouldn't I have found their, er, dirt, if it was mice?"

Gerry nodded. "Yup, I always check my pans before I use them. Anything stored in the lower kitchen cabinets gets washed first." She shrugged. "Old houses, you know."

"But there haven't been any more thefts from stores," Heather pointed out.

"That's true," Gerry mused. "I guess the thief got what he wanted."

"Or moved on," said Hilary.

"I saw something in Lovering yesterday," Cyndi began. "Nothing to do with theft. But I saw two bank employees escorting a customer out of the bank, forcibly. He was yelling and taking swings at them, but they had a good hold of him."

Gerry perked up. "What time was this?"

Cyndi frowned. "Well, I was late for a hair appointment." She shook out her freshly dyed and trimmed blond hair. "So, maybe a bit after one? Why?"

"What did the guy look like?" Gerry continued.

"Tall, skinny. Had on a parka. He was really angry."

"I think I know who that is," said Gerry slowly. "I gave him a lift to the bank yesterday. He's the hitchhiker you often see on the road."

"Ian Murchison," said Christine.

Gerry turned to her with astonishment. "How did you know?"

"His old house was on the same road as my mother's. I grew up watching it fall down around him. Sad."

Gerry nodded. "I dropped him off around that time. It must have been him. Can you believe he lives in a tent in the woods?"

Christine sighed. "Like I said, sad."

"And no family?" Gerry asked.

"He had a younger sister, but she married and left Lovering, I think."

Gerry pondered for a moment. "I wonder what made him so mad at the bank."

Hilary said matter-of-factly, "The only thing that would make me mad would be if I couldn't get my money out. Or to find out my husband had cleared out the account." She changed the subject. "I'm going for this last brownie if no one else wants it."

Heather smiled at her. "We wouldn't dare, Hil. Now that you've said you want it."

As she bit into the brownie with gusto, Hilary mumbled, "I know, I was just being polite." She paused as they laughed. "What? I'm polite! Sometimes."

Bertie Smith opened a section of his newspaper wide, then began folding it elaborately, so eventually only a quarter of a page was revealed. "Care to hear your horoscope?" he asked his companion.

Gerry, sketching the snowy wasteland punctuated by fence posts and hedgerows outside the train window, sighed and rested her hand. "Hit me," she requested.

"It's always three sentences. Have you noticed that?" He read, "'Consider applying yourself to what you don't already know. Upgrading skills may pay off. A significant other holds the key to your happiness.'"

Gerry said uncertainly, "The first two seem contradictory. And isn't the happiness thing true for anyone?"

"You have put your finger on it," Bertie said with satisfaction. "Listen to mine: 'Review a financial arrangement. Don't be swayed by emotion when organizing your affairs. This is a good time for re-evaluation.' I mean, it's so vague." He unfolded the paper noisily and then refolded it. "I don't know why people bother to read them."

Gerry smiled. "And yet you do."

"Every day," he admitted cheerfully. "I must be an idiot."

An idiot he was not. Edward Albert Smith—antiques dealer and café owner—was a self-made man, the son of a single mother who had spent years serving cakes and meat pies from the basement bakery counter at Eaton's. He'd started out as a picker for other dealers before opening his own shop in Westmount, Montreal's most upscale neighbourhood, in mid-life. It was that very shop he planned to visit that day, to check in with the manager and have a word with the second-floor tenant, a woman who ran an art gallery. Though he still kept his third-floor apartment, he rarely stayed there.

Gerry resumed sketching. "Are you seeing Marion today?"

"I said I'd pick up some lunch and eat it with her at her place. You want to join us?"

"I *could*," Gerry said slowly, thinking of leaving the warmth and quiet of the conservation department and venturing out into an overcast February day (snow was forecast) in boots and coat. "Let me call you later when I decide." She added, "What are you going to eat?"

"Aha! So your company is dependent on the menu?" Gerry just laughed. "I better come up with something good then. I'm thinking about deli smoked meat sandwiches with mustard, dill pickles on the side, coleslaw and fries."

Gerry groaned. "I'm in. Of course, I am."

Now it was his turn to laugh.

Gerry watched carefully as Sue Two demonstrated scraping just hard enough at the many layers of gunk to reveal the separate feathers of the eagle's plumage, but not enough to scratch into the surface beneath. The eagle had been removed from the top of the frame of Napoleon's portrait for ease of cleaning. "Just deep enough so the lines pop," said her mentor. "Okay?"

"Okay," said her student, taking over. "Judging by how the rest of the frame looks, we're almost finished this stage?"

"Uh huh. I'll start applying the base layer next week. After the gesso."

"What's in the base?"

"It's a mix of red clay and rabbit skin glue."

"Rabbit skin glue?" Visions of trappers skinning rabbits and boiling their skins in large pots in backwoods log cabins to make glue for artists boggled her mind.

"It makes a nice sticky substance. Pure collagen. We thin it with water. You'll see."

"I can't wait," Gerry said wryly. "This is stuff they don't teach you at art college."

Sue laughed. "Did I mention, if the glue stinks after you've added the water, it's spoiled? Throw it away and get a fresh supply."

Again, Gerry visualized a grizzled old bearded man tromping back out to the woods to hunt for more rabbits. "Noted," she said, and resumed her picking and scraping at Napoleon's eagle's feathers.

Gerry and Bertie walked through swirling snow the short distance from the museum—where he'd met her with a savoury-smelling bag—to Marion's apartment.

"When was the last time you saw Marion?" Bertie asked her as they struggled across an intersection, the road surface rapidly becoming a grey slushy mess.

Gerry had to think. "Well, at the museum last month. But before that, gosh, it must have been last summer, wasn't it? When she came to stay at Fieldcrest for a couple of weeks?"

Cathy Stribling's B&B, where Marion had vacationed several times, provided not only a comfy bed and excellent cuisine, all in a tattered country ambience, but a built-in faithful hound—Cathy's dog Prince Charles—who was more than devoted to Marion. Perhaps "besotted" was the word for the way he followed her every move, possibly because, whenever he was in attendance on her, food seemed to slip from her arthritic fingers, either to the floor or directly into Charles's mouth.

Bertie continued, "So you must have noticed a bit of a change since then. I saw her two weeks ago and I was shocked."

Gerry said only "Mm," and prepared herself. She hated how the bodies of her most elderly friends ultimately betrayed them. Yet, having lost her mother at forty-four, and her father at sixty-two, she was comforted by some of her friends' examples of longevity. Marion must be in her mid-eighties now and still managing on her own. She'd looked smart at their museum lunch, even if she was now in a mobility scooter where she'd once managed with a walker.

She *thought* she'd prepared herself.

Marion's building was a mid-twentieth-century high-rise—an expensive place to live—one of several built on the lower slope of Mount Royal, on a narrow strip of land between the end of Westmount's shops and the beginning of the mountain's rising woods. The lobby was furnished with glass coffee and end tables and mirrored walls and painted in turquoise and pink with black trim—art deco style. And Marion's apartment, on the nineteenth floor, was similarly furnished, or over-furnished, with what must have been the latest fashion in the 1940s and '50s when Marion and her late husband had set it all up.

Her wardrobe was from the same era—once chic and expensive, now retro but still elegant. And Gerry had never seen Marion anything but elegant. Today was to be the first exception.

When they got off the elevator, their friend was not at the open door to her apartment, which had been the protocol heretofore. When they entered her space, they caught a glimpse of her retreating in a wheelchair down a long hall.

Gerry thought of Dot, bouncing into life in her baby walker, and the contrast brought a lump to her throat. "Hello, Marion," she called down the hall as she and Bertie took off their coats and boots.

"Dining room," was what she thought she heard in reply.

Gerry followed Bertie into the room where Marion was waiting and felt the lump in her throat intensify.

The table was carefully laid, not quite as if for a formal lunch, but almost. Three large plates were surrounded by more cutlery than Gerry would have supposed necessary for smoked meat sandwiches and fries; each place had a water and a wineglass; and cloth napkins had been rolled and placed in silver napkin rings. Gerry burst out with, "Oh, Marion, how lovely! I'm used to baby mush splattered everywhere with cats patrolling under the table for scraps."

Marion raised herself from the wheelchair and slid into a chair. "Ow," she said, unabashedly. "Bertie, make yourself useful and get the wine."

No Chanel suit or beret today; Marion was dressed neatly in slacks, a blouse and a cardigan. Marion at home looked a deal older than the public Marion visiting the museum had. Gerry didn't think she'd ever seen her friend without makeup and some kind of head covering, but today there was neither—Marion's face was pale while wisps of hair barely covered her pate. Yet the voice was the same. "Well, Miss." She addressed Gerry in stern tones as Bertie poured a fizzy white wine into their glasses. "What do you have to say for yourself?"

Gerry, who knew this gruffness disguised affection, was not put off. "Er, I'm hungry?"

"Hah! When are you not? It does smell good, though." The women watched as Bertie served them their lunch. For a while, after the clinking of glasses, they addressed themselves to the succulence in front of them.

Marion ate very little, and that with a knife and fork, before pushing her plate aside. She gestured to Bertie to top up her wine. When she caught Gerry looking at her almost full plate, she said, "Don't worry, I'll eat this again tonight. And maybe tomorrow if there's any left. Meat, starch and—" She poked at her pickle with her fork. "A vegetable. Balanced meal. Cheers!" She drained her glass. "Ah, alcohol, the milk of the elderly." She watched the others as they continued eating. "What I meant before was, what's new? Got any mysteries to solve? Any murders out there in Lovering?"

"N-no. Thefts at some businesses, but no murders," Gerry said slowly. "And things, mostly little objects, have been going missing from people's houses."

She told them about her drawing implements; Hilary's household items, given to her by her mother, now found; Cathy's various containers—a tin, a bowl, a tray; and Heather's jewellery from her husband.

"Oh, yeah," she concluded. "And my friend Christine, who's very particular about her food, organic and fair trade and all that, is missing some packages of nuts and stuff. So almost everyone. Except Cyndi." She turned to Bertie. "You and Prue haven't noticed any mislaid things at home or at work, have you?"

"Nope," he replied, topping up their glasses. "Nice Gewürztraminer, Marion." He perused the label. "I must get some."

She dismissed him with a wave of a hand. "Well, I knew the alternative would be cola so I took the initiative." She gestured at the three cans of cherry soda pop sitting, unopened, on the table. "Everybody delivers nowadays, even the liquor store."

"The cola was included with the meal," Bertie protested. "But this is much better."

Gerry, who'd enjoyed the slightly sweet fruity wine, agreed. "Yes, thank you, Marion. And thank you, Bertie, for the food."

He rose and cleared the table. As he worked in the kitchen, Marion leaned toward Gerry, and, in a low voice, asked, "What does Prudence say?"

Gerry was surprised. "You mean about the missing stuff? I'm not sure she knows about all of them. I mean, she's aware my cat Monkey seems to have been hiding pencils and crayons at my house. I think I told her about Hilary. Maybe Cathy as well. I can't recall. Why?"

"Well," replied Marion. "Because of what went on at your house when she was house sitting for you during your trip to Europe. Two autumns ago."

"What went on?" Gerry asked in a wondering tone.

"You know—when she found the trapdoor under your dining room rug."

"Oh. *That*. But that was just because she had to move the rug out of the way of the guys who installed the woodstove."

Marion leaned back. "*I* see. So, she never told you about all the other things that happened during that month?"

"What other things?" interjected Bertie, returning to the table with a teapot and three cups.

Marion favoured him with a sour look. "Have you been eavesdropping?"

"Eavestroughing?" he said blandly, looking around him. "I didn't think apartment buildings *had* eavestroughing."

This earned him a grudging smile from his hostess. "Well?" she asked him again. "Have you?" Gerry also smiled, listening to this exchange.

Bertie answered. "Marion, it may have escaped your notice, after your fifty or so years inhabiting this space, but the kitchen is all of six feet from where you're sitting. I've heard every word. I admit, it's possible that when I noticed you lower your voice, I stopped making noise myself and started listening more carefully. What other things might or might not my wife have mentioned to Gerry?"

"I think I've said enough," Marion said with a satisfied air. "Ask her yourself." She turned to Gerry. "Tea?"

All that afternoon, as Gerry worked on her task, and later during the train ride home (she was alone—Bertie had taken an earlier one), she kept wondering what Prudence could possibly have told Marion a year and a half ago that she hadn't told her.

She resolved to beard the lioness, as it were, in her den, and, the next day, Saturday, proposed a visit to Prudence's place of work. "Just for fun," she said brightly to Doug at the breakfast table.

"You, me and Dot?" he asked skeptically. "In a restaurant? Fun?"

"Yes, why not?"

He wiped the mush off his arm, where it had mostly sprayed after Dot sneezed with her mouth full, and said, "Uh, because of things like this? I thought you said she was at an awkward age for restaurants—too big to be stuffed in a carrier and too, um, unpredictable to take out in public."

Dot smiled adorably at her parents as Gerry fumbled for an excuse. "It's just that I haven't been to the café for ages and I'd like to see what they've done to the place. And meet the new employee, if she's there."

"Oh! A surprise inspection. Now I get it."

Gerry didn't contradict him.

He thought for a moment. "How about this: we all drop in, say hi to Prudence, have a quick snack, then, if Dot seems restless, I can extract her while you carry on with—" He gave his partner a quizzical glance. "With whatever you have on your agenda."

Gerry gave him a small smile. "You know, for a divorced person, you're actually very good at interpersonal relations." She kissed him softly on the lips. "Very good."

Dot chose this moment to speak very clearly. "Da-da." Neither of her delighted parents noticed that, as she said the word, she was looking over their heads.

The curtains, drawn back, swayed, and Monkey appeared from behind them. She moved to sit between the window and Dot's chair, looking up in the same direction.

10

True to form, Dot behaved just long enough to gobble down some egg custard—typically used as filling for chocolate éclairs—a special order brought by a beaming Bertie. She grinned at fellow customers as she messily masticated the delicious treat. Then, no doubt feeling trapped in the café's high chair, she began vocalizing her displeasure, lifting her torso and slamming it back down repeatedly.

"Told you," Doug muttered as he released his daughter. But since letting Dot loose among patrons trying to enjoy a relaxing Saturday morning coffee wasn't an option, he stuffed her back into her snowsuit. "We'll meet you at the community centre."

Gerry helped, looking innocent, when what she'd counted on happening, had. She kissed them both goodbye and settled down to finish her café au lait and almond croissant. She enjoyed looking around at the interior of Maggie's Café, formerly Coco Poco.

Where the front area had been the entire café, and the larger rear room the owner's office and coffee roasting emporium, Prudence and Bertie had knocked down the wall that had separated the two. Now the front—furnished with coat racks and a couple of benches, the coffee-making apparatus and the cash—was where patrons arrived and placed their orders, whether take-out or eat-in. The back, glass-walled on its south and west walls, painted white on the others, accommodated small tables for two to four people. The large black-and-white floor tiles and the hanging plants were minimal decorations, but they created a cozy atmosphere.

Bertie joined her at her table. "Phew! A lull." He sipped his Americano. A young barista stayed at her station behind the cash.

"Does Prudence know you're slacking off?" Gerry teased.

He pretended to be offended and waved a hand expansively as he said grandly, "All is well in the kingdom. Or should that be queendom? Anyway, Ginger has it under control."

Gerry looked at the barista and smiled. Ginger, who'd worked part-time at the café for several years, smiled back. Her short hair, which had been gelled so it stood straight up, had, over the years, moved through a gamut of colours. Today it was cotton-candy pink. The tiny jewelled stud she usually wore in one nostril had been replaced by a small ring. Gerry quietly asked Bertie, "Any new tattoos?"

"What? That's a very personal question!"

"Not you! Ginger!"

"Ah, well, I could not say. There was some talk of a new one in a place where I shall hopefully never view it." He leaned closer. "You should have seen the size of the first nose ring." He shuddered. "My wife intervened and offered to pay for the smaller one you see today. Thank goodness the girl respects her."

"Everybody does," Gerry said matter-of-factly. "We lesser mortals can only watch and learn."

The woman herself, Prudence, appeared in the front of the establishment and exchanged a few words with Ginger before approaching their table. "Hi, Gerry. I can't stay. I'm baking. Want to come up?"

Bertie rose and obsequiously cleared the table and others nearby before returning to stand meekly next to Ginger. He winked at Gerry as she and Prudence passed.

They climbed the staircase to the second floor. Here, where the previous owner had lived, a professional kitchen had been installed, all gleaming stainless steel. At the rear were two small offices. A delicious smell wafted towards Gerry's nose. "What's in the oven?"

"Chocolate chip muffins. Have a seat."

Gerry sat on a sofa facing a coffee table flanked by two chairs. Prudence asked, "Can I get you anything?"

"I'm good. How are you?"

"Oh, you know," Prudence said absently. "The weekend. Busy, busy." She opened one of several oven doors, inspected her muffins and closed it. "You?"

"I'm fine. The new baker not in today?"

"Tomorrow."

"Oh. I had lunch with Bertie at Marion's yesterday, as I'm sure you know."

"Mm hmm." Prudence flopped down on the sofa next to Gerry.

"And, uh, Marion mentioned that, uh, besides discovering the old storeroom under the dining room table at my house, when you were cat-sitting last fall, I mean, two falls ago, you also, er, had some other occurrences? Unusual ones? Possibly of a poltergeistery—or whatever the word is—nature?" She stopped.

"The word you're looking for is supernatural," Prudence said drily. A timer buzzed and she rose. "Excuse me." She removed the muffins and switched the oven off with evident relief. "There, that should hold us for today. I'll give you a few when you go."

"Great," Gerry said enthusiastically, then, her voice changing to a more tentative tone, added, "Er, Prudence? You didn't think to tell me before? About stuff going on in my own house?"

Prudence rejoined her on the sofa with a cup of coffee. She put her feet up on the table. "That's better." She sipped, then said, "I guess as the signs were meant for me, I didn't think it mattered. I mean, you already knew The Maples can be a bit spooky at times."

Gerry nodded. "Do you mind telling me about them now? I have a good reason for asking."

"Okay. It was just as though someone wanted to get my attention and kind of messed up little things in the house. The silverware in the dining room armoire drawer was all jumbled together instead of neatly laid out. The curtains in the foyer were rolled up instead of hanging. Some of my wool—remember I was knitting that orange sweater for Dot?—was cascading down the stairs one morning."

"That's it?" Gerry felt a little disappointed.

"Oh, I forgot, wood for the woodstove, or was it the poker? It was the poker—it had been knocked over from where I'd propped it. And the main thing was, when I'd gone down the ladder into the storeroom, the trapdoor slammed down. I'd pulled it all the way back so it couldn't have been an accident."

"You must admit though, that some of the objects moved around could have been by the cats. The wool, and the poker."

"Well that's what I thought too, but they couldn't have lifted a heavy wooden trapdoor. I don't care how many of them there might have been."

Gerry laughed, picturing all the cats—some standing on each other's shoulders—massed together with a common goal. Bob would have been foreman. She laughed again. "No, you're right there. There's a reason for that expression 'It's like herding cats.' They are a bunch of individuals for sure. So, did you get to the bottom of it?"

"Oh, yes," Prudence said slowly. "I got a call from Mrs. Smith."

"Mrs. Smith?" Gerry said in wonderment. "But *we* call *her*."

Mrs. Smith was Prudence's medium, inherited from her mother, who'd been so stricken by Prudence's father's death that she'd been unwilling to let go. Constance Catford had found Mrs. Smith and visited her faithfully for many years, happily chatting away with her dead husband and others. And Prudence, faithful daughter that she was, accompanied her mother when she was able, becoming convinced of Mrs. Smith's sincerity and veracity. When her mother died, Prudence continued regular visits. In the three years they'd known each other, Gerry—though initially skeptical—had occasionally accompanied Prudence, and had even once consulted Mrs. Smith on her own. The connection ended the year Prudence's ex-husband died, she having no wish to be in touch with him from beyond the grave.

Prudence replied, "Well, I don't anymore, but when she contacted me, I could hardly refuse. Besides, I was curious."

"And?"

"And it turned out the repositioning of items was done by my mother. Somehow. I think she wanted me to make up my mind about Bertie. And give up housekeeping. She and my dad always thought I'd do better than that."

"So, the misplaced objects were a spirit trying to communicate," Gerry said slowly, thinking of all her other friends who were experiencing similar occurrences. Then she commented on Prudence's remark. "It doesn't matter what you do, just strive to be the best at whatever it is. *My* dad used to say that."

"He was in finance or something, wasn't he?"

"Yeah. I never could get a precise job description from him. 'Money,' he'd say. 'I'm in money.' Like his father, I suppose. Anyway..." Gerry rose. "I should go look for my family. Thanks for telling me about the weird happenings at The Maples. At least we know Dot's crayons and my pencils were levitated by a naughty cat." She laughed.

Prudence gave her a half dozen muffins in a bag and watched her descend the stairs. As she tidied her kitchen, she felt pensive. Then, dismissing the conclusion to which she was jumping, she said, "Nah," and returned to her café.

Back at The Maples, enjoying a quiet hour while Dot napped—perhaps finally getting the hang of it, her parents hoped—Gerry and Doug tuned in to an English Premier League soccer game. It was the kind of thing you could talk through, so Gerry told him what she'd learned from Prudence.

A few cats, sensing warm human bodies, had joined them, though most were sleeping snug in boxes or near the woodstove in the next room. After all, afternoons were meant for naps.

Bob kneaded Gerry's lap while Jay lay on the sofa back's top, batting at Gerry's curls.

"Madame, you are surrounded," said Doug and put his arm around her. Jay turned her attention to the arm, lying on her side and grasping Doug's shirt softly with her front paws while kicking with the back ones.

"So, what do you think, Doug? About what happened to Prudence here while we were in Europe?"

"Well, could be, I guess. If she says so."

"I know, right? She's the most sensible one of all of us."

Doug knew that by "all of us" Gerry meant their extended family and close friends.

"Oh, I almost forgot," he said. "I bumped into my aunts. At the art show at the community centre where I was showing off my daughter."

"Did you? How are they?"

"They look fine to me." Jane and Bette were both considerably older than their brother, Sydney, who had died recently. "Considering they're pushing eighty," he added. "But Uncle Sydney was their power of attorney, and since he's passed, they've asked me if I would fill his shoes, so we're going to the lawyers and then to the bank to make the arrangements.

She snuggled into his shoulder. "That's very good of you."

He smiled. "I know. I'm a good guy." He kissed her, and the next half hour passed pleasantly, until Dot's wails pierced the air.

Gerry retrieved Dot, swapped the soccer for a film featuring singing vegetables, and Doug was just about to nod off at one end of the couch with Jay curled in his arms while Dot jigged in her baby walker in time to the music, when a loud knocking at the front door disturbed their afternoon. Gerry got up. "Who on earth—?"

She peered through the window to the side of the front door. The figure in a parka was tall and had his back to her. She opened the door and Ian Murchison spun around. She hesitated then ushered him in.

He looked around the spacious foyer, at the wide staircase rising to a landing before splitting into two side staircases and continuing up and out of sight. His body gave a quick shiver.

Gerry felt ashamed. Her foyer was the size of a large room in many people's houses. And this man lived in a tent with a bunch of cats. "What can I do for you, Ian?" she asked in a soft voice.

He stuttered. "R-r-ran out of cat food. Again. Not enough money in my account. You s-s-said—" He paused and again gave that quick shiver.

Bob padded in and sniffed Ian's legs before caressing them with his body. "My cat likes you," Gerry said, smiling. "And, sure, I can give you some cat food. I just bought a big bag."

Doug appeared, holding Dot. "Hi, Ian, how's it going?"

Ian mumbled a reply.

Dot pointed at Ian and said, "Da-Da."

Gerry said, "Don't mind her—she's calling everybody Da-Da lately, remember?"

"I don't mind," he said faintly. He looked exhausted.

"I'm going to give Ian a bit of food for his cats," Gerry explained to Doug.

"Oh, sure. I'll drive you home, Ian. Save you the wear and tear on your boots."

All three looked at Ian's footwear, and an awkward pause followed as they collectively realized the boots had long outlived their usefulness.

"Will you stay for a cup of tea?" Gerry offered.

He shook his head. "Gotta get back to the cats."

"I know the feeling," Gerry said ruefully. "They do complain when meals are late, don't they?"

Five minutes later, Doug and Ian drove off, with most of the new sack of kibble, and as much tinned human food as Gerry could cram into a plastic bag along with a loaf of bread.

When Doug returned, he looked grim. "It's not right, Ger. There but for the grace of God, you know? I helped him lug the stuff in, and he's got all these tarps layered over the tent and he's cooking over an open fire in a big metal container—" He gave her a tragic look. "I feel terrible, all warm and cozy here."

"I know, hon," she said hugging him. "When I fed the cats, I noticed your second-best pair of workboots were gone from the back porch. That was kind of you." He shrugged. "The ones one of the cats—and I'm naming no names but it probably begins with an 'M'—chewed on; one of the tongues was a bit raggedy. Where is Ian's tent, exactly? You said somewhere near Prudence's?"

"Up Station Road about halfway, a bit past her house and across the street. There's a phone company servitude. You just walk in."

"Huh. Oh, just so you know, we're out of bread. We can shop tomorrow."

But Doug remained unsettled, and she heard him muttering as they prepared supper together, "It's not right. It's just not right."

A week passed. Snow fell and drifted. Doug was kept busy ploughing driveways and shovelling out his older customers' walkways. And on Friday, Gerry took the train to work at the museum.

Perhaps, given the freezing rain—which turned the drive to the station into a cautious creep and even slowed the train—she would have been better off staying home.

The Montreal sidewalks were dangerously slippery. Sometimes she walked along the edge of the road where grit and salt gave her boots some grip—but also put her at risk from irate motorists and bus drivers.

With some relief, she settled at her workbench. Today's task was to continue applying bole on top of gesso on mostly flat surfaces between the frame's many intricately carved raised ornaments. The ornaments—the bees, the honeysuckle, lotus and lily blossoms, the bay leaves—would receive different treatments. Precision was required. She'd been working for about ten minutes when the lights went out. She looked up in dismay.

The room had plenty of natural light from windows and skylights. Gerry glanced uncertainly at her boss Susan One, who sighed and got on the phone. Then she said, "All right, ladies, we wait an hour, then we go home. Protocol. Insurance, workplace safety—you know."

They worked on.

Shortly after 10:00 am, Gerry found herself standing on the well-salted museum steps with many hours to kill before the next train back to Lovering. Bertie hadn't made the trip in that day, so she couldn't go hang out at his nearby antiques shop. And the elevator at Marion's apartment building probably wouldn't be running. There was no way she would be hiking up nineteen floors!

She decided the train station was her best bet. Perhaps there were backup generators there and she could keep warm. The freezing rain rattled on surfaces around her as she made her way gingerly back to the station. She bought a coffee, and a sandwich for later, and sat down to sketch some *Mug the Bug* ideas. An hour passed and she was eying the sandwich when she heard "The crooked heart / leaning, tilted / pumped and smiled / still pumps and smiles– / crooked little heart." A little piece of paper was dropped in front of her.

After her initial start, Gerry listened to the poet, smiled and said, "Eeks! I've been poetry ambushed. Hi, Yvonne. Thank you for that. Join me?"

"Wait. Every customer gets two." Another little piece of paper joined the first. Yvonne added in a lower tone, "If they wait around after the first one." She recited the second poem from memory. "So many odd dreams, the strangest: the butter dish, a glass rectangle, backing out the driveway, a full-sized vehicle of some sort, because, I suppose, the butter wanted to go for a drive." She grinned.

Gerry hooted. "Surreal! I love it! Do you require payment in food like before, or cash?"

Yvonne looked at Gerry's sandwich. "When's your train?"

Gerry grimaced. "Not until 3:30, I'm afraid."

"Why don't you come over to my apartment? We can do better than a cold sandwich. I've got a gas stove. It'll be warmer than this drafty place. And you can meet Wanda."

Imagining Wanda to be Yvonne's partner and always up for an adventure, Gerry agreed. After all, the woman knew or had known Blaise. And Gerry was curious. "Okay. Is it far?"

"From here? Usually, no, but with the power out, we'll have to walk to the bus instead of taking the Metro."

Gerry stuck out a foot. "Fortunately, I wore my winter hiking boots, so I should be good." It was only as they began their trek that Gerry wondered, what on earth will we talk about? She began with the weather: "At least freezing rain brings a milder temperature, eh?"

"I like the cold," said Yvonne, striding briskly. "Lets me know I'm still alive."

"Before I had my daughter," Gerry confided, "I cross-country skied and snowshoed. Now I just pull her sled."

"Soon she'll be able to ski with you."

"I hadn't thought of that. She's just started walking."

There was a pause. "So, what brings you downtown?" asked Yvonne.

"I'm doing an apprenticeship at the museum. In art conservation and restoration. Only one day a week but it's fascinating."

Yvonne grunted. "I bet."

They walked up the hill from the train station and turned east, passing the gates of McGill University. "Not too far now," said Yvonne.

"What neighbourhood do you live in, Yvonne?"

"Well, they call it Mile End now but when I first moved there, we just called it the Plateau."

"You and Wanda?"

Yvonne laughed. "No. Long before Wanda. I moved there when I got married in 1976."

Adjusting to the possibility of there being a husband as well as Wanda, Gerry asked, "And have you been in the same apartment all that time?"

"Yup. Look—the freezing rain has turned to real rain."

Both were getting soaked, but Gerry hadn't really noticed, concentrating as she was on not slipping. Yvonne stopped at a corner. "And here's our bus. As ordered." She showed a pass as Gerry fumbled for change. The bus was half empty. When Yvonne took a single seat, Gerry took the one behind her.

The bus trundled up Park Avenue, soon leaving the downtown, built-up area. The expanse of Mount Royal Park rose to the left, a grey-white mass, its woods masked by mist. The park ended and a commercial/residential mix of buildings presented itself; they passed a gas station and a movie theatre, but mostly attached brick apartment buildings, low-rises, some with shops on their ground floors.

When they got to Saint Viateur, Yvonne rose from her seat and exited. Gerry quickly followed. "Let's get some bagels," Yvonne said. They crossed Saint Viateur and Gerry smelled heaven. They joined the queue in the tiny bakery. The brick wood-fired oven was aglow and the room toasty warm. Yvonne quipped with the workers as she ordered two black and two white, which Gerry observed meant two poppyseed and two sesame seed. She bought six of each to take back to Lovering where the only bagels available were a sad commercial travesty of the real thing.

They jaywalked across Saint Viateur to get back to Park Avenue and continued a few buildings south of the bus stop. Yvonne stopped. "We're here." Here was a small laundromat with a steep staircase to one side. "*Merhaba*, Mr. Sydin." Yvonne waved at the balding man standing in the doorway looking anxiously out at the rain.

"No power, no customers," he said glumly.

"Tomorrow," Yvonne promised.

"Tomorrow," he echoed, turned and went inside.

"Hold on to the railing," Yvonne commanded. Gerry held. The steps were coated with at least an inch of ice, now made slick by the falling rain. Yvonne paused on a small porch and unlocked the door to the right. Gerry followed her up a flight of carpeted stairs. Yvonne unlocked another door. "Welcome."

Gerry stepped in as Wanda came to greet them.

11

"Hello, darling!" Yvonne said happily and clasped Wanda tightly. Wanda's tongue vibrated as she panted with joy. Fawn, with black face and ears, she was a perfect pug.

"Er, hello, Wanda," said Gerry, and scratched Wanda's head. Wanda closed her slightly bulging eyes. Gerry added, "I love dogs."

"Good!" said Yvonne. "Now you've been introduced, take off your stuff and I'll heat up some soup."

Gerry did as she was told, looking around at the apartment. Straight ahead and to the right was the L-shaped kitchen and eating area. On her left, the large living room was separated from the kitchen by an open series of built-in irregular shelves from floor to ceiling, upon some of which Yvonne had placed her pots and crocks, with more delicate ornaments higher up. Many houseplants were ranged in the living room's bay window, which overlooked Park Avenue. Gerry sat down at the cheap dinette set. The gas stove was lit, and shortly homemade lentil soup, sliced bagels, butter and cheese were set in front of her.

"I'm a vegetarian," Yvonne announced. "Forty years now."

"Wow," Gerry said politely, inwardly doubting she'd ever be able to eschew such delights as hamburgers and barbequed chicken. "That's great. And your soup is delicious." She looked down at Wanda who was politely looking up. Her short tail, curled closely to her rump, wagged hopefully.

"No food for Wanda, please. She's a svelte fifteen pounds and I want to keep it that way."

Like woman, like dog, thought Gerry. Without her coat, Yvonne was revealed to be youthfully slender. She'd dragged her shoulder-length grey-brown hair back from her face with a scrunchie and looked—almost—elegant.

"It's not hard to be a vegetarian in this neighbourhood. There's a health food store just past the bagel shop, an Italian bakery on the corner, and loads of restaurants: Greek, Mexican, Ethiopian, Indian, Chinese, Middle Eastern."

If she hadn't already been eating, Gerry was sure her mouth would be watering hearing the list of cuisines. "That's so great for you. I miss that—I grew up in Toronto—out in Lovering there isn't that much choice. There's Chinese and Indian, that's it."

They ate for a bit longer. "Your apartment is nice and warm, even with the power off."

Yvonne nodded. "Heat rises so I'll always be the warmest. I bet the radiators are still a little warm. Power's only been off a few hours. Tea or coffee?"

"Tea, please."

Yvonne made a pot and they moved to the living room. Wanda jumped onto the sofa next to her mistress so Gerry sat in a chair facing them and the bay window. Gerry noticed Wanda was only a bit bigger than her biggest cat.

"So," asked Yvonne, "what do you do when you're not restoring art or pulling your daughter through the snow?"

"I'm a cartoonist," replied Gerry, and went off on a tangent about *Mug the Bug* and her children's books, and about her longing for something more.

"And you think conservation might be the something more?"

"Not exactly, but it brings me closer to the fine art I feel I should be doing. I mean, cartooning is fine, but..." She let the pause extend before lamely concluding, "I just feel I want to *leave* something. Behind me. After I'm gone."

Yvonne nodded. "I get it. Time's breath, breathing down the back of your neck."

"Is that a quote?"

"Not really; I'm paraphrasing a saying. You know—when people say something like 'My mother is breathing down my neck about homework.' Or, 'My boss is breathing down my neck to finish that project.' So, when time, or mortality pressures you, it can be intense. I feel it. As if I have to get as many poems as possible published before…"

The pause extended a few beats before Gerry asked, "Have you published a lot? I mean, I don't know how it works for poets. Blaise has published a few books and he still submits poems to magazines. And he's ninety-five!"

"Does he? Good for him." Yvonne rose. "Let me show you my library."

She led Gerry to a small room off the side of the living room. An easy chair and a narrow desk with a typewriter were surrounded by bookcases. A filing cabinet stood next to the desk. "I mostly write sitting on the sofa, but here is where I get organized. And here are my publications." She gestured to a couple of shelves next to the desk. "Magazines, anthologies, chapbooks."

"Impressive," Gerry said, admiringly. "But what's a chapbook?"

Yvonne handed her a slim volume, its binding a piece of wool threaded through two holes in the cover's spine. "One or more poets put together some poems, too few for a book, and make a chapbook. Some poets don't bother with them, but I've done a few. It's mostly only other poets who read poetry. And we read to each other at events."

"Interesting," Gerry said politely.

Yvonne fiddled with a folder on her desk. "Look," she began. "I like you. But could I ask you to do me a huge favour?"

"If I can," Gerry said cautiously.

"Take these poems and show them to your friend, Blaise Parminter. Ask him what he thinks. My phone number is in the file, if he feels like calling me."

"I don't know," Gerry said slowly. "He's getting frailer, it seems to me."

"I'd appreciate it," Yvonne pleaded. "And if he doesn't have anything to say about the collection, that's okay. I won't have lost anything."

"Then, sure." Gerry took the poems. "How long will it take me to get back to the train station?"

"Better allow an hour." She smiled. "The buses aren't necessarily always on time, but it's 2:30, so plenty of time to catch your train. I hope your coat has dried out a bit."

"It has. Goodbye, Wanda. It's been nice to meet you."

"Be careful on the outside stairs," Yvonne called as Gerry let herself out.

As she stared out the bus window at the rain, she realized that after the first brief mention, Yvonne hadn't talked about her husband at all. But neither had Gerry about Doug. Or the cats.

"Wake up, sleepyhead. It's your birthday."

As Doug kissed the top of her head—the only part of her not wrapped in the warm cocoon of bed covers—Gerry murmured, "Mmph," and snuggled in deeper. She felt the bodies of some of her cats nestled close, and she hoped their warmth would help her go back to sleep.

Doug said in sing-song tones, "I brought you a present."

There was a soft thump as something heavy landed on the bed, followed by the sensation of someone poking at Gerry's head. The pressure from the cats ceased—they had presumably leapt to safety. They knew better than to compete with the "present."

"Ow. Let me guess. Does it weigh eighteen pounds?" She uncovered her face and squinted in the bright winter morning light. "Does it have red curls?" Dot laughed. Gerry's arms suddenly shot out of the bed and grabbed her. "Does it want a wrestling match?" They rolled around giggling as Doug watched. Gerry sang a nonsense song. "I'm rolling the kitty! Rolling the kitty! I'm rolling the kitty! Roll, roll, roll!"

Gerry sat up. Dot, on all fours, prowled the bed, meowing. Doug commented, "I guess it was inevitable—our daughter thinks she's a cat."

"She's pretending! What's for breakfast?"

"Bacon. And eggs. Maybe croissants. Or toast. Or bagels. You coming?" He gathered Dot up. She meowed in his ear. "I already fed the cats."

"Thank you, sir. Yeah. Just give me ten minutes, okay?" She sank back down onto her pillow and thought, wow! Twenty-eight years old! Two more years and I'll be thirty! Eeks!

A cat jumped onto the bed, circled, kneaded, then curled up near her feet. Gerry half sat up. "Monkey? You never come up here. What's up?"

Low and guttural, "A-woo-oo-oo-oo-oo" came from its throat. Gerry's hair stood on end. The cat began to retch, and, before Gerry could jump up and remove her, threw up on the bed.

"Argh!" Gerry shot upright—just as Monkey began retching on the bedside carpet, then in the hallway. Gerry rushed after her, trying to contain the damage. Halfway down the stairs, the cat stopped abruptly and began grooming herself. Gerry sat on the step beside her and watched. "Are you done?"

Monkey blinked and hopped slowly down the rest of the stairs. After waiting and listening for a few more minutes, Gerry returned upstairs to begin the cleanup.

After three years living with many cats, she was a pro. A little more than ten minutes later she slid into her chair for breakfast.

Dot was eating scrambled eggs, a dish she relished, with her fingers. Doug brought coffee. "Here you are, birthday girl. What kept you?"

"Cat puke," she said between bites of toast and bacon.

"Yum," he said lightly. "Who?"

"Monkey. Again. Little pieces of white stuff mixed in. Could be plastic. I dunno."

"She's certainly a gourmet. Dot—in your mouth, love, not your eye." He wiped her face.

Monkey entered the room and took up her usual position by the back wall near the curtain.

"She looks a little thin," said Gerry.

"I'm not surprised if she's eating garbage instead of food."

"Maybe she needs to go to the vet," Gerry replied, reaching a hand down to her pet. "Eh, Munks? You sick? I wonder how old she is."

Doug shrugged. "Check Maggie's files. Now, do you have room for more coffee?"

"Yes, please!"

After breakfast, dishes, dressing Dot, and cleaning the cat boxes—chores Gerry and Doug shared—Gerry went upstairs to check on the bedspread in the washing machine. She transferred it to the dryer, threw a load of clothes into the washer, and headed to her office—one of three small rooms that had once served as bedrooms for the house's servants. In the old days when there *had* been servants.

She pulled out the cat files her aunt had kept, which contained itemized descriptions, behaviours, dates of visits to the vet, adoption details and ages. "M, M, M," murmured Gerry. "Jinx, Kitty-Cat, Lightning, Marigold—aw, Marigold." She paused, thinking of her aunt's favourite at the time of her death, a petite calico with an iron will who'd only survived Maggie by a few months, but had made her way into Gerry's heart. Gerry moved to the next card. "Oh, man, this is hard." The next card belonged to another deceased cat, Min-Min, a gentle soul, who'd died when Gerry was pregnant. "How about," she murmured, "I put the files of you dead cats at the back. That way, I won't have to feel sad every time I look in here. Not that I'll forget you."

Next came Monkey's file—not much to read. Born in 1999, she would turn seven sometime this year. She had been adopted from CRAS at the age of one. CRAS—short for Cat Rescue and Adoption Society—was a group Gerry had occasionally been involved with, donating both time and money. Her cat Seymour, with his single eye, velvety black coat, and sweet disposition, had also come from CRAS.

Then, at the bottom of Monkey's single page file, Gerry read in her Aunt Maggie's neat grade-four-level cursive—"Trouble."

"'Trouble'?" Gerry said to herself. "How trouble? You couldn't have been a little more specific, Aunt Maggie?"

She returned downstairs to the den where Doug was reading yesterday's big weekend paper while Dot watched cartoons and played with her toys. "I'm going to dash over to Blaise's. He said to visit him on my birthday."

"Dash away," Doug said absently.

"I'm doing a load of laundry—if you could shift it into the dryer in about half an hour?"

"Got it." He looked up at her. "Sorry, I'm distracted." He showed her the page he was looking at. "I'm engrossed in this serious stuff." The page was, of course, the comics.

"Bye, nuts," she said. "I love you."

She let herself out the front door, Yvonne's poetry file tucked under her arm. Unlike in other seasons, when she simply cut across her and Blaise's backyards, winter made the road the safer option—especially today, with Friday's ice now frozen solid and hidden beneath a layer of fresh snow, creating treacherous conditions for walking. At least the road had been salted.

Blaise let her in with a joyful cry of "Gerry! Happy Birthday! Come in! Come in!" His cats—Graymalkin and Ariel—hovered in the background, but after they'd recognized Gerry, they came forward.

"And how are the two luckiest cats in the world?" Gerry asked.

"They're fine. Just fine."

They settled by the electric fireplace in the large living room. The remnant of Blaise's breakfast was on a tray by his easy chair. "I live in front of the fire in winter."

"Don't we all," Gerry replied. "Or we'd like to. I was in Montreal when the power went off on Friday and took a long walk in the freezing rain to get to a friend's apartment. It was quite uncomfortable. The walk, I mean, not the apartment.

"Remember I said I'd met another poet? And that she knew you? From long ago when you used to go to Montreal for poetry readings?"

He thought for a moment, then appeared to remember. "Yes. What was the name?"

"Yvonne Punt. That was the friend. She lives in a third-floor flat in Mile End, at the corner of Park Avenue and Saint Viateur. She has a really nice pug named Wanda."

"A rug? Named Wanda?"

Gerry raised her voice slightly. "Sorry. Did I say rug? I meant to say pug. A pug dog. Anyway, Yvonne gave me this." She put the file on his lap. "It's full of poems, and she wondered…"

"My, it's a long time since anyone asked me to look at their poems." The former English teacher beamed and opened the file. "Let me see—table of contents, about a hundred pages. Well, if I do a poem a day, I might be finished by May. I hope she's not in a hurry."

Gerry smiled at him. "I didn't get that impression. Just anxious to publish."

He nodded. "I know the feeling. For most of us poets, no one cares about our poems once we're dead. So we flog them relentlessly while we're still alive. At least I do."

Gerry nodded. "That's more or less what Yvonne said—that only other poets are interested in poetry."

He laughed. "Well, some others read it, but she's almost right. Do you require tea, Gerry?"

"I just had breakfast, Blaise, but I'll make a pot. Why not?"

When she returned, a package had appeared where she'd been sitting—a package and a cat: Ariel was busy trying to untie the ribbon. "The woman in the gift shop wrapped it for me," Blaise said. "Ariel, leave the ribbon alone. She can't resist anything stringlike."

Gerry gently lifted Ariel onto Blaise's lap. Graymalkin, who was already wedged next to one of Blaise's thin thighs, batted his companion half-heartedly on her rump. Ariel opened her mouth in a silent fake snarl and settled comfortably, but still keeping an eye on the ribbon.

Gerry, wise to the problems ingested ribbon could cause cats, put the temptation into her pocket, opened the smallish box and carefully unfolded the tissue inside. A ceramic sparrow perched on a lump of green looked cheekily up at her.

Blaise spoke: "I liked his expression. He looks a bit of a rogue. And he makes me think of that psalm: '"Yea, the sparrow hath found an house, and the swallow a nest for herself, where she may lay her young."'

"It's beautiful, Blaise. Thank you. And so is the psalm. I guess I'm a sparrow or a swallow, eh? That would make a nice name for a house—The Swallows' Nest."

"I'm glad you like it. Put The Swallows' Nest in one of your books. Now, let's drink our tea."

When she got home, Gerry placed the sparrow on the windowsill in front of her artist's table. It was too late to go this Sunday, but the words of the psalm lingered in her mind, and she resolved to attend church soon. Perhaps she'd take Dot and explore Sunday school.

Around one they headed over to the Parsley Inn for lunch. They'd decided to chance it with Dot after all. Doug, in particular, had urged the reluctant Gerry to give it a go. The owner, Phil Parsley, seated them in a corner by windows overlooking the frozen lake. On a little island not far from shore, someone had stuck a Christmas tree and decorated it. As she strapped Dot into the high chair and offered her a breadstick, Gerry said, "I guess we're segregated because of you-know-who. Far away from other diners."

"Mm," said Doug and opened the menu.

Looking around, Gerry saw one of Doug's neon artworks mounted on the wall over the long buffet table. She pointed and said, "Oh, that's nice; I didn't know they put it there in the winter."

Usually, the piece adorned the inn's lawn down by the water.

"Yeah," Doug replied, looking pleased. "And the newest one is in the bar."

"Really? I'll go look in a minute."

Soon enough, Gerry realized the real reason they'd been seated in the corner: friends and family began arriving, and amidst laughter and chatter, began filling the nearby tables—some of which they pushed together. Prudence and Bertie came first, followed by Cathy, Bea, and Cece. Then came Doug's sons and James's girlfriend, Julia. Gerry was greeted with warm hugs, kisses, and gifts. The last to arrive were her Aunt Mary and her boyfriend, Ed.

Everyone ordered their drinks and meals, and that corner of the restaurant quickly turned into a party. People stood with drinks beside one another's tables, chatting and laughing, while

Dot—clearly eager to be in the thick of the action—was passed around and taken for little walks by everyone in turn.

Gerry had her favourite hamburger (okay, one of them)—the one with blue cheese and caramelized onions—and then sauntered into the bar to visit Gregory, one of her former kittens and sibling to Jay. He'd been adopted by Phil Parsley, the inn's owner. She found the cat reclining on the bar counter and gave him a scratch on the head while exchanging pleasantries with Phil. Behind the bar, Doug's neon art was on display: orange, red, and pink segments blinked in a slow, intricate progression. Gerry had only ever seen it in the drawing stage before.

Back on the restaurant side, and after congratulating Doug on his work, she was just about to ask what was for dessert when two of Phil's four teenaged kids (all of whom worked in the family business) entered the room pushing a trolley with a large flat chocolate cake, ablaze with candles. While everybody, including the restaurant's other patrons, sang "Happy Birthday," Doug leaned over and whispered in her ear, "Happy Birthday, love. Prudence made the cake."

She gave him a big kiss and whispered back, "I'm so lucky." She and Dot blew out the candles together and cake ensued.

"Best birthday ever," Gerry announced to the crowd. As she opened her gifts, she thought of Blaise and the ceramic sparrow in her studio, its head cocked, bright eyes looking upward.

PART 3

PRUE

Gerald Coneybear moved listlessly from room to room of the house he'd called home so long ago. The house he'd left in disgrace in his twenties. The house he'd taken for granted would be his one day, until his father had told him otherwise. The house he'd brought his wife home to only after his parents had died; the house inherited by his youngest sister Maggie. And, later, brought Deborah and young Gerry to when she, Deborah, was dying—steadily, slowly dying from ovarian cancer.

He'd thought he'd been done with the place after that. He hadn't gone back to Lovering after Deborah died in Toronto. He'd done his best with Gerry, but any zest for life he might have had, had gone with Deborah.

It had been hard to live through the eight years after her passing, though he'd tried to be cheerful whenever in contact with Gerry; to boost her whenever she seemed down; to cheer when she found commercial success with her first comic strip; to stifle whatever disappointment he felt that she hadn't taken a more classically creative path. Drawing cartoons seemed such a waste of time.

But secretly, he'd been counting the days. He sometimes neglected to take his insulin or to eat properly. He wasn't heartbroken, just so damned tired. Of trying to please people, of his many mistakes. And Gerry didn't really need him. So—he just—let go.

He'd felt bad she'd been the one to find him. With detachment, he'd watched her stunned reaction, tears. But dying hadn't seemed real; his apathy continued after death. And in the time after, it seemed he was stuck with it.

And then his child gave birth to her daughter, and he wasn't present in the flesh to be a part of their lives. And he felt regret.

He paused in front of one of Gerry's landscape paintings, the one in which two wolves pause, their moonlit tracks on snow showing they've just crossed the frozen lake. They stand by the edge of a road, their yellow eyes gleaming as they look at the beholder. Why didn't she do more of this, he wondered?

He looked down at the little cat who seemed, of all the cats in the house, to be the most attuned to him. "Well, whatever your name is—Dot calls you Trouble, doesn't she?—well, Trouble, whatever you do, don't take life for granted, or slight it. Because the afterlife is just that: after life. And there's really nothing satisfying about it. Not for me, anyway."

He thought of some of the others, spirits who seemed content to flit around the house; Maggie, anchored by the place itself and her many cats, some alive, some dead; and Deborah, now unwilling to leave the house which cradled not only her daughter but her granddaughter. Their emotions ran in straight lines where his—his were conflicted. Staying where he'd so spectacularly disappointed, failed, hurt, and been hurt. But going was no longer, or at least not yet, an option. Not until—

He paused outside what had been his bedroom. He was aware of the child asleep within. He looked down at Trouble. "Now listen, cat, here's what I need you to do."

Ian felt bad. He usually felt bad—negativity was just how he operated, he reflected. But when people were nice to him, like that couple had recently been—giving him a huge sack of cat food, plus their own food and a pair of winter workboots—for some reason he felt worse.

He stared up at his roof. Smoke made the air hazy. He felt his cats ranged at his sides, all of them keeping each other and him warm. Home heating partly running on a six cat-power engine, he thought affectionately.

He knew what it was: he felt guilty about the thefts. Not the actual taking—he'd taken what he needed—the tarps, the bowl for *a fireplace, the money to make up the shortfall at the bank—but the breaking in. He knew that was a violation. That meant hours of aggravation for people as they repaired broken locks and window glass. He regretted the inconvenience he'd caused.*

But if that bastard at the bank hadn't been so… He shut down the humiliating memory of losing control, of being manhandled out of the building. Of people staring. Always staring. At weird Ian, going mental.

There was less money in his account each month—he knew it. No matter how they tried to explain it away, no matter how often they told him he was imagining things, he wasn't. He had less to spend. It ran out before the next deposit. He wasn't imagining it. Or was he? He sometimes didn't know what day it was, and in winter, the days all blended into a white continuous hell. If he had to choose between the cold of winter, the short dark days, and the heat and mosquitoes of summer, he'd vote for summer every time. Maybe his black moods were getting the better of him, making difficult what most people could manage—the simple fact of surviving.

But he hadn't imagined what he'd seen one of the nights he'd been skulking around Lovering in the dark looking for an opportunity to break in somewhere. Cash—he was always short of cash.

He'd been across the street from the seniors' residence, screened by a row of shrubs that edged the lawn of a café. He'd watched a van slowly pull into the entrance to the retirement home, reverse, then back up to the main door. A person got out of the van, then another, then another. One of them went in to the glassed-in vestibule where the residents' names were printed next to their call buttons. He must have pressed a button and been buzzed in because he then opened the inside door.

Whoever it was beckoned to the others. One of them brought something to wedge the inner door open. Ian moved closer, taking cover between parked cars. That's when he saw all three were wearing balaclavas. They entered the building. Two of them came out several times, dragging rolled-up rugs and loading them into the van.

Thieves, he'd thought—like me—and never considered raising an alarm. He'd noticed how their movements grew quicker, more furtive, as all three struggled to drag and lift the final rug.

He remembered how, as the van shot past his hiding spot, one of the passengers pulled off his balaclava, turned, and looked straight into Ian's astonished face

12

"I think I know what Monkey was eating that last time she threw up," Doug said, holding out his hand.

Gerry prepared herself to recoil. She was surprised to see a strip of white plastic. She handled it. Bendy. "Yeah, I guess if that was chewed up into little bits, that could be it. What is it?"

"Follow me."

He led her to the downstairs bathroom, where the cats' seven litter boxes were lined up along one wall. No one in the household used the downstairs tub anymore; with that many litter boxes, the room had long since been abandoned as a bathing space in favour of the fresher-smelling upstairs bathroom. The tub served as storage—currently holding several sealed boxes of fresh cat litter.

"Look," Doug said, pointing down.

Gerry peered. There, where the pale green tub met the beige floor tiles, was a gap in the caulking. "Seriously?" she asked.

He nodded and pressed the piece he held back into place. It filled part of the gap. "I think so. She was just leaving the room when I came in. And it gets better, or worse, I mean." He drew back the shower curtain.

Gerry's eyebrows went up. "Good grief!" Here the damage was extensive. Obviously, Monkey had been at work for some time on the bathtub caulking where it met the tiled wall. "The little monkey! Now I know why Aunt Maggie noted 'Trouble' at the bottom of her file."

"It's easy to fix, but will she just do it again?" asked Doug.

"I'm calling the vet," Gerry announced. "Enough is enough."

So, the following Monday—while the Markovs cleaned The Maples—Gerry found herself at the veterinary hospital with Dot, watching as one of the two partners examined Monkey. Dot sat quietly in Gerry's arms, gravely observant.

Gerry concluded the list of substances—wood, paper, wax crayons, caulking—known to have been ingested by Monkey by saying, "And I think she's lost weight."

"Hm," said Dr. Perry, a roundish middle-aged man who exuded calm. He probed with gentle fingers. "She *is* thin. Not dangerously, though. Does she go out?"

"I don't let the cats out in winter," Gerry said with an inner sigh. It was already the first week of March, and in Lovering, winter still held on—while in Toronto's milder climate, she knew, the buds would be starting to swell. She shifted Dot to the other hip. "Our neighbour's cat was attacked by a fisher one winter, so I keep them in."

"I remember that; I operated on him. Big grey cat." He ran his hand down Monkey's spine. "So we can rule out worms then. Making her thin. You *did* worm her last fall?"

Gerry nodded. "Her and the other eighteen!" This yearly task, accompanied by much chasing (by Gerry) and much running and foaming at the mouth (by the cats) had to be one of her least favourite cat-related duties.

Dr. Perry smiled and put Monkey on the scale. "Does she eat?"

Gerry frowned. "It's hard to tell. There are so many of them. But I count them when they're feeding—I was told my aunt used to do that—and no, nobody has been missing at mealtimes."

She looked around for the room's one chair and sat down; her arms were tired from holding Dot, who, having been uncharacteristically silent, now took her finger out of her mouth and said, "Ba, ba. Da-da. Tubble," before reinserting the digit.

Dr. Perry looked admiringly in her direction. "Somebody's almost talking. How old is she?"

For a moment Gerry felt confused. "You mean Dot? She's fourteen months."

"My daughter was chatting away at eighteen months." He regarded Monkey for a few more seconds. "What I'd like to do is keep her in—just overnight. Do some blood tests and get a reliable stool sample." He grinned. "Unless you want to loiter near her litter box and hope you grab the right lump."

Gerry grinned back. "I guess I'll pass on that. Okay. So...I pick her up tomorrow?"

He nodded and lifted the cat, who began to struggle. "Anytime."

They left the examining room and Dr. Perry disappeared with Monkey. It must have dawned on Dot that they'd lost one of their crew, as she began shrieking and stiffening in Gerry's arms. It was with a red face that Gerry left the building.

"It's okay, Dot, it's okay," she kept repeating as she tried to strap Dot into her car seat. One of Dot's booted feet flew up, catching Gerry in the lip. "Ow," Gerry said flatly, holding the lip. Dot calmed, went limp, and by the time they'd reached home, was asleep.

The day had begun sunny and cold, but as the afternoon passed, Gerry noticed clouds moving in. Snow began falling at teatime and Dot fell asleep again on the sofa in the den. Gerry wedged her in with a couple of pillows, got a mug of Earl Grey and *The Candy King* and sat next to her on the sofa to continue where she'd left off.

All would have been well if it hadn't been for Kevin the Corgi.

For the first and second days of William's sidewalk candy shop, Kevin, a hound even more low-slung than Prince Charles, kept his distance, accompanying his lady on her daily shopping, waiting obediently outside the various commercial establishments of Bubbly-Sauceton.

On the third day, Kevin's business brought him to the cobbler—the matter of a slightly chewed boot to be repaired. The cobbler's shop was next to The Furtive Beagle. Kevin's mistress gave William a smile and went into the cobbler's. Kevin sat down and looked at William and the prince through slitty eyes, panting a little. "Soooo, Charles, what's all this?" he asked slowly.

A patron of the pub came out onto the pub's front step, consulted with William, made his purchase with a laugh, and walked away, his candy wrapper rustling. Both dogs' ears twitched at the enticing sound. They caught a whiff of peppermint.

Charles lifted his head, which had been resting on the pavement, and said gloomily, "Commerce." He repositioned his nose between his paws and sighed.

Kevin cocked his head to one side. "Commerce?"

Charles lifted his head again, but only by an inch or so. "High. Finance." Again, his chin met cement.

Kevin cocked his head to the other side. (His mistress always cooed 'How cute!' when he did this, and he was hoping it would have an effect on Charles. Or William.) He took in the scene. The boy sat quietly, counting coins first, then the number of candies remaining in a large bowl.

Kevin smirked. "Looks like a lot of fun. Not."

Charles just shifted his head so it pointed further away from Kevin's gaze. Kevin's lady came out of the cobbler's, bought a handful of sweets from William and put them in her purse. "Kevin, stay," she said, and entered the pub.

"I'm staying, I'm staying," Kevin said rather peevishly and raised his front paws one by one as he rocked from side to side. Then he composed himself and lay down near Charles.

"All right there, Kevin?" William said kindly. Kevin's response was to yawn. William went back to taking inventory.

"So, Charles," Kevin said quietly, "is he going to give us any?"

Charles paused, then said painfully, "No."

"No?" Kevin sounded astonished.

"No." Charles looked around then whispered, "He doesn't even eat it himself."

"You're kidding. Why not?"

Mournfully, Charles said, "Profits."

"Profits?"

"Profits."

The dogs contemplated how profits, whatever they were, could be better than eating candy. The concept continued to elude them. All Kevin could think to say was, "Too bad." He edged a bit closer to Charles. "Say. Charles. You ever think of, ah, *stealing* the candy?"

Charles lifted his head abruptly and said in a growl, "Stealing? Stealing William's candy?" His fur bristled along his spine.

Kevin sat up then stood. Though it scarcely made any difference in his height.

"What is it, Charles? Why are you growling at Kevin?" asked a bewildered William.

At that moment, barn cats—Big Eyes, Middy and Tigs, and some of their relatives— sauntered around the corner of the pub. They weren't sure why William had suddenly developed this urge to hang out in front of the pub instead of in the back and were eager to satisfy their curiosity.

Charles staggered to his feet.

"Heh, heh," said Kevin. "I didn't mean *steal* steal. I meant just kind of nudge the bowl a bit, so the candies fall on the ground, sort of."

As Charles continued growling, Kevin began to back up. Thinking to distract his erstwhile friend, he pretended he'd just noticed the cats.

"Oh, look, Charles, cats. Let us give chase. Tally ho. Forthwith and anon. Toodle—"

But Kevin never got the chance to say "pip" for Charles was bugling. "You-oo-oo-oo-oo," breath. "Cuh-uh-uh-uh-uh," breath. "M. Oh-oh-oh-oh-ver-rr-rr-rr," breath. "Heerrrrrre!" breath. "To-oo-oo-oo," breath. (Well, you get the idea.)

Incensed at Kevin's daring to impugn Charles's fidelity to William (even if he didn't share the candy), Charles sang the loudest, longest song the environs of The Furtive Beagle had ever been exposed to.

Kevin cowered. The cats' ears went back but they were nevertheless enthralled. People popped their heads out of windows. Passing motorists slowed. A lady on a bicycle braked so hard she almost fell off. Pub patrons spilled out the front door, holding their pints, their sandwiches. And finally, William's parents emerged, red-faced.

"Right!" said his mother, snatching up the bowl of candy. "The shop—is—*closed*!"

Kevin's owner snapped on his leash and Kevin dragged her home as fast as he could. Charles subsided into a tired, thirsty puddle of a dog, and then William, accompanied by his drooping canine and herd of excited cats, sadly dragged the bits of wood that had been his store back behind the pub and into the barn. Tigs wove his body between William's legs.

"Oh, Tigs," said William plaintively, "it was going so well."

"Never mind," purred Tigs. "Perhaps they'll let you get a paper route instead."

And that's exactly what happened.

THE END

Gerry couldn't believe it; she'd actually finished her book. Well, the text anyway. She'd do the illustrations as she could find time, fitting them in between her other obligations.

On the sofa next to her Dot stirred. "Dot! Dot! Mommy finished her book! Yippee!" Dot stretched and smiled sleepily at her mother. "Hungry, sweetie? Oh, my goodness! Look at the time! We better start thinking about supper, eh? Want some lovely macaroni? That's fast. Come on. Let's get it all ready for Daddy when he comes home."

After feeding the cats—and while they were still eating—Gerry dragged Dot's high chair into the kitchen doorway, plopped her in, and handed her a little pot and a wooden spoon. Dot took turns stirring imaginary macaroni as Gerry stirred hers, and serenading her mother (and the cats) with her improvised instruments. Meanwhile, Gerry peered out the kitchen window at the snow piling up on and around her car. She wondered where Doug was. If he was going to be late, he usually phoned her.

To the melody of "The wheels on the bus go round and round," she sang, "Daddy must be plowing snow, plowing snow, plowing snow," winding up with the refrain from "All Through the Night."

"I think I blended two songs, there, Dot." She added some frozen broccoli to the pot of boiling pasta and got a jar of pesto out of the fridge. "Protein, protein," she muttered, then brightened: she opened a can of tuna and grated a small mountain of cheese, giving Dot a lump on which to gnaw.

The cats, unaccustomed to so much activity during their suppertime, grew excited—and by the time Gerry drained the pasta and began scraping tuna from the tin, they were feverish.

"This was a mistake," she hollered, "letting you guys stay in here while I'm cooking! Shoo! Shoo!" She moved Dot's high chair back a bit and put the tub of cat kibble near the table in the next room. Some of the cats followed the kibble; some followed their noses, jumping on the counter near the tuna and cheese.

"Aaagh!" said Gerry, grabbing cat bodies and plopping them on the floor.

"Aaagh!" said Dot, imitating her mother and dropping her pot and spoon likewise on the floor.

The kitchen phone on the wall next to the fridge rang. "Yes!?" Gerry said as she continued to sweep cats from the counter.

It was Doug. "Hello, Ger." He sounded awfully quiet.

Gerry hissed at Winnie, who had his head in the pot of pasta and tuna, and the cat was so surprised, he leapt off the counter and out of the kitchen.

"Did you just hiss at me?" Doug said in surprise.

"I'm defending our supper," said his mate.

"Uh. About that. I'm going to be late."

Only now did she realize that he sounded quite miserable. "Why, what's wrong, hon? Are you working?"

"Well, I was. Now I'm at Prudence's."

"Prudence's?"

"Yeah. Actually, I parked in front of her place and went to bring Ian some food and stuff, and—"

"Doug?"

His voice cracked as he told her. "Gerry, Ian's dead."

13

Gerry gently applied gold size to one of the eagle's wings, her gaze focused intently. Sue Two leaned over for a closer look.

"Good. Just do a few inches at a time. Wait!" Gerry had been reaching for a sheet of gold leaf. "It takes about fifteen minutes for gold size to dry to the right stickiness. Just enough time to clean your brush. It's hell to get off if it hardens. Want a tea?"

Gerry nodded as she rinsed the glue off her brush. Sue, middle-aged, comfortably plump, pushed her salt-and-pepper hair behind her ears and waited for the kettle to boil. "Any news about that poor fellow who died?"

Gerry shook her head and frowned. Lost in her task, she'd forgotten all about Ian Murchison, beaten to death in his shack in the woods. It had cast a pall over the people of Lovering, in particular Gerry and Doug.

She looked down at the emperor's frame. What did it matter—applying gold leaf to plaster and wood—when some people (like Ian) were so vulnerable? Never had she felt so strongly that art was useless in the "real" world.

Sue brought over their tea. "I put your milk and sugar in."

"Thanks." Gerry sipped. "Hey," she said, leaning over her work table, "it's changing colour." The size was fading from bright white to a duller hue.

"Perfect," said Sue. "I'll do the first bit." She tore off a small corner from a square of gold leaf. "Your fingers must be dry," she murmured as she bent over, patting the leaf into place. "Otherwise, you'll be gilding yourself." She picked up a tiny brush and reversed it, using the rounded tip of its handle to push the leaf into crevices between the carved feathers. "Be sure to go gentle, or it'll tear." She leaned back. "You try."

Gerry copied Sue's actions. "You're a natural," Sue said. "Okay, I'll leave you to it."

Gerry finished that small section, applied size to the next, rinsed the brush, and drank her tea. Her thoughts drifted back to the previous Sunday.

A shaken Doug had returned home late that evening. As the one who'd discovered the body, the police were keen to question him. To Gerry he'd described parking in Prudence's driveway, telling her and Bertie he'd be there for only a few minutes while he took food to Ian, then crossing the road and walking into the woods.

Though it was after dark, the path in the snow had been easy to see. Doug had brought a loaf of bread, some canned soup and stew, and a sack of cat food. When he reached the tent, he'd called out: "Ian? It's Doug Shapland. Got some food for your cats." There'd been silence. A cat ran out of the shack and into the woods.

Doug opened the tent flap and called again. "Ian? You asleep, man? It's Doug." Two more cats fled into the darkness. He stepped in.

By the dull glow of a dying fire, Doug could see Ian lying on his back on the tarp that served as a floor. Blood was spattered across his face, head, and the tarp beneath him. A black cat, crouched at Ian's side, hissed. Doug knelt, putting a hand on Ian's chest. No motion. He removed one of his gloves and felt the skin on the side of Ian's face. Cold. Very cold. He stumbled away, back to Prudence and Bertie, and called the police.

Gerry and Doug had spent the following five days quietly, feeling guilty and sad. Ian's abode was a crime scene, but Doug had gone back every day to leave fresh cat kibble outside the police tape, assuming Ian's cats were still sheltering nearby, or perhaps in the tent itself. The plan was to catch the cats, but special traps were needed for that. Gerry had contacted her friends at the Cat Rescue and Adoption Society, scheduling Saturday for that operation.

"Six weeks until the exhibit opens," Sue Two called from her bench. "Still lots to do."

Gerry took this as a gentle rebuke for daydreaming and settled in for the afternoon's work.

Meanwhile, back at The Maples, they were trying home therapy for Monkey, who had been diagnosed with pica—the compulsive eating of non-food items. Dr. Perry had found nothing physically wrong with her and suspected she was simply bored or sad.

Now, whenever one of the humans happened upon her, they initiated play, followed by praise and affectionate contact. So far, Monkey had remained impassive—deigning to extend an occasional paw when a toy mouse on a string came her way and seeming to tolerate caresses rather than enjoy them.

Saturday morning, as Doug wrestled a reluctant Dot into her snowsuit and boots, Gerry engaged in a bit of wannabe feline bonding, using that classic toy, the rolled-up ball of aluminum foil, whipping it in the direction of the sitting Monkey's front paws. The cat seemed more interested in observing the Doug-and-Dot interaction, which was punctuated with cries of "Dot, please!" and "Gah!"

Gerry got down on her hands and knees and approached the cat, batting the foil between her hands. Monkey tore her gaze away from Doug and Dot and pounced on the foil. She put it in her mouth and trotted away. Gerry followed, but bipedally.

Monkey, having reached the hall, restrained the ball with one paw while she tore little bits off of it. She didn't seem to find it appetizing, spitting out wet silver flecks.

Gerry pounced. "No, you don't! Oh my goodness, Monkey, you do make everything difficult!" She picked up the flecks, confiscated the ball and scooped up the cat. Kissing her on the head, she returned to the living room, where Dot was having a full-blown tantrum. Doug was ruefully holding his jaw.

"Kicked you with a boot, did she?" Gerry asked grimly.

"I'm afraid so. Well, obviously we can't take her like this."

Dot, red in the face, was thrashing and shrieking. Doug released her from the boots and the suit and she lurched away, plunking herself on the hearth rug and handling the blocks from which she'd been so rudely torn away.

Her parents exchanged a look. "Flip you for it," Doug suggested.

The winner of the coin toss, Gerry, was still chortling to herself as she backed her Mini onto Main Road. The look on Doug's face when he'd lost! Coin toss or not, she'd been determined that she should be the one to meet the intrepid members of CRAS. Cat trapping, she mused, and her mind slid sideways. Rabbits trapped for glue for art restoration; now feral cats for their own sakes. Or maybe the rabbits were raised for their skins domestically. On rabbit ranches? How big was the market for rabbit-derived glue, anyway?

She pulled into Prudence's driveway. There was no car, of course—on a Saturday, both Bertie and Prue would be at the café. She got out and hopped around in the cold. A medium-sized grey sedan slowly approached. Gerry waved. The car parked behind hers and she grinned as its two occupants, all bundled up against the cold, alighted.

"Hello! Thanks for helping me with this. Gosh!" She looked into the car's back seat where collapsed metal cages were stacked. "So many!"

The car's driver, a stout elderly woman named Jean Delamar, who ran CRAS almost single-handedly, replied. "Well, we may also catch a wild animal or two and we don't want to waste time. Not in winter."

"Hi, Gerry," said the other woman, middle-aged, small. She smiled pleasantly.

"Hi, Heather. Where's Miriam?"

Miriam was Heather's teenaged daughter and usually accompanied her mother at the cat-adoption events where they'd all met.

"Gerry, it's the weekend. She's sleeping in, of course."

"Of course," Gerry replied. "Silly me. And no doubt she's done this before. But it's my first cat safari! I'm excited!"

Jean pulled a sour face. "You won't be when you have to check the cages first thing every morning and then deal with what's inside. These aren't going to be your nice housebroken kitties, you know."

"Actually, I don't know," Gerry slowly responded as they unloaded the cages. "I mean, I don't know if Ian had some of the cats from when they were kittens. They may not be really feral."

Each grasping two cages, they crossed the road. Jean kept lecturing as they trudged the snowy path into the woods. "If you do catch one, absolutely no touching until it's been to the vet. And don't even bring it into your house, whatever you do—it might infect your cats with a virus. Well, will you look at that!"

They paused as they had reached Ian's shelter. Gerry, who'd only heard it described by Doug, looked around.

That there was a tent under the overlay of several tarps, she took on faith. What was obvious was that without Ian to remove fresh snow from its roof and sloping sides, the shack was collapsing under the weight.

"It's igloo-shaped," commented Heather.

"Someone lived here," Jean said, shaking her head. "Sometimes, I really don't know—" What she didn't know, she left unsaid, but the other two got the gist.

"I guess it's okay to cross under the police caution tape?" Gerry queried. "It's been about a week—"

Jean made the decision. "Well, I'm not going to leave trapped animals at the mercy of the elements, not when there's a structure that they've been used to calling home." She passed beneath the yellow tape with her two cages and entered the tent. Heather and Gerry followed.

Inside was sadder. Another tarp was half-draped over a filthy-looking nest of blankets and sleeping bags. Some suitcases, open, with clothes spilling out, occupied one corner. A large metal bowl mounted on a rock pedestal contained charred bits of wood.

Silently, they arranged the six traps on and around the bedding. Gerry watched as Heather held down the metal ramp inside one cage. Jean filled a shallow dish with kibble and handed it to her. Heather placed the food at the far end of the cage and removed her hand. "See," she said, "they have to step on the ramp to get to the food; it goes down, then when they step off it, it snaps back up. Trapped." They repeated the process, giving Gerry a chance to try her hand with the remaining five cages, then Heather went back to the car for the last two.

Gerry looked around. Ian had had tools: a saw, an axe, and—a large staple gun. "Oh," she said.

"What?" said Jean, busy preparing two more dishes of kibble.

"Oh, nothing, I just realized something. About Ian." Gerry looked more closely at Ian's "fireplace." The metal bowl looked like the same type of stainless steel one Prudence had upstairs in her bakery kitchen. "I think this is a mixer bowl."

"Yes? Ingenious use of it. He wasn't stupid, apparently." Jean nodded at one corner of the tent where there was a pile of paperback books.

"No," Gerry said slowly. "No, he wasn't that."

Heather returned and the women quickly set up the remaining traps.

"There," Jean huffed as she straightened. "Now, even if you catch a fox or something, there'll be the other cages, hopefully full of cats."

Gerry doubted a fox could fit into one of these cages but you never knew: if one was hungry enough, it might manage it. Jean was speaking: "—tonight and then in the morning. And remember, straight to the vet or put them overnight in a shed if you have to. You have a shed?"

Gerry nodded. "I have a shed. And thank you very much. I'll let you know if we catch any critters. Um, you go ahead home. I'm going to stay here for a few more minutes."

With smiles and waves, the good ladies from CRAS tromped away through the snow.

Feeling guilty, but deciding that as long as she kept her gloves on she wouldn't *really* be contaminating evidence (and wouldn't the police have already taken anything they thought was of interest?), Gerry began to go through Ian's possessions. Besides his clothes, books, tools and cooking implements, there wasn't really much else. She found two items that fit the description of what she was looking for, hesitated, then picked them up. One tin contained a pouch of tobacco and rolling papers. One was empty. Might be. She carefully put them back, took a final look around, and left.

When she got home, she found a note: *Gone to Legion. Match at 11:30!!!* She smiled, picturing Doug—if Gerry happened to be late—pushing a curling stone with Dot tucked under one arm. She had plenty of time. In the strangely quiet house, most of her cats were dozing. She made a coffee, put it in a travel mug and left.

Doug handed Dot over with relief. They'd been loitering in the lounge next to the curling rink, which was raised about four or five feet above the ice. A long glass window at one end offered a view down the sheets—five in total—allowing for five matches to take place simultaneously. At the far end of the lounge, opposite the entrance, was a bar. Off to one side of it, a door led to the kitchen. You placed your food order with the bartender, who then passed it along to the kitchen staff. Sometimes Doug was the bartender and sometimes the cook, and, as he also groomed the ice and kept the place clean, everybody knew him.

"Remember our first date?" Gerry said in his ear.

"That wasn't a date; that was getting-to-know-you," he murmured back. "And it turned out pretty well, don't you think?"

"*Pretty* well. I'm still evaluating," Gerry said demurely.

"Huh. Well, wish us luck."

"Luck," she said lightly. He headed past the bar and to the right where a short flight of stairs would take him to the rink. As he appeared on the ice, she said, "Look, Dot, there's Daddy," and held their daughter up to the window. Doug slid over, patted his daughter's hand from behind the glass. The match began.

Dot seemed happy enough, standing, nose pressed, her breath making little patches of condensation on the glass. Gerry leaned back, lifted her legs and rested her feet on the ledge that ran underneath the window frame, as nearly everyone else who was watching was doing.

She thought about the stolen objects she'd seen in Ian's tent: tarps and a staple gun from the hardware store; a mixing bowl from the town bakery; a tin (probably) of cash, now empty, from this very Legion. But no rugs, Persian or otherwise. She lowered her feet and leaned toward the woman sitting next to her who was minding two kids, one about four, the other about two. She knew her slightly as another curling club wife.

"Barb, do you mind watching Dot for a minute?" Barb nodded. Gerry sauntered over to the bartender, a skinny old guy called Larry. "Hey, Larry. How's it going?"

He put down the can of ginger ale he'd been sipping from and shifted closer. "Good, Gerry. What can I get you?"

On his breath, she could smell the sweetness of pop mixed with some strong liquor. "Um, I'll have two hot dogs, one all-dressed, one, er, undressed, and a bag of chips." She waited as he stuck his head in the kitchen door, repeated her order, and returned. She paid. "Larry, do you happen to know what the bingo petty cash box looked like? The one that was stolen?"

Larry looked blank for a moment. "Yeah, sure. This is where they play. And sometimes they leave the box in the till here. Or under the counter if the till is locked. But why do you wanna know?"

"Oh." Gerry paused. She didn't want to blame Ian for something he may not have done. She thought fast. "Uh, I was just at the rummage sale and bought a tin, and wondered…"

Larry cackled. "Afraid of receiving stolen goods, eh?"

"Well, something like that," Gerry muttered, feeling foolish.

"It was originally a chocolate box, I think, all shiny gold metal with a purple ribbon in a bow stamped on it. Is that the one you bought?"

"Gosh…well…no. Nothing like it." The kitchen door opened and a smiling woman handed her two hot dogs and chips. "Oh, thanks. Thanks very much."

As she returned to her spot by the rink with lunch, she thought, *so, Ian really did break in here. He must have been desperate.*

"Here, Dot," she said to her excited-to-see-food child, "have some bun while Mom breaks up your hot dog." To Barb, she muttered, "Choking hazard, eh?"

"You don't have to tell me; I've got to watch these two like a hawk. Raisins, grapes, nuts; they just don't chew…"

Between mangling Dot's hot dog, listening to Barb and watching Doug play, thoughts of Ian Murchison faded. But only temporarily.

14

"And which Heather is this? Cat Lady Heather or shrink Heather?"

Gerry replied, "That's true. I know two Heathers now. And two Sues. Cat Lady, of course—that's who I saw today, setting cat traps. And my other Heather is a psychologist, not a shrink."

Doug grunted. They were all in the cab of his pickup truck. After curling, they'd gone home to watch TV, do some chores, and take naps. Now, feeling refreshed, they were on their way to Prudence and Bertie's for supper.

"It's perfect," said Gerry. "After we eat, we can check for cats in the woods."

"Or any other animal," he said. "What if we catch a skunk?"

"I hadn't thought of that!" She remembered getting skunked in the woods not long after she'd moved to Lovering, and how she'd had to leave her coat outside for days before washing it. "Let's hope not!"

Dot—perhaps because she was riding up front, or thanks to a long afternoon nap—was *not* performing her usual trick of dozing off during car rides. Gerry prompted her: "Who are we going to see, Dottie?" Silence. "You remember—Prue."

Dot sucked in a breath then said, "Poo!"

"Um, not what I was hoping for, but I'll take it. Right—Prue. And Bertie."

Doug commented. "Bertie's probably too big an ask, don't you think?"

Dot repeated herself. "Poo!"

Doug laughed.

"Okay then," Gerry said ruefully. "Poo it is."

They enjoyed their meal. Prudence had made a shepherd's pie and Dot was intrigued by the textures of minced meat and mashed potatoes, though she made a face as the peas from the dish's middle layer entered her mouth. Dessert was an assortment of pastries, cookies and muffins from Maggie's Café, cut into pieces so everybody could try a bit of everything.

At the end of the meal, Bertie leaned back and clasped his hands over his stomach. "I better watch it, or this good life will start to show."

"Start?" Prudence said, raising her eyebrows.

He sat up straight and sucked in his belly. "I'll have you know, Madame, that I have the same figure I had forty years ago."

Dot chose this moment to hold out a bit of cookie towards Prudence, saying, "Poo!"

"Appropriate," said that lady, "considering what your Uncle Bertie's been saying." She leaned toward the hand and pretended to nibble the offering. "You eat the rest, Dot."

"Well," Doug announced, standing up. "I'm off to check cat cages. Who's with me?"

Bertie, pretending to be hurt, said, "I obviously need the exercise, so I'll join you."

Gerry jumped to her feet. "I want to go too! Can we leave Dot with you, Prue? You don't want to go into the woods, do you?"

Prudence smiled thinly. "I can think of things I'd rather do on a Saturday night, but you three enjoy yourselves. Dot and I will start loading the dishwasher."

A dishwasher was one labour-saving device Bertie had insisted on having installed when they'd married, along with a clothes dryer. Prudence had been hang-drying her small amount of laundry outside in the summer and inside on a wooden rack near a base heater in the other seasons. She'd drawn the line at a microwave, however, vowing that such an abomination should never share the same kitchen with her. And Bertie had known when to give in.

Dot smiled horribly at them all, her mouth hanging open, full of cookie crumbs.

In the time it took the three adventurers to suit up and pull on their winter boots, they had already crossed the road and reached the remains of Ian Murchison's home. By now, a well-packed path led the way. It was a cloudy night, so Gerry used a flashlight to scan the snow around the shelter.

"I don't see any cat tracks." She stepped off the path to look behind the structure. The snow had that heavy dense feel of old snow, many layers of which had fallen in the last four months. She reappeared around the other side. "Nothing."

"It may take a while, love," Doug said encouragingly. "Or they could already be—gone."

Knowing he probably meant dead—frozen or eaten by wild animals—she silently entered the shelter first. "No one in here."

Doug knelt by one cage. "Shine the light, please?" She did. "Look. Most of the food in this cage is gone. Must be small animals, mice or chipmunks. They could fit through the gaps in the metal."

"Are they all like that?" Gerry asked, flashing the light around from cage to cage. There was food in about half of the remaining cages. "Okay," she said doubtfully. "But whoever checks here tomorrow morning better bring more kibble."

Bertie volunteered. "I could do it," he said. "And we still have kibble from when Luc stayed with us. Though it might be a bit stale by now."

"Thanks, Bertie, that's really kind of you," Gerry said, remembering Prue and Bertie's other kindness in looking after a relative stranger's cat while its owner recovered from a stroke. "If they're hungry, they won't care."

They began the return walk. The night was cool but not cold and Gerry felt a bit better, thinking of cats out in it. She looked around. Maybe Ian's cats were watching them right now.

"And if there is someone in a cage, call us, okay?" she cautioned Bertie. "The women at CRAS said not to touch any wild cat without gloves on and not to bring it or its cage inside. Call us and we'll take it right to the vet for testing. Cats can get some fatal viruses, you know. Fatal to other cats, that is."

"Got it," he said as they reached the door of his and Prudence's house. "And now, what about a nice game of Scrabble?"

Gerry and Doug groaned. Prue or Bertie always won. Doug said, "The price of our supper, is it?"

As they entered the house, Bertie called, "I've brought two victims, I mean Scrabble lovers, dear."

Prudence laughed and replied, "The board is already set up."

After a quiet Sunday with Bertie and a not-too-hectic Monday morning of babysitting, Prudence finally had a chance to tackle a small task she'd been meaning to get to for ages. With Dot down for her nap and Gerry happily working in her studio, Prudence sat at the dining table at the east end of the living room, finishing her tea as she gazed out the window at the lake.

Gerry had purchased a new frame for the Coneybear family photo, which had once hung in Dot's room. Now, with the broken glass long since disposed of, Prudence turned the still-framed photo face down and carefully slit the brown paper backing—likely cut and pasted by Maggie or her mother, Ellie—that had been added to protect the photo from dust. Prudence smiled as she saw the paper had been cut from a grocery bag; there was the familiar store logo. A thrifty lot, her relatives.

She peeled back the paper and saw her own name—Prudence Catford Cruck—written on an envelope, once white, now yellowed, that had been taped to the back of the photo. Below her name had been printed in block letters: PRIVATE.

The cat Monkey jumped noiselessly onto the chair next to Prudence's. She seemed content to sit and watch from calm yellow eyes as Prudence's lips pressed together grimly. She expected no good to come from something so secret. She picked up the knife again, slit the envelope, and skipped to the end of the letter that was inside.

So! The photo hadn't been framed by her cousin Maggie or her aunt, but by another one of her many cousins, Gerald—Gerry's dad. She returned to the beginning of the letter and read.

July 27th, 1992

Dear Prudence,
    I'm writing you this so you, if only you, may know the truth of what happened concerning Alex and I.
    I had no plans to return to The Maples or even to Lovering. It's been almost twenty-five years. I only returned this summer at Deborah's request.
    As you know, she's dying, so I couldn't refuse her. I suppose she hoped that I might find some—comfort? closure?—by visiting the old place. I have found neither.
    Or maybe she wished to create a memory for us, for Gerry. Sadly, it won't be a happy one. She's in so much pain…it can only be months now.
    How to begin…you know Alex and I were great friends, first as boys, then as teenagers, and got into all sorts of trouble. We did all the wrong things together: drank and smoked, stole cars, broke into people's houses. Sometimes we got caught, but my father, convinced that

> it was Alex, from a poor semi-literate farming family, who was leading his nice respectable well-connected son astray, always managed to get us off.
>
> But *you* remember how easygoing Alex was, a follower. I was the one who was bored, who craved the thrill of being a bad boy. I led; Alex came along for the ride.
>
> This pattern continued for some time, eroding my relationship with my parents. They tried to keep it from my sisters, but I think Mary knew. I *hope* Maggie, so much younger than I, and more innocent, didn't. Not at that time, anyway. I'm not sure what she's guessed or learnt since…

It was disturbing for Prudence to read the words written by someone long dead, especially when they referred to others—most of them now gone as well. What disturbed her most, though, was reading about her former husband. She continued to page two of the letter.

> Anyway, after one incident involving the burning down of a hay barn, and in which the horses in a nearby barn narrowly escaped, my father gave me an ultimatum: shape up or get out. This had the required sobering effect and I stopped seeing Alex and other disreputable (not that I wasn't) friends. I went to university, dropped out after a couple of years, then got a job at my father's company. High finance, they call it. Boring as hell.
>
> One Friday night, I happened to meet Alex at the bar in Lovering—The Castle. He seemed down. He told me you and he had called it quits. He had no job. He didn't know what he was going to do. We got drunk. We got drunk a lot over the next few weeks. And I started to get restless again. *More* restless.

At work I had access to lists. Lists of bank branches. And timetables. Of when money would be trucked to and from various branches. And a very bad idea began to ferment in my beer-soaked brain.

Our first robbery was at a little branch way out in the sticks near the Ontario border. It was too easy. Alex had shotguns at his family's farm. He sawed one down and we were in business.

You must know that the gun was never loaded. It worked though; scared bank employees handed over the cash. We waited six months before we did it again. This time we went up north and east of Ottawa. Piece of cake.

We never did get caught. Not at the banks, anyway. *I*, however, did, stupidly hiding my share of the loot in my room. I never thought my mother would burrow right down to the bottom of the blanket chest at the foot of my bed. She was looking for spare sheets, I suppose.

She took the money to my father, I guess; she and I never spoke of it. But *he* and I did, or rather, he spoke, I listened. He was white-faced as he told me what he thought of me. He asked if I'd used privileged information from our mutual workplace and turned even whiter still when I admitted it. There was a pause as he swallowed his profound disappointment, then I was dismissed. Once I became a parent, I realized he must also have felt sorrow.

The next day he told me his decision. I was to quit my job on the premise of wanting to move away. He didn't care where, he said—he suggested out of the province—that was for me to decide. But—and on this point he was crystal clear—I was never to return home while he was alive. And, in case I was in any confusion about the gravity of what I'd done, he was about to change his will, telling me that neither house nor wealth would come my way.

I leave it to you to guess at how I felt. And yet— wasn't this what I'd secretly wanted? To have adventures; to get away from my oh-so-respectable life, from dull little Lovering?

All this to say,

Prudence heard Gerry's studio door open then close. As Gerry breezed by to the kitchen, she said, "Tea or coffee, Prue?"

And Prudence, now sitting on the letter, her heart pounding, answered, hoping she didn't sound as dazed as she felt, "Uh, coffee, please. Thanks."

Over supper that night, Gerry commented to Doug, "Prudence was a bit distant this afternoon."

He spooned some sweet potato at Dot's open mouth. "Distant?"

"Yeah. Like, at lunch she was normal Prue. Then, when we had afternoon coffee, she was different."

"Distant *and* different. Hey, she's eating it!"

"She's pretty good with the sweet vegetables. Not a fan of the green stuff yet."

"Got her mother's sweet tooth," he teased. "Maybe Prudence was just tired. It's not easy looking after this one for a whole day."

"Tell me about it," Gerry agreed. "I hope she's not getting sick of babysitting."

"Could be other stuff going on," he offered. "Running a business is no joke."

"But she's got Bertie to do the business part; he's experienced at that."

The telephone rang. Gerry got up and answered it.

"Hello?" Gerry opened her eyes very wide at Doug. "Oh, hi, Prue. What? Oh, that's wonderful! Do you—I see. I see. Okay. That works. If you don't mind. All right. All right. Wednesday. Thank you very much. Bye."

"She's coming Wednesday?"

"Yup."

"So I guess she's not sick of babysitting?"

"No." Gerry sat back down at the table. "That's good. And Bertie's just retrieved a cat from the woods. That's why she called."

"Yay!"

"Yeah. But not from one of the cages. Apparently, it dashed out of the tent and ran up his leg! He was so surprised, he just clutched it. It's at their house now."

"So much for keeping your distance. Do they want us to come get it?"

"N-no. They're willing to take it to the vet tomorrow."

"Well. A result."

Gerry smiled. "Yes. It sounds like one of Ian's cats has come to a decision." She paused in thought. Ian's cats reminded her of something she'd noted earlier when she'd visited his tent. "Doug, there were no rugs at Ian's place."

"No. Not that I noticed. Just the floor of the tent overlaid with tarps. Okay, Miss Dot, you're done." He wiped her face then let her out of the high chair. He turned to Gerry and gave her his full attention. "Why?"

She spoke slowly. "Because the rugs stolen from the seniors' residence are the only stolen things unaccounted for. All the other stuff was found at Ian's."

"I see. You checked, did you?" he said wryly.

She sounded defensive when she replied, "I may have, when we brought in the cages." She reflected for a moment, then added, "But Ian had no way of moving big things, like rolled-up rugs.

He'd hardly drag them away then abandon them. Anyway, if so, they'd have been found."

"Not if he stashed them elsewhere in the woods."

"He wouldn't have done that. He stole stuff for his use."

"Maybe he had help," Doug said. "Someone who had...has a vehicle." He joined Dot on the rug in front of the fire and began handing her blocks.

"But Ian was a loner, wasn't he? No friends, no family."

"He had a sister, but she moved away years ago."

Gerry said jokingly, "You're not suggesting Ian's long-lost sister showed up to rob rugs with him, are you?"

"No, of course not. You're right, he was a loner."

Gerry retrieved a package of white chocolate chip cookies and handed them around, seating herself on the sofa. Immediately, cats began to make their moves lapward. "I got white chocolate so Dot wouldn't stain her clothes."

"Good idea." Everybody munched.

Gerry stared at the fire. "How did things go with your aunts?"

"Fine. We met with the lawyer and then went to the bank to sign some paperwork. Uncle Sydney left them a little money in his will, so I suggested the bank set up a tax-free savings account for them."

"Brilliant! They're lucky to have you with power of attorney taking an interest."

He flushed. "They were very grateful. They wanted to give *me* some money. I said no, of course."

"Of course." She thought some more. "Your going to the bank reminds me of something—Ian. Any idea why he would feel shortchanged by the bank?"

Doug shrugged. "He wasn't stable, mentally. Maybe he failed to jump through some bureaucratic hoops. And he probably didn't even own a calendar, so how could he have a solid sense of time passing? He'd just spend his money until it was gone."

"Yeah. I guess so. Well, it's my turn to bathe Dot, so *you* get to tidy up the kitchen." She rose, to the disgruntlement of Jay and Seymour, who'd just gotten comfortable on her lap. "Meet you later in—" she glanced at her daughter "—the t-e-l-e-v-i-s-i-o-n room, okay?"

"Okay."

As she was tucking her now sweet-smelling daughter into her crib, Gerry saw the photo of her grandparents with their three children had been neatly reframed and rehung above Dot's bureau. She made a mental note to thank Prudence on Wednesday.

15

"Who wants more cake?" Cyndi called from her kitchen. The moms groaned. Their children played on the rug at their feet.

"If I have to," Hilary said reluctantly. "No cake goes unloved when I'm around." Gerry snickered. "Yes, Miss—Miss I-Lost-All-My-Pregnancy-Weight-And-Now-Am-Cuter-Than-Ever!"

Gerry snickered again. "I'll have another piece, Cyndi. It's so good. And I still have ten pounds to lose."

Cyndi appeared in the doorway into the family room. "Ah, the famous last ten pounds. Two slices of pecan coffee cake coming up."

Hilary and Gerry held out their plates. "Not for me, thanks, Cyndi," said Christine politely. She leaned forward and pointedly picked up a piece of raw broccoli from the crudité tray in front of her.

Hilary said to Gerry, "Live fast and die young, eh, kid?" before diving into her cake.

Gerry laughed and coughed. "I'm going to get some more coffee," she croaked. "Anyone?"

Hilary held out her cup. Christine determinedly drank from her enormous water bottle, the water infused with slices of cucumber.

Gerry regarded her friend while eating her cake. Christine Smith was a little older than the other moms—in her early forties—

so, Gerry thought, maybe that was why she was meticulous about her diet. And exercise. Christine golfed and played tennis and had kept up the yoga that Gerry had stopped after Dot's birth.

Something occurred to Gerry: "Christine, you knew Ian Murchison's family, I think you said?"

Christine nodded. "The kids were way older than me. Ian and Rebecca. Rebecca was a lot younger than Ian but she left home first. Not that he ever did."

"I saw a death notice in the paper," Gerry said. "But no funeral announcement."

"Not enough family or friends to have one, I guess. There's an aunt, his mother's sister; she's still around." She paused. "My mother says she thinks Rebecca left home because Ian was so weird. Their parents focused on him, maybe too much. My mom had a long time to observe the family—them being neighbours."

Gerry was silent for a moment, then leaned forward and spoke softly. "Doug said Ian was badly beaten—I assume to death. But there's no mention of it elsewhere in the paper, not even under police news. I wonder why?"

Christine also leaned forward. "I heard—well, my mom heard—that he died of a heart attack." She sat back upright and took a big swig of cucumber water, looking pleased, probably at being in possession of insider information.

Gerry mused, "So, an older man, undernourished, a smoker, is getting beaten up, feels terrified, no doubt, and has a heart attack. Is it murder? Manslaughter?"

"Probably the former," said Hilary. "Murder is intentionally causing the death of a human being. But, if, say, someone beat someone else up and left, not knowing the victim was having or would soon have a fatal heart attack, it's still murder, though possibly not intentional."

Gerry looked over at Christine whose eyes had glazed. "You look how I feel, Christine—confused! Why murder, then?"

"Because," Hilary continued, "of something called 'murder in the commission of an offence'—in this case, the beating, which is illegal, right? That makes it first-degree murder, even if intent can't be proven."

"Still confused," admitted Gerry.

"That's why we have lawyers," Hilary said cheerfully. "To figure out what and how to prosecute. Maybe that's why the cops are being close-lipped about the cause of death. Not that I'll be in the mix for the next little while. We decided I'll extend my parental leave until Noah is ready for preschool." Noah, hearing his name, gave his mother a lopsided grin.

Christine, who'd already decided to stay home for a while after Jane's birth, nodded. "Once you have three, it's just too much to juggle with a full-time job." Her daughter toddled over and climbed onto her mother's lap. Christine lifted up her shirt and Jane latched on. Of the moms, only Cyndi was also continuing breastfeeding her toddler.

Gerry spoke: "I haven't had any more art supplies go missing lately. The cat we think was hiding them has pica and the treatment is love and attention, which seems to be working."

"Huh," said Hilary. "I thought only pregnant women got pica, craving clay or even dirt. Some kind of mineral deficiency, I thought."

"Well, the tests on the cat didn't show any deficiency so the vet went with mental or emotional causes."

Cyndi snorted. "Too bad Heather isn't here. She could analyze your cat!" Heather was away, pleading a professional appointment.

Hilary continued. "I think I told you that I found what I lost, too. The oven mitts and apron were under some old tea towels scrunched up in the back of a drawer, and the scarf and earrings were under our luggage in the basement. I couldn't believe it when I lifted up the cases—there they were."

"How was the trip to Florida?" asked Christine.

"Unbelievable. First time we'd been alone together overnight in years. We were both asleep half the time. Luxury is waking up whenever."

"How about you, Christine?" Gerry asked. "Those bad mice still making off with the macadamias?"

"Yes. But still no mouse dirt. And it's not Lawrence—he's got his junk food, his chips and cheese puffs." She sniffed.

"I wonder what it could be?" said Gerry. "I should ask my friend Cathy if her little boxes have shown up at the B&B. It would be strange if they have."

"'The Case of the Temporarily Missing Objects,'" quipped Hilary. "It must have been my two oldest playing some game, but I decided that was one battle I wasn't going to win and let it go."

Christine mused, "I don't know what to do—organic food is so expensive."

"Can you lock it up?" asked Hilary.

Christine laughed. "Raw nuts have to be kept in the fridge. I can just see how locking that would go over with my crew."

"Hm, no," they murmured.

Dot began to wail. Sydney, Cyndi's daughter, had taken one of the plastic rings Dot had been laboriously fitting over a cone. Sydney kindly offered Dot the ring back. Dot took it and promptly hit Sydney with it. Gerry swooped in. "Okay, someone's tired. Sorry, Sydney. We'll skedaddle, I think. My place next week?"

Prudence hadn't come to sit Dot the previous Wednesday after all, so Gerry hadn't been able to get much work done. Thursday Dot napped after playgroup, and Gerry did a little cartooning, but by Friday morning as she sat on the train, she was wracking her brain for ideas.

Outside, the March landscape was misty; the land was warming, its snow beginning to melt around the edges. "St. Patrick's

Day," she murmured and began sketching the tropes: Mug the Bug quaffing beer wearing a bowler hat, hunting for shamrocks, meeting a leprechaun. Too late for this year, she thought, and no good anyway. She crumpled the page. "Snakes," she muttered.

"Pardon?" said Bertie, snapping his newspaper to straighten the pages.

"Snakes," she repeated more loudly. "St. Patrick and... For *Mug*."

"Ah. As in, the casting out from Ireland by said saint."

"Correct." She sketched Mug sitting on a wriggling serpent. "Bertie."

"Mm?" He snapped his paper again, briskly. The person sitting in front of him visibly jumped.

"Where could one sell hot rugs?"

"Hot rugs?" He sounded incredulous.

"*Stolen* rugs," she said. She added a bowler and mug of beer to the Mug seated on the snake.

Bertie relaxed his newspaper onto his lap and watched her work. "I take it you're referring to rugs for floors and not—" He nodded ahead of them where the back of a large bald head was on display.

Gerry giggled. "No, silly: carpeting, of course." She stopped drawing and gave him her attention. "You're the expert."

He stared down at his lap. "Well, it would depend where I'd stolen them from and how valuable they were. If taken from a private residence, I'd be likely to be very discreet; try to sell to a private buyer. If they were brand new and I'd taken them from an importer or store, I'd move them far away before trying to sell."

"And if you took them from a seniors' residence?"

He turned to look at her. "From the common area in a seniors' residence in, say, a small town?"

"Yeah. Like that."

He straightened in his chair and focused on the bald head in front of him. "Well, that's different. Assuming no one was able to describe the rugs very well to the police, their original owners being probably long gone, I'd feel I could offload them pretty much anywhere."

Gerry groaned. "That's what I thought. Thanks anyway."

"Not a problem," he replied and returned to his paper again, giving it a good snap. The bald man jumped again and this time, turned.

Gerry, still applying endless amounts of gold leaf to the Napoleon portrait's massive frame, smiled as she recalled how Bertie had raised his paper as a shield and shrunk down in his seat when the man sitting in front of them had glared. He wasn't really afraid, she thought, he was just playing. That's probably why Prudence loves him—he knows how to play. She sighed. I used to know how to do that—do that more.

She reached for the sketch pad she kept beside her work station and quickly drew Mug the Bug in Bertie's place on the train, snapping a tiny newspaper. Sometimes the mindless work at the museum made her brain bubble with ideas. And sometimes not. She yawned and stretched, then ambled over to watch Sue Two repairing the painting of Napoleon. "Do you think I could ever do that?"

Sue straightened. "Yes. Of course. Why not?"

"Don't you ever get nervous? That you might make a mistake and wreck it?"

Sue smiled. "No. This is my field of expertise. I *know* what I'm doing. Are you lunching in or out?"

"Out. A friend is coming to get me. I should go."

Minutes later, a pensive Gerry stood shivering in the damp air on the museum steps. Lost in thought, she started when Yvonne Punt touched her arm. "Oh, hello. How are you?"

"Good," Yvonne said curtly. "Hungry?"

"Always."

"Like spicy?"

"Not *too* spicy. Why?"

Yvonne smiled. "You'll see." They walked to a cross street, turned and headed south.

"Is it far?" asked Gerry, almost trotting to keep up with Yvonne's long legs. They turned again and began heading east.

"Nope. In fact—" Yvonne pulled open a door. "We're here."

Gentle reggae music and fresh food aromas wafted toward them. "Mm. Smells good," said Gerry. They each grabbed a tray and looked at the menu choices overhead. When Yvonne ordered a chickpea and veggie roti with red sorrel to drink, Gerry did the same. The sandwiches were quickly constructed (one with lots and one with a bit of hot sauce) and soon they were seated by the long glass window watching passing foot traffic. Gerry, who knew sorrel as that green perennial plant in her garden that she didn't know how to cook, was surprised by the red drink. She sipped cautiously. "Mm! It's nice!"

"Hibiscus flowers," said the succinct Yvonne. "Sugar, spices."

"And the roti is yummy too," said Gerry. "I used to eat rotis in Toronto but to be honest I'd usually get chicken or goat. Thanks for introducing me to veggie food."

Yvonne splattered her roti with even more hot sauce then offered the squeeze bottle to Gerry.

"No, thanks. This is funny, going for Jamaican food on St. Patrick's Day. And me half-Irish."

Yvonne mumbled, "Not very important to me, I'm afraid."

"No. Me neither. And I don't like beer, so—" They munched. Outside, a thin drizzle had begun and walkers were hunching and hurrying. "You mentioned you had something to show me, Yvonne?" To be honest, Gerry was expecting more poems, so was surprised when none appeared.

"Sure. Yeah. We have to walk to it."

They finished their lunch, returned their trays and left. Yvonne led them to the corner and turned south. They walked steadily downhill for about five minutes. Gerry was glad she'd worn her lined raincoat with its hood. Yvonne wore her usual long winter coat with a baseball cap that kept her face and glasses dry. "Nearly there," she said encouragingly, and, a few minutes later, stopped.

The neighbourhood, like the sloping street they'd traversed, was clearly going down. The buildings, some with plywood boards covering doorways and windows, were narrow, one address pressed against the next, except where a skinny alley or recess accommodated garbage and garbage receptacles. And people. Mostly women, they were clustered around one front door in particular.

Hi, Yvonne, or, Yvonne, *bonjour* was heard from a few. "*Bonjour*, hello," Yvonne replied, then went up the building's few front steps. Gerry followed. Inside, it was clear that two or three buildings had been combined—on the left of the narrow hallway stretching ahead was a vast dining area. Women sat at long tables, talking, a few laughing. Yvonne jerked her head for Gerry to follow her down the hallway.

It ended in a kitchen where other women were working. "All right, Yvonne?" one asked, raising her head from her work table and smiling.

"All right, Cherie?" Yvonne replied. She handed Gerry an apron and they got to work.

None of this was new to Gerry; as a child, and before her mother got sick, she and her parents had used to volunteer at a food bank once a month, packing boxes and bags for its clients. And her father had occasionally served at a men's shelter downtown, though he'd rarely let her or her mother accompany him.

"Gets pretty rough sometimes," he'd cautioned. The one exception was on Christmas morning, when the clients could be expected to be on their best behaviour. Gerry remembered skipping from table to table with sugar bowls and milk jugs while grizzled men trembled and picked at their food, some of them feeling too ill to eat, contenting themselves with coffee or soup while their full plates of Christmas dinner went cold.

After her mother died, her father had stopped volunteering. Now she wondered: was he only doing it because he wanted Mom to think he was a good guy? And set me a good example? Or, she thought sadly, remembering how they had seemed to drift apart after her mother died, maybe he was still going, but just didn't tell me.

Dirty dishes had to be cleared from the dining room into the kitchen. When places opened up, Yvonne would go to the front door and return with new diners to be served. The clients behaved themselves. One woman who raised her voice at another got a slit-eyed look from Yvonne and something said in a low hiss that quelled her.

Gerry kept an eye on the big clock high on the wall, and when it said 12:50, she approached Yvonne. "I should get back to work. But thank you for showing me this place."

Yvonne nodded. "You okay to walk back alone?"

"Oh, sure." Gerry grinned. "I'm from Toronto, remember?"

When she got her coat from the back of the kitchen, she nodded to Cherie who said, "That Yvonne, she's good with them, eh?"

"Seems to be," Gerry said cheerfully.

"They listen to her." Cherie stopped chopping carrots and spoke more quietly. "Because she used to be like them." She paused then added, "Like us." She went back to her work. "See you again, maybe."

Uncertainly, Gerry said, "Maybe."

16

That same lunch hour, Prudence was feeding Dot, who—when she wasn't chewing—was engaged in a long conversation with the cat, Monkey, perched beside the living room's drawn-back curtains.

The cat wasn't saying much. But her eyes followed the trajectory of Prudence's hand from bowl to Dot's mouth and back. Dot alternately leaned over the side of her high chair to address the cat and looked up at the curtains to grin and wave her hands.

Not for the first time did Prudence compare the toddler's behaviour to that of schizophrenics portrayed in film and on TV. The unpredictability was what was so disconcerting.

Finally, the bread and cheese and banana were, more or less, consumed, and the welcome nap time beckoned. Prudence tenderly lifted Dot from her chair, held her close, then let her loose while she cleaned the area.

Dot toddled over to Monkey and sat next to the cat, putting a hand firmly on its back. "Tub!" she crowed.

That's a new one, thought Prudence, who, that morning, had heard enough iterations of her own name, abbreviated—"Poo! Poo!"—to last a lifetime. How did Dot get Tub from Monkey? And what will happen when she learns the words for bathtub and poo?

She continued to muse on language acquisition as she finished wiping and carried Dot's dishes into the kitchen. Dot followed her and crouched next to the cats' tub of kibble, stirring its contents with her hand. Another tub, thought Prudence. Looking straight at Prudence, Dot conveyed a few pieces of cat food into her mouth.

Prudence moved silently and swiftly, inserting a forefinger into the mouth and retrieving the choking hazards. "No!" she said firmly. "Cat food. No good for children." As Dot's face crumpled and she prepared to wail, Prudence scooped her up. "Come on, Tub, let's get this little one into bed."

Monkey, however, was content to remain by the kibble, crunching.

Dot was soon down, and a relieved Prudence sat to eat her own lunch. She was tired, but it was more nervous exhaustion than anything else. The five days since she'd found and read Gerald Coneybear's old letter to her had passed slowly. The truth about her dead cousin weighed on her, more for Gerry's sake than her own. She wrestled with her conscience. Should she tell Gerry about the letter, even let her read it? It would only bring her sorrow, and, as her father was dead, closure wasn't ever going to be possible.

Prudence took the letter out of her purse where she'd been keeping it—she hadn't shared it with Bertie—and skimmed through it again, paying special attention to the end.

> I leave it to you to guess at how I felt. And yet—wasn't this what I'd secretly wanted? To have adventures. Get away from my oh-so-respectable life, from dull little Lovering?
>
> All this to say, that when I heard Alex had later been caught and sentenced to 30 years for a violent bank robbery, my soul shrivelled and I blamed myself. I know you've already separated, but I want to apologize to you if I played a part in ruining your marriage.
>
> And, if Alex is still alive and you are in contact with him when you read this in who knows how many years, would you please apologize to him for me? I know my

weakness helped wreck his life. I think about him every day and live in constant regret.

Yours, Gerry

The fury Prudence had felt when she first read the letter surged back. What was the point of it now—this letter, discovered so late, when all the key players were dead except her? Had Gerald Coneybear's ghost reached out to her months ago? Had he somehow made the photograph fall from the wall so the letter would be found? But why her? Surely Gerry or Doug would have been more likely to come across it. Was he asking her to decide whether to tell Gerry? How dare he?

On impulse, she crumpled it up, laid it on the cold hearth and set it alight. Monkey was sitting on the rug and watched the process. As the letter's words became ashes, Prudence looked over her shoulder and asked, "Are you satisfied now?" And down the chimney came a cold draft sounding like a sigh.

As she went into the kitchen to do the dishes, the cat followed her with her eyes.

"And are you a new member?" the very old lady asked gently in a Scottish-accented voice. "I haven't seen you in here before."

Dot, her eyes still barely reaching above the counter even after Gerry helped her onto the low stool, was for once silent.

Gerry said, "We're joining today. Both of us."

"Oh, good. If you would just wait a moment while I—"

With a few comments on the weather, she stamped the books and card of a middle-aged woman before returning to Dot and Gerry. How archaic, still checking out books manually, Gerry thought as the woman opened a drawer and extracted two cards: one blue and one green. She looked down at Dot. "Name?"

Dot stared up, unblinking.

"Dot Coneybear," Gerry said.

"Address?" Gerry gave it.

Still speaking to Dot, the woman said, "That'll be ten dollars."

Gerry paid. The woman slid the blue card over to the top of Dot's head. "Five-book limit. Two weeks. Late fees apply."

She went through the same procedure with Gerry, taking fifteen dollars. Then she smiled. "Welcome to the Lovering Library. Let me show you the children's section."

She led the way to the back of the large room, where low shelves lined the walls. With a wave of her hand, she indicated the sections for toddlers through young adults.

Dot went to a little table where some books were laid out. The woman, who'd been hunched a bit, straightened. "I knew your grandmother," she told Gerry. "I'm assuming you're Ellie Coneybear's granddaughter?" Gerry nodded. The woman continued: "She used to volunteer here too."

"Volunteer?"

"Yes. We're almost completely volunteer-run. Ellie was upstairs, like me. I'm Elspeth McCrae."

"Nice to meet you, Elspeth. Upstairs?"

"Downstairs volunteers work organizing the rummage sale in the basement. Up here we just sell used books, but down there you'll find old clothes, dishes, jewellery—odds and ends. Whatever people donate. The rummage sale funds the library."

"Oh, I've donated, dropped stuff off in the cupboard at the side. But I've never, er, rummaged."

"You should come with your daughter. Children love it. There are lots of toys. I see I have another customer, so excuse me." She addressed Dot: "Enjoy yourself," she said before leaving them.

Gerry sat down on one of the little chairs near Dot. "Gosh, Dot, your great-grandma used to come here."

Suddenly, looking at her daughter, Gerry realized how deep her and Dot's roots went in this town. And she was glad she'd finally joined the library. After all, she'd already worked her way through most of the books at The Maples.

After they checked out their books—an assortment for Dot and some mysteries by Edwina Murray that Gerry hadn't yet read (and which reminded her, she hadn't visited Edwina for some time)—Gerry took a brief detour on the way home. In fact, she went in the opposite direction along the river road, turning left at the first side street.

This part of Lovering, on the heights above the Ottawa River as opposed to the lowlands where The Maples was located, was where many of Lovering's original families had lived or were still living. And on this particular road, the houses were pleasant, oldish, and set back on large, treed lots.

Christine Smith had mentioned this street—her mother's, where their family home stood—and that Ian Murchison's house there had been torn down a few years earlier and replaced with a new building. And there it was: glaring white stucco with heavy brown wooden beams. It was unusually tall, likely three or four stories, with a tower at one end and a brutally bulky wooden gate by the road. It was the only obviously new structure on the street. Mock Tudor, indeed. Gerry shuddered at the architectural travesty. "That must be the spot," she murmured, slowing the car.

Dot, flipping through pages of one of her library books, was talking to herself. Gerry looked at her in the rear-view mirror and wondered how a child, raised on such a street in Lovering, could wind up living in a shack in the woods fifty years on. Living and dying in a shack with only cats for company.

"The cages!" she exclaimed. Maybe CRAS needed their cages back. Bertie was checking them evening and morning, but no further cats had turned themselves in. Yes, she had better call Jean when they got home. She turned and grinned at her daughter. "Okay, Dotster, time for lunch." Dot thumped her feet against her booster seat with enthusiasm.

"*A Most Tempting Offer. A Most Tempting Offer.*" Edwina Murray looked perplexedly up at the ceiling of her sunken living room. "Now, which one was that?"

"*You* know," Gerry said confidently, having just read the blurb on the book's inside front cover and the first hundred pages, and thinking, if the author doesn't remember, who can? "The one where the girl goes to work at a tropical resort, a guest is murdered, and she tries to figure out who dunnit?" Lunch and Dot's nap having gone smoothly, they were next door having tea with Edwina.

Dot toddled around the room then decided to explore. She began to crawl up the four wide steps that led to a raised hallway that ran the length of the room. Gerry retrieved her and sat her down on the rug, handing her some wooden animals she'd brought.

Giving her mother an indignant look, Dot once again headed for the stairs. Shadow, Edwina's majestic black Labrador retriever, raised his head with its soulful eyes and looked at Gerry. "Would you?" she said to him. He rose and followed Dot's progress up the stairs.

The esteemed author was still staring at her ceiling. "Um," she said. "I don't—

"*You* know," Gerry repeated, now a bit desperate. Had she misremembered the book? "The heroine lurks around the resort, flirting with the men, chatting up the old ladies, then we learn that she has a past."

Still nothing from Edwina, who said, lowering her gaze, "So, who dunnit?"

"Well," Gerry said doubtfully. "*I* don't know, do I! Someone by the pool with a cocktail that was part rum, part pineapple juice and part antifreeze!"

"Oh, yes, the antifreeze." Edwina laughed. "When Roald and I were in the tropics one time, I remember trying a planter's punch and thinking that it tasted as if it was made with antifreeze—sweet but deadly. I took a sip then gave it to Roald to finish. Yes, she did it. The old it's-the-would-be-sleuth-herself-as-the-murderer routine. Too bad you can only use them once," she mused.

"Use what once?" asked her bewildered guest, ruefully aware that the author had just spoiled the rest of the book for her reader.

"Tricks like that. Plot devices. Having the most sympathetic character be the murderer. Or the narrator as murderer. I've used that one too."

There was a pause. Dot had successfully mounted the stairs, with Shadow beside her, and was now leaning against his side, their heads level. Shadow winced—perhaps from the pain of tiny handfuls of fur being tugged loose—and moved away in some haste to the right, down the hallway toward his lair: his late master's den, now converted into a sunroom. Dot gave chase.

Gerry, engrossed in the conversation of trade secrets, and with her back to the hallway, didn't notice. Edwina, seated facing the action, did, but wasn't bothered. She counted on her fingers. "*Dangerous to Know, Purple Angel, Home to Roost, The Case Against Norman Crumbles, Wild Blood* and *Murder Among the Dahlias.* Six, not including my *really* old ones, like *A Most Tempting Offer.* That was with the publisher before this one."

Dot appeared from the right, moving rapidly now to the left, with Shadow in pursuit.

"Those must be the ones I got from the library, the old ones. I got—" Gerry listed the ones she remembered, concluding with, "And one I can't recall but on the cover there's an island in a bay with a tiny cottage on it. *Without... Without—*"

Dot and Shadow disappeared to the left where Edwina's office was located.

"*Without Mercy,*" Edwina completed the title. "A metaphor for my marriage," she concluded drily.

Gerry said nothing but "Mm," as what could one say about a husband who was both a sponge and a philanderer and made no secret about being either. She became aware of her daughter's absence and turned in her seat in time to see first Shadow, then Dot appear from Edwina's office and move with dispatch along the hallway.

"They've been chasing each other back and forth for a few minutes," Edwina said, smiling sweetly. "I'm glad; he rarely plays."

Like his owner, thought Gerry—then reconsidered. Edwina's face lit up when she talked about her books; she became animated. Like me, she plays while she works. Since Dot seemed fine, Gerry asked, "What are you working on now?"

"I've got two going. They liked *Murder Among the Dahlias* so I'm doing another in that Garden Club Mysteries series. And the Bed and Breakfast one is almost finished. It's called *Between the Sheets*." Edwina looked at Gerry. Gerry looked at Edwina. Then they both burst into laughter.

"You're bad," chortled Gerry. "You don't look it—but you're bad."

Edwina—tall, thin, bespectacled, her grey-brown hair pulled back in a loose bun—blinked rapidly. "Thank you. I try to have fun. You could call me a player in disguise. All in my head, of course."

"Of course. What's the second garden one going to be called?"

"Well, it's not final, but probably *A Delicate Flower*."

Gerry snorted. "I take it that's ironic?"

Edwina grinned. "Perhaps, perhaps not. Er, a character resembling your Aunt Mary may or may not feature heavily."

Gerry groaned. "Now I *know* it's ironic."

A crash from the sunroom brought both women to their feet. What they found when they arrived was not a dire scene:

two wing chairs with a small table between them. In one chair, Shadow was curled up, feebly wagging his tail. In the other, Dot was leaning forward over the table, from which several objects had just fallen.

"I'm so sorry, Edwina. I'll pay for them."

"No need. Just some of Roald's old pipes I keep there for the dog to smell. Only the china ones are broken. I'll get a dustpan."

Oh, the mysteries of marriage, thought Gerry. Keeps them for the dog to smell, eh? She sat in Dot's chair, corralling her child in a loving embrace, and reached across to pat Shadow. "Good dog. Good dog."

When Doug came home from work that night, Gerry gave him an extra-long hug.

"What's that for?" he asked, returning it.

"Just because," she said.

"I'm not complaining." After a minute, he said, "Hey, I got some old sap buckets today and I thought, as I won't have time to run lines from buckets to the sugar shack and we don't even have a viable sap boiler up there, we could just tap the maples here at the house. That way we can just carry the cans into the house, empty them into a big pot, and boil it down as we go."

"Fun!" she said. "Let's start tomorrow."

That took care of Sunday afternoon. That evening, they had Cathy, Markie, and Andrew over for supper. They kept it simple: boiled ham, mashed potatoes, and peas, with a fresh strawberry and whipped cream layer cake from Maggie's Café, which Doug had picked up. After supper, Dot—kept awake all day helping with the maple tree tapping in the fresh air—gracefully conked out, leaving the adults free to relax by the fire.

"Cathy," Gerry said, bringing her friend a second cup of tea, "I've been meaning to ask you: did you ever sign up for that Asian cooking course?"

Cathy beamed. "I *did*, and it starts in April. Four cuisines: Indian, which really could be a separate course on its own, there are so many regional specialities, Japanese, Chinese and Thai."

"Oo," said Markie. "We volunteer to be guinea pigs when you do your homework."

Everyone agreed. "Well, what I'm *hoping* to do, once I've mastered the recipes, is to start offering themed evenings, or even teach myself."

"We'll sign up for that," said Andrew. "Me for the dinners and Markie for the classes."

"Ho," said Markie. "It's never too late to learn something new. Like cooking. You might surprise yourself."

"*I* need to take cooking lessons," said Gerry, "but nothing fancy."

Cathy leaned over and patted her knee. "Based on what you served us tonight, dear, you're already there." She leaned back suddenly and covered her mouth. "Oh! I didn't mean—"

Gerry laughed. "No, no, you're right. They were my words. And I'm glad I'm at the 'nothing fancy' level already. It has to be food Dot will eat, too."

Cathy held up one hand. "And I have something else to announce. I've been going to exercise class in the church hall and *I've lost five pounds!*"

There was general applause and congratulations. "That's great, honey," said Markie, the thin athletic one, and kissed her plump sister. "You already look fine, you know, but I'm glad you're getting out and getting healthier."

While Markie, Doug and Andrew discussed what would have to happen in order to reactivate the family sugar shack and syrup operation in the woods, Gerry quietly asked Cathy another question. "Did you ever figure out what happened to all your little containers? The ones that went missing?"

Monkey came into the room and sat down near the rear windows. Gerry went over and picked her up to give her some love, but the cat had other ideas, jumped from her arms and returned to her original position. Gerry shrugged and sat back down.

Cathy clucked her tongue. "I must be going senile. I found them all in the smallest bedroom, one I rarely use as you can barely fit a single bed in there. They were lined up on the window sill, as though I'd been trying out an arrangement. Why?"

"Why? Oh, nothing. Nothing at all." She had a glimmer of an idea but was distracted from pursuing it when the phone rang. It was Prudence.

"Gerry, listen," she said, "Bertie thinks he's found the rugs."

PART 4
MEOW

Gerald didn't understand it. The missing crayons and pencils hadn't been sufficient hints to change his daughter's trajectory from commercial to fine arts. He flitted around her studio, taking in the cartoons, the sketches of cats, the ideas for children's picture books.

He was alone. The door to the studio was usually closed and this night was no exception. So his feline companion had to wait in the foyer.

He heard voices coming from the living room; his daughter was entertaining. He let his mind slip back to the first fifteen or so years of his life, before the devil, as it were, had gotten into him.

He remembered wonderful family parties, when his aunts and uncles and numerous cousins had gathered at The Maples. His Uncle John and his wife Isabelle, Prudence's aunt, had lived across the road so had been in and out of the house as had many of the neighbours, including the parents of Cathy and Markie Stribling who were in the house tonight. And the young man who was his granddaughter's father was descended from an aunt on his, Gerald's, mother's side.

All those Coneybears and Catfords, Parsleys, Petherbridges, and Shaplands. They were still around; living and dead. Lovering was still a fine place to raise a child—he stopped his aimless circling. Why, then, had it gone so wrong for him?

And why was he trying to interfere in his own daughter's life? He hadn't, much, when he'd been alive. Was he trying to make up for some past inattentiveness? What did it matter that she was, in his opinion, squandering her talent? As long as she was happy.

He exhaled and saw the cold grey mist which was all he was, re-form in the air in front of him.

At least the other matter had gone more or less according to plan. Less, if he considered that his friend Alex was no longer alive to be apologized to. He wondered where his ghost had got to. Still, he was glad Prudence had destroyed the letter.

He returned to the foyer where Trouble was sitting. "Well, little friend, shall we join the party?"

Ian walked the path to his house as the sun set. Especially in winter, it was better to be in, chores done, trying to conserve heat, before dark. He carried a bag of food and he had two packs of cigarettes in his jacket pocket. He was all set.

As he approached the shelter, he called "Catscatscatscatscats!" a sibilant sound his cats had grown used to. "Hey, you guys, you all here?" He counted them as usual. One, two, three, four, five, six. "Hello, my special girl," he said softly to Mandy as she curled her blackness around his legs. "We've got cans tonight."

He hummed as he opened one large can of cat food and thwacked it out onto a pie plate. All six cats, their whiskers touching and twitching, fed communally. He watched their grey-striped, orange-striped, white and black splotched, and black fur undulate around the dish.

He kindled a fire in his makeshift firepit and opened another tin. This he thwacked into a pot. Soon he was wolfing down beef stew with bread and margarine.

All fed, he built up the fire, and he and his cats lay down. As usual, he kept his clothes on, even his new boots. Later, when he warmed up, he would remove them, a few layers of clothing. He reached for a Kurt Vonnegut novel and began to read.

He dozed then awoke when he heard the sound of feet crunching in snow. "Who's there?" he called.

Someone was feeling around the outside surface of the shelter. The zipper for the tent was underneath all the tarps and improvised framework. Ian got up and called again.

"What do you want?" His cats had disappeared, hiding. *I wish I had a dog,* he thought, feeling frightened.

The sounds outside intensified. He could see from inside that someone was tugging at his house. He looked around for a weapon. His axe. He picked it up. A ripping sound came from the front of the shelter. He saw a large knife blade. Someone was cutting their way in. He raised the axe.

A face appeared. Then another.

Ian let the arm holding the axe drop to his side and asked, *"What are you doing here?"*

17

"All right, let me see if I have this straight." Doug lifted Dot from her high chair onto his lap, from where, he hoped, she'd be more amenable to eating her toast soldiers dipped in soft-boiled egg.

It wasn't that she didn't like this comestible—she did. But lately, being strapped in a high chair had seemed to weigh heavily on her fourteen-month-old shoulders as some sort of an injustice. Today her father's lap proved an acceptable perch and she opened her mouth.

Doug continued. "When you and Bertie visited Madame Ménard at the seniors' residence last fall—"

"It was at Christmas, actually," Prudence corrected.

"Okay, Christmas. She buzzed you in and you went up to the second floor where there's a…what do you call it?"

"A large hallway and communal living area. The apartments are so tiny that when people move in, they're downsizing and they often donate some of their furniture to the residence—including rugs."

"Including rugs," Doug echoed.

A small, nervous black cat sat on Prudence's lap—the only one of Ian's cats rescued so far, the one that had attached herself to Bertie in the woods. Bertie, for some reason, had named her Lili, after the song "Lili Marleen," he said. Lili shifted uneasily, likely because several unfamiliar cats were staring at her.

Doug, Prudence and Dot were at the table where Doug and Dot were finishing breakfast. Gerry, who'd heard some of the rug-finding saga on the telephone the previous evening, had yet to make an appearance. As Doug had explained to Prudence, after their guests had left the previous night, Gerry'd gotten going in her studio and was still working when he went to bed.

"So, Bertie and I are walking through this common area on our way to the hallway that leads to Mme Ménard's apartment, when suddenly, I realize I'm walking alone. I look back and there's Bertie on his knees with a corner of a huge Persian rug flipped over, his loupe in his eye and his face about four inches from the rug."

Doug chuckled. "I can just see it."

Prudence nodded primly. "Anyway, there was some stuff about knots per square inch, KPSI, as it's known."

Gerry shuffled in. She looked blearily at her loved ones. "Coffee," she croaked, and continued into the kitchen.

Prudence called in that direction, "I've just gotten to the KPSI part."

Gerry returned, cradling a large mug that featured a red Dalek from the TV show *Doctor Who*, a gift she'd given herself a few years earlier. "Go on," she croaked again, pointing to the mutant. "I feel like one of these. No, that I've been exterminated by one."

News of an interloper having no doubt spread by cat telepathy, more of The Maples' crew joined the party in the living room. Lili prodded Prudence's lap painfully, shifting so she faced Prudence's stomach.

"Ouch," said that lady, pulling claws from her person. "Maybe this wasn't such a good idea, bringing her here. I was worried, as she's used to living with other cats, that she'd be lonely when we're both out of the house all day." Lili seemed to calm down, so Prudence continued with her story.

"Well, Bertie was counting out loud, and when he got to twenty, he said, 'Very interesting;' to thirty, it was 'Hum;' and at forty, he just let out a 'Whoop!' Then it was stuff about wool, natural dyes, little wear, intricate and unique design and so on. That it was probably made in northwestern Iran, formerly Persia, and should be authenticated by an expert.

"Of course, I was there to visit Mme Ménard and Luc, which I did, while Bertie went off to the building manager's office to tell her to keep people off the rug. As if she could. I don't know what happened after that."

"And this is where it gets interesting," Gerry said, stealing a toast finger off Dot's plate. Dot, full, handed another one to her mother, seemingly charmed by her eating them.

"Because that rug was stolen shortly afterward—along with several others," Doug said slowly. "Huh. Almost as if the thieves knew it was there, eh?"

Prudence nodded. "Exactly. But then it was Christmas, then New Year's, and we were busy at the café, so by the time Bertie got in touch with one of his expert friends, that rug, and others, were gone."

"Until yesterday," Gerry said triumphantly.

"Until yesterday," Prudence repeated. "Bertie likes to treasure hunt—picking, it's called—so yesterday we drove to the flea market down by the canal.

"So, we're sauntering around and I'm looking at some pretty china plates—you know, for the café—and I realize I've lost Bertie."

"Again," snickered Gerry from the kitchen. "Toast, anyone?"

"No, thank you. Yes, again. And I see he's crossed the aisle behind me and is talking to a rug dealer, and I can see, though he's trying to look cool, he's excited."

Gerry returned with a plate of fresh hot buttered toast and began to crunch.

"The rug," said Doug, jigging Dot on his knee. Cats, cruising for crumbs, and becoming used to the stranger on Prudence's lap, surged closer. Lili, trying to sleep, opened one eye, her slender black tail beginning to thrash.

"Yes. Anyway, Bertie informed the dealer that the rug had been stolen. The poor man was crestfallen at first but then admitted he hadn't paid much for it anyway. He'd only bought that one rug from the seller, who—cleverly—seems to have spread his goods around. And according to the dealer, the seller was medium-height and stocky, not tall and thin, so it wasn't Ian Murchison. So, the seniors' residence will get one of its rugs back, and maybe—if the original donor or their heirs can be identified—someone might be in for a nice surprise."

Winston, Franklin and Joseph chose this moment to surround Prudence and place their front paws on the perimeter of her lap, cleverly boxing in its inhabitant, all the better to smell her.

It was too much for poor Lili, who suddenly launched herself into the air. Her nearest refuge was about six feet away—the fireplace mantel, where top cat Bob lay fast asleep. She might have made it, too, if Bob's senses hadn't kicked in. He reared up, ears flat, mouth open in a hiss, baring his fangs and raising one paw. Lili twisted mid-air and landed instead on the hearthrug—right on top of Mother, Ronald, Seymour and Lightning.

It wasn't pretty. The appalled humans eventually found Lili in the next room, on top of the kitchen cabinets. Doug retrieved her with the help of a stepladder. A rueful Prudence loaded her cat into its carrier and drove her home, promising to return. Doug left for work—today he was helping a local farmer fell dead trees—while Gerry and Dot headed upstairs to get dressed.

"Pee-ew! You need a diaper change, girl!"

Gerry held Dot so she was sitting on the top of the room's bureau, with her feet in the open drawer where Gerry one-handedly rummaged for a clean diaper, wipes and zinc ointment. Dot twisted around and placed a finger on the photo of Gerry's dad's family. "Da!" she said.

"Oh, Dottie, you call all the men 'Da.'"

Gerry looked at the photo and with a pang remembered Dot calling Ian Murchison "Da Da" in the car. "Poor Ian," she murmured, changing Dot on the bed, and thinking that now, at least, they knew he probably didn't have anything to do with the theft of the rugs.

18

"Meow." A pause. A rustle. "Mew. Mew."

Gerry prowled the dining room slowly. "Where's Dot?" She suddenly bent over and looked under the table.

Dot was in one of the larger cardboard boxes, which were meant for two cats at a time. Her face was turned away. "Meow," she said.

"Dot, where are you? All I can see are cats." It was true: various felines were curled in boxes, taking their ease. Gerry straightened up as Doug entered the room. She pointed underneath the table.

Doug played along. "Where's Dot, Ger? It's time to go."

"Well, Doug, I'm afraid—" Gerry paused for effect. "I can't see her. She *may* have turned into a cat."

Doug grinned and pulled out a chair, sitting at the table. "How did that happen?"

Gerry also pulled out a chair, or tried to—it was occupied by Harley, in all his immensity. Gerry left him where he was and instead sat on Doug's lap. She spoke in a hushed voice. "Well, you know what happens when people go into the Cat Lands."

Another meow, this one a bit quieter, came to their ears.

"Cat Lands?" asked Doug.

Gerry dropped her voice an octave. "You know—that special place, under the table."

"Oh, under the table." Doug raised his eyebrows and pointed to his wrist.

Gerry continued. "Sometimes people crawl under the table to see their friends, and they forget that they're little girls. They really, really, really think they're cats. And sometimes, they are!"

"What? You mean they turn into cats?"

"Yup. So, I don't know where Dot is. All I see—" Gerry slid off Doug's lap and began searching under the table on all fours. She stopped at Dot's box. "Are cats!" As if to prove her point, Cocoon in one box, and Max in another, woke up and raised their heads.

Then Dot's head popped up. "Ma!"

"Dot!" said Gerry.

"Can we go now?" Doug asked, peering at them.

"Daddy!" Gerry said indignantly, while crawling out with Dot. "It's April Fool's! It's Dot's April Fool's joke on us." She concluded, less confidently, "Or something."

Doug picked Dot up and swung her into the air. "Dot doesn't know April Fool's."

Dot giggled.

Gerry switched into efficient mother mode. "Right. Have you got everything you need? Diaper bag? Drinks, snacks?"

"Yeah, I already packed the chips and beer," the former alcoholic joked.

He and Dot were off to meet his sons. The spring thaw had come and the men of the family had decided to celebrate with a trek. Doug had been used to camping and hiking with his sons, and today was to be Dot's initiation into the Shapland tradition. They were all going on an expedition to climb Royal Mountain, the local ski hill, now closed for the season. It was only seven hundred feet high so it made for a nice walk. "Are you sure you won't come?"

"I am so sure!" Gerry replied. "Instead of a day alone to do whatever I want? After the cat boxes, dishes, laundry. *Then* whatever I want."

"Okay," he said, smiling. "Next time it's my turn to stay home, all right?"

"Deal." She kissed them. "Say hi to your brothers for me, Dot," she called as they left.

I hope they take lots of photos, she thought, as she went about the house doing chores. Lucky Dot's got all those guys to carry her when she gets tired.

She sat down on the sofa in the living room with her second coffee and stared at the cold hearth. She closed her eyes and took stock of her life.

Dot was walking. It was official. She rarely crawled anymore, unless she was being a cat. And bottles, like breastfeeding, were had become things of the past; sippy cups were now leaking all over the house as Dot tipped, shook and otherwise experimented with them.

At the museum, the frame on which Gerry had focused for the last two-plus months was nearly completed. All that remained were the distressing techniques she was beginning to learn.

She imagined the newly gilded frame—it shone. But apparently, that wasn't the goal; it had to be dulled down by applying lacquer and wax with a brush or cloth until it looked slightly stressed.

Her eyes opened. Strangely, she was alone. No, wait, that *was* strange. Where were all the cats?

She remembered. The cat flap was now unblocked. They must be outside. She got up to look out the back window.

There were her cats. A nose here, a tail there. An orange one sat under the hydrangeas—Mother, she thought. A fluffy grey and white one was on the pink flagstone path that abutted the narrow wooden deck that ran along the back of the house—that was Cocoon. Away by the shore were three grey blobs and a white one—the three brothers and their sidekick Ronald. Up to no good, no doubt. At least where birds and mice were concerned.

Gerry savoured her coffee. It felt smooth in her mouth. She took a deep, slow breath and looked up. Something up in a bare maple caught her eye. "I wish he wouldn't go so high," she muttered, remembering one occasion when Bob had plummeted from a different tree, the willow, into the swimming pool. Today, he was stretched out, serenely observing his kingdom.

Someone brushed against Gerry's calf. "Oh, hello, Monkey. You not outside with everybody else?" She picked up the cat and for once, it allowed her to. Gerry buried her face in the cat's fur then tilted its head up. "Look at Bob, Monks. Isn't he a nut? You and me would never go that high, would we?"

Monkey appeared to look up for a moment, then let her gaze drop back down. And Gerry felt a sudden rush of love. For it all: the cats, her home, her family. Her *family*. That she had one was due entirely to Aunt Maggie leaving The Maples to her. Otherwise, her parents dead, Gerry would be living her life alone in Toronto. No Doug. No extended family of cousins and friends. No *Dot*.

Which made her tear up. Dot. Dot would be fine. Even if there was no Gerry to look after her. Dot had a father and three big brothers. And honorary grandparents, uncles and aunts in Prudence, Bertie, Bea, Cece, Andrew, Markie and Cathy. And even Mary. For the first time since Dot had been born, Gerry felt her maternal anxiety ease. Just a bit.

She kissed Monkey's little head and put her down. "Boy, I need today, Munks. Let's wander into the studio and see what tickles our fancy. I *think* I know…"

What she was most eager to work on now was finishing the last few illustrations for *The Candy King of Bubbly-Sauceton*. The final one—maybe for the back cover—would be a long view of the fictional town's main street, showing William from behind as he delivered papers, just as her father had, with Prince Charles stumping alongside. And maybe a few cats peeking out here and there. But before that…

She lost herself in creating and worked until she felt hungry. Monkey had kept her company all morning, sedately sleeping on the studio's sofa, and now accompanied her to the kitchen. Sandwich in hand, she returned to the studio and switched projects. For a long time, she'd wanted to complete a little homage to Aunt Maggie, who'd written curious short pieces about Lovering and its characters—all real people she'd known as a child—and all written for Maggie's English composition class in elementary school.

Gerry had illustrated a half dozen so far, but, as each composition only warranted one or two drawings, there was not yet enough material for even a slim book. She pulled out one of her aunt's scribblers, lay on the sofa and began to read. Monkey hopped up and deigned to nestle.

Miss Partridge

Miss Patridge is very old. Miss Partridge is very stiff and walks slowly. Miss Partridge has white patches mixed up with regular skin colour on her arms and face. Miss Partridge used to be a nurse.

Miss Partridge lives in a nice flat grey house with bumpy walls and white trim. Her gardens are very nice. Not like ours, but still, quite nice.

Like us, she has little blue flowers scattered all over her lawn in the spring, and fat pink balls called peonies later in the spring. And fine mums in the fall. In between she has annuals.

Annuals are plants that are planted annually. That means once a year. They die in the fall. Like bugs. This is sad, but my brother Gerry says they, the flowers and the bugs, have one fun year and that that's enough for them.

Annuals are the reasons I know Miss Partridge. I plant hers for her. My brother used to plant them, then he got too busy with other stuff and I got the job.

I ride my bike over to Miss Partridge's on the last Saturday of May. I've done this twice now. Miss Partridge pays me five cents for every plant I plant. She comes outside and tells me which plants to plant where. And then we count the empty containers and she pays me.

The plants have nice names like marigold, sweet alyssum, salvia and coleus. Miss Partridge likes bright colours, so her flowers are red and orange and purple and yellow. I like them too.

Miss Partridge used to be an army nurse. She says that soon, when it all gets too much for her, she's going to live in the big veterans' hospital in the next village.

I don't know what 'it' is, but I know when I asked my mother what happened to Miss Partridge's skin, she looked sad and said Miss Partridge is a heroine and I must never, ever mention it. The skin, I mean, not the other 'it.'

Like all her aunt's youthful literary efforts, this one ended abruptly and, Gerry thought, in this instance, poignantly.

She went and sat at her artist's table, which faced the road, and contemplated the little story. It would be kindest, she decided, if, when doing the illustrations, she gave Miss Partridge long sleeves and a turned-away face while she supervised young Maggie in the garden. Yes, let the reader imagine—the crunch of tires pulling into the house's circular driveway broke into her reverie.

"What the—? It can't be Doug back already!" She peered through the window and saw her Aunt Mary's large expensive car. "Oh, rats! Rats, rats, rats! I only wanted one day! Just one!" She calmed herself. "It's okay. You haven't seen her in ages. She's your only aunt. She's been ill. Give her some time. Breathe. Breathe." She heard Mary at the front door and went to let her in.

"Gereee! Let me kiss you!" Air kisses were exchanged.

"Come in, Aunt Mary. I was just—" Gerry winced internally at the lie. "Going to take a break."

"Oh," her aunt said loudly, stepping into the foyer, "are you *working*?" (This from someone who never had.) "I just assumed, because it's Saturday—" She took in the silence of the house. "Where is everybody? I didn't see Doug's truck."

And that's probably one of the reasons you dropped in, Gerry thought sourly. She led the way to the living room. Mary dropped her purse on the coffee table and flopped onto the couch, sending the more sensitive cats—Lightning and Seymour, who'd been sleeping there—flying from the room. A more stolid individual, Max, stood his ground, staring at the intruder. "Oof, I'm a bit tired. It smells nice in here. Kind of sweet."

Gerry went into the kitchen and called, "We've been taking the sap from the trees at the house here and boiling it down pretty regularly. Doug tells me it's almost finished now. It's getting too warm for the trees. Tea or coffee?"

"Coffee. I need the pep."

Gerry stood in the kitchen doorway. "Are you tired from something in particular or in general?"

"General. But these drugs they give you aren't great." She was referencing her breast cancer post-surgery, post-chemo medication.

"How long do you have to take them for?"

"I'm not sure. Five years, I think—or until the cancer comes back." The last words were edged with bitterness, and for the first time Gerry felt a genuine flicker of sympathy for her aunt.

The kettle boiled so she turned away. "I'm sorry you've had such a rough year, Mary," she called over her shoulder. She brought the coffee and some cookies.

"Yeah, me too. But it's over now. The worst is over, Ed says."

"How is Ed?"

"Oh, *he's* fine. Excuse me." She reached under her shirt and made an adjustment. "This thing is really heavy. I call it my cannonball."

Gerry didn't know what to say. "Er, that sounds uncomfortable."

There was a pause, then Mary said, "Your neighbour has invited me over for tea next week."

"Which one?"

"Edwina Murray. The writer. Says she wants to pick my brain for her next garden club mystery. I *do* know a lot about gardening."

"Oh, yes." Gerry, remembering how Edwina had hinted that her next epic—*A Delicate Flower*—might, or might not, be based on her aunt's character, just barely managed to keep a straight face. She hurriedly changed the subject. "I, ah, was just reading one of Maggie's little stories—one called 'Miss Partridge.'"

"Miss Partridge? I remember her. Gerry—your father—did her yard work for a while until he got fed up with it. Then Maggie did some little jobs for the old lady, not cutting the lawn of course or anything major. They wanted me to take over from Gerry, but really—" Mary looked at her white hands and well-maintained, polished nails. "Can you see it?" Mary's idea of gardening was from the design-point-and-command school.

Gerry managed another noncommittal "Er," before asking, "so, how old was Miss Patridge? She was a veteran?"

"Yes. I guess in the 1950s she was already in her sixties. Not what we'd call old today." She patted her wig complacently. "But she'd served in both world wars and had been bombed or something. Or was it a plane crash? I forget. Anyway, she'd been burned. I remember, when she moved away, Maggie helped her pack. And got given quite a few porcelain ornaments for her trouble."

"She must have liked that."

"*That's* better," Mary said, finishing her coffee. "Anyway, I just wanted to ask you if you all want to join Ed and me at my place on Easter Sunday? Casual. The usual ham and so on."

"I'll check with Doug, but I don't see why not." Sensing her aunt's business concluded, Gerry began to clear up.

Sure enough, Mary stood. "Well, better get going. Things to buy, you know." She trilled her rather brittle laugh and once again, Gerry felt sorry for her unlikeable aunt.

19

All of the CRAS cat traps, but one, had long since been returned to the society. The remaining trap was still being faithfully checked each day by Bertie. Gerry, her creative train of thought broken by Mary's visit, decided she might as well retrieve the last cage that afternoon. Then she'd call Jean Delamar to arrange its return.

I wonder if my family is coming back down Royal Mountain now, she thought as she drove the short distance to Prudence's house. After she parked, she noticed a rusty red Honda at the side of the road next to the start of the phone company's servitude.

Walkers, she supposed, and went along the half-frozen path.

She began to hear a most frightening noise.

She knew what *that* was. She quickened her pace, but one foot encountered a patch of ice hidden under a puddle and down she went, jarring her left elbow as she landed.

She lay dazed for a moment before sitting up. She rubbed the elbow. Not broken. She waggled the ankle that had twisted and winced. "Rats," she said, but quietly, thankful that no one had seen her fall.

Cautiously, she rose. The ankle was only sprained, by the feel of it. She limped toward the noise, which was intensifying. She ducked under the police tape and flipped back the tarp that hung across the tent entrance, noticing for the first time a long tear to one side of the canvas, and looked inside.

What sounded like a mountain lion was just a cat. A very large, grey-striped cat. In the cage. That Gerry would now have to carry. She went in.

The cat's ears were flat to its head. Its yellow eyes were huge. And the sounds it was making reminded Gerry of Bob and Blaise's cat Graymalkin mixing it up.

It must be terrified, she thought. "Hey, buddy," she said softly. "Is it okay if I call you Buddy? Hey, Buddy, did you at least have something to eat?"

She bent over the cage. No food visible, so, assuming Bertie had loaded the trap that morning, at least the cat had fed.

"Who're you?"

Gerry jumped and spun around. A woman stood in the entrance.

"What are you doing to that cat?"

Gerry straightened. "Ah, nothing. Nothing. We, I, we're trying to rescue Ian's cats."

The woman appeared to be thinking this over. She was tall, about fifty, and wearing jeans and a heavy men's khaki jacket. A black tuque was pulled low over her forehead.

Gerry asked, "Are you a town inspector, or something?"

The woman laughed. "An inspector!? Nah. I'm the sister of the guy who used to live here."

"Oh, you must be Rebecca." Gerry examined her face. It managed to be puffy and drawn at the same time. Her eyes were bloodshot.

The woman nodded, looking surprised that Gerry knew her name. She gruffly said, "I just came to have a look around."

They both looked at the dirt and disorder, the ripped canvas. Gerry said, "I'm Gerry Coneybear. I live on Main Road, not far from here, and I knew Ian a little. Just to give rides to. And we both liked cats." There was an awkward pause. "So, I'm very sorry for your loss." Another pause. Gerry realized she should make her exit. "Well, um, is it okay if I take a blanket to cover the cage? I'll return it if you want." She turned to look at the cat who was emitting a continuous low growl. "I'm afraid of it scratching me even through the cage, and I forgot my gloves."

Rebecca waved a hand. "Yeah, yeah. Take whatever you want. It's all junk." She seemed disgusted and kicked at the rubbish on the floor.

Gerry chose a stained quilted comforter and laid it over the cage. The cat quieted. "You don't want it, do you?"

Rebecca seemed taken aback. "Me? God, no." She laughed again. "Our German shepherd would eat it for lunch!"

Gerry awkwardly picked up the whole bulky object and limped past Rebecca. "Be careful when you go, eh? I slipped on the path a moment ago."

Rebecca said nothing further. Gerry wondered where the woman had been when she'd arrived. Then she grinned. Probably having a pee behind the tent. She crooned to the now silent cat, "Okay, Buddy, time to get you to the vet."

But when she got there, it was after 4:00 pm on a Saturday and the absence of cars in the parking lot meant that not even a technician was still working. No point in hammering on the door.

Back home, she parked next to Doug's pickup. She carefully unloaded Buddy, slid open the big door to the woodshed, and brought the cage in, resting it on the floor. As it was spring, there was little wood left, about half a cord, and her voice, when she spoke, rang hollowly in the space. She twitched a portion of the comforter away.

"I'm sorry, Buddy, you're going to have to stay in there. How miserable for you. I'll get you something nice to eat—oh, no, I can't." She envisioned dropping bits of canned cat food through the wire. "No, that would be too messy. I'll get you some more kibble. And I'm afraid you'll just have to be thirsty until tomorrow. No! I have an idea!"

She entered the house, shouting, "We caught one! We finally caught one!"

Doug appeared moments later. "Shush! She's asleep in her playpen in the den. Conked out on the drive home, woke up, cried a bit, then went back to sleep. What did you say? Why are you bashing up ice cubes?"

"Come on—I'll show you. We've trapped a cat."

They left the house. "Okay, I'm curious. The ice?"

"Well, if we open the cage, he'll escape for sure." They paused in the open doorway of the shed.

Buddy was emitting weird, long-drawn-out yowls and looked to be in full attack mode, every hair standing on end. "I see what you mean," Doug said cautiously. "But the vet's open tomorrow, right?"

She nodded. "Yup. We just have to get through tonight." A yowl from behind them made them turn. Bob was crouched on the parking pad asphalt outside the shed, ears flattened, tail fluffed, body tensed in pre-spring readiness. "Oh, thank God the other one's caged," Gerry said. "Can you imagine if it wasn't?"

Both cats suddenly hushed. Bob inched closer. Behind him, reinforcements appeared: Winston, Franklin, Joseph and Ronald. "Okay, then," Doug said. "Ice?"

Gerry began dropping bits of ice through the top of the cage, aiming for the empty dish inside. "He's eaten whatever kibble Bertie left in the cage but he must be thirsty. Let's leave him alone for a bit." She put the cover back over the cage, left the shed, and closed the door. "He must be used to ice and icy water, living outside since Ian died. I'll take him some more kibble later."

Bob and the other cats looked confused. Bob got up and carefully sniffed all around the shed door, the other four watching. The boys and Ronald soon lost interest, but Bob, as Gerry noticed later from a kitchen window, made himself comfortable in front of the door, grimly keeping guard.

He was still there when, an hour later, Gerry returned with a cupful of kibble. "Sorry, Bob," she said, as she closed the shed door in his face. "Buddy might have a disease." Inside, she rained dry cat food on Buddy's large head.

For he was a big cat, almost as big as Harley and Kitty-Cat. Probably hadn't been fixed either. "Well, that's gotta be done at the vet's, for one thing," she told him. "Regrettably for you.

At first the cat wouldn't eat while she was there, but once she'd moved away and found a large enough log to upend for a stool, it began crunching. All the time, she kept up a light banter, explaining how things went at The Maples.

"That's another big guy outside, the one you were trash talking with. He's kind of the boss here. I wonder if you were the boss of Ian's six. You were? Huh. Well, you and Bob are going to have to work it out if you're going to join our gang. Work it out with Bob and the others will probably all fall into line. Except maybe for Lightning. She's another tough one."

The door slid open and Doug came in carrying Dot. Bob leapt toward the doorway, but Doug's foot prevented his entry. Doug slid the door closed.

"Meow!" Dot said, pointing at Buddy. Doug put her down and she toddled towards his cage. Buddy put his ears back and hissed. Dot laughed. "Meow! Meow!" Then she hissed back, quite realistically. Both her parents' faces expressed surprise. Even Buddy seemed taken aback.

Gerry intercepted Dot before she could stick her fingers through the wire. "His name is Buddy, Dot."

Doug sounded resigned as he said, "You're keeping it, aren't you?"

Gerry grinned sheepishly. "I'm afraid so. But he has to not fight the others. And pass all his tests at the vet's."

They all looked at Buddy. Buddy hissed again. "Let's give him some privacy," Gerry suggested as she prepared to open the door, "Stand by to repel boarders!"

They did—repel Bob, that is—and everyone trooped into the house to prepare supper—except for Bob, who took up sentry duty once more, even missing his own supper.

Nor did he appear on Gerry and Doug's bed that night, apparently having spent the hours in front of the woodshed's sliding door. It was with relief for her exhausted favourite that Gerry took Buddy to the vet the next morning, where he would be quarantined for at least two days.

When she returned, she found Bob asleep on the mantelpiece, and when she fixed herself a coffee and settled on the sofa with a book, he hopped off and subsided on her lap, alternately snoring and purring for the rest of the morning.

Cat drama over—at least temporarily—Gerry found herself thinking about Ian Murchison's sister, Rebecca. She certainly hadn't seemed sorry about his death. Gerry said as much to Doug at lunch.

"I guess," he replied, "if they hadn't seen each other for a long time, it kind of makes sense."

"Or if she resented him, which people who knew the family seem to think," Gerry mused.

They both looked at Dot in her high chair, eating fruit with her fingers. "Do you think we should have another child?" Gerry asked, timidly. "So Dot isn't alone growing up—like you and I were? I mean, the boys are old enough to be her father. Fathers. You know what I mean."

Doug paused, then said, "We should consider carefully, I think. I don't have an immediate response either way. It would be my fifth child." He smiled sweetly. "I guess if you wanted to, I wouldn't say no."

"Oh, great! So, it's *my* decision!?"

He seemed taken aback. "No! I just meant—as it's your body. And you seem so tired, and always saying you don't have time for work—where are you going?"

Gerry was up. "I don't know. For a drive. Or a walk. A walk." In an instant she was out the door and striding down the road. It was only as she slowed, that she realized she had the answer to her question. For now, at least.

She walked past St. Anne's church. Soon the little flowers Maggie had written about would blue the churchyard's nascent lawn. She thought about all the family members buried there, about families in general.

She had a vague plan of walking a big loop, as far as the train tracks that would take her back towards The Maples, then cutting through the woods behind Cathy's, but she was startled when a vehicle slowed behind her and a gruff male voice called, "Gerry!"

It was Charlie and Rita, Prudence's friends and neighbours. Rita leaned across her husband. "We're just going to Prue's café. Want a ride?"

"Sure. Why not?" She crossed the road and hopped into the pickup truck's cab next to Rita. A talk show blared from the radio. "—build the damn hospital but can't hire enough people to staff it!"

"What's new?" Rita asked.

"Nothing. You?"

The radio show's host asked, "Caller, what do *you* have to say about—"

"Bringing some bread to Prue. She's going to try sandwiches."

"Oh? That's why the cab smells so good. You looking for a job?"

The radio interrupted. "It's been five years and we still don't have a—"

Rita laughed and turned to Charlie. "Gerry asks if I'm looking for a job."

Charlie, who was a bit deaf, said, "Eh?"

"A job! Gerry asks if Prue's going to give me a job."

"Prue's giving Gerry a job?"

Rita thundered in his ear. "No! Me!" She reached and turned the radio down. "No," she said at a lower volume. "Me. A job baking for Prue. You know—we talked about it."

She turned back to Gerry. "But from home. We don't have any pets and I would wear a hair net."

Charlie's voice rumbled. "Terrible about that Murchison guy in the woods, wasn't it? Prue said you were helping him. He always looked frightened when I saw him."

Rita glanced at her husband and sounded exasperated when she said, "Well, you did shout at him to stay away from the yard that time, didn't you?"

"I have a lot of tools and machinery lying around!" Charlie replied indignantly.

A junkyard was how Gerry remembered Prudence describing her neighbours' backyard, which was next to the woods where Ian had lived.

"Well, anyway," Rita said calmly. "Charlie was worried about me too, being alone in the house sometimes."

Gerry could see how it might make a difference to how one felt about him, if the homeless man was camping right next door.

As they passed the community centre, Gerry saw Rebecca Murchison emerge, following a man. Her head was bowed, and she was shuffling. Had she been at the Legion bar? The man strode to a pickup truck and got into the driver's seat, slamming the door behind him. A white van pulled up beside the truck, and Rebecca's husband—if that's who he was—appeared to be talking to someone inside the van. Rebecca got in the other side of the pickup, but by then Gerry was past the centre and Charlie was turning to park at the café.

Inside, Gerry asked Bertie, who was working the front, if she could use the phone. Proudly he pulled a mobile out of his back pocket. "Use this, m'dear," he said grandly. "I just got it. It's the future!"

As Gerry looked blankly at the little glass screen, he showed her how to input the number. She told Doug where she was. Stepping away from Bertie, she said softly, "I'm so sorry. It was all me. Not you. Me."

She returned the phone to Bertie and, to her surprise, found him deep in conversation with Charlie—about lawn mowers, of all things. *Lawn mowers? Bertie?* Looking around the café for a quiet corner where she could unruffle her feathers, she spotted one already occupied by her friend Christine. She waved and walked over. As she approached, she noticed that, for some reason, Christine looked guilty.

A younger Gerry would probably have said something like, "Oh, ho!" on spying the remains of a *pain au chocolat* and a large coffee on her health-conscious friend's table.

Grown-up Gerry merely smiled and asked if she might sit down. "I'm just waiting for Doug and Dot to meet me here." She looked around. "Is Lawrence with you?"

Christine shook her head, wiping her lips with a paper napkin. "No. He's with the kids. Mom's little getaway." She laughed self-consciously. "It's funny, that's what my dad used to say when my mom went out by herself, shopping, or meeting a friend. He'd encourage her to get herself something extravagant. He's been dead for five years now."

"Oh, my dad too. My mom died long before him. You're lucky you still have your mom. And good for you," Gerry said. "We all need a little treat sometimes." She sighed. "Actually, I just had a spat with Doug and walked out." When Christine looked concerned, Gerry hastened to add, "No, no, not *walked out* walked out. Just, you know, went for a walk to cool down. I overreacted."

She grinned. "Do you ever do that, Chris? Overreact? You're usually so calm."

Bertie brought Gerry her favourite almond croissant and a latte. "Your usual, Madame." He turned to Christine. "Anything else for you? No?" He winked at Gerry and left.

Christine sipped her coffee. "I suppose. I'm going through an early menopause and I just feel so *angry* all the time."

Gerry was shocked. "Really? But you're so young-looking!"

Christine laughed. "Thanks. I try. I'm forty-three; it's not unheard of. Jane must have been my last egg."

Gerry felt disturbed. "Gosh. That's what Doug and I—maybe it's too personal—I don't know—we were discussing whether to have any more kids."

"You're right—it's very personal. I can't advise you. I'm done—that's for sure!"

Gerry cast about for something else to talk about. "We're at your place for playgroup this week, aren't we?"

Christine nodded then smiled. "Don't worry; I'll get some good things for us to eat. It won't be all lettuce and sunflower seeds."

Gerry laughed. "I'm grateful." She lowered her voice. "Hey, I just saw Rebecca Murchison stagger out of the community centre. With, I'm guessing, her boyfriend? Husband?"

"Her husband, Rick—Richard Graham. High school sweethearts." She shook her head. "Rebecca had—has—a drink problem."

"Oh. That's too bad. I saw her in the woods yesterday too. At Ian's place. I was retrieving a trapped cat and she was checking out his stuff, I guess."

"She's his heir, I suppose. Oh, there's Doug and Dot."

"I better go." Gerry rose.

"I'm going too. See you Thursday."

"See you Thursday."

20

Easter Sunday at Mary's passed pleasantly enough. Mary had them all outside squelching around on her wet lawn looking for Easter eggs. Gerry and Doug had already performed the exercise with Dot at their house earlier that morning, so they let Dot toddle off with her big brothers, who took turns lifting her up to retrieve eggs from window ledges and the crotches of trees.

Easter Monday Prudence came to babysit as the cleaners, the Markovs, had taken the day off. Doug went to the Yacht Club; some early birds were eager to get their boats into the water, and boat-craft was another of his areas of expertise.

When Gerry came out of her studio around eleven in search of refreshment, she found Prudence in the kitchen with Dot, both in aprons. Dot's, denim with a baby elephant on its front, fit her perfectly. "Prudence, wherever did you get it?"

"Lucy makes them." Lucy Hanlan was one of Prudence's oldest friends and owner of Lovering's fabric store.

Dot, standing on a chair with one of Prudence's arms steadying her, was stirring something vigorously.

"It's sweet. Thank you. What are you making?"

"Wait and see," Prudence replied smartly. A puff of flour enveloped the small baker. Prudence smiled. "Remember when I first taught you to bake?"

Gerry laughed. "Flour everywhere. Well, at this rate, Dot will be able to take over the cooking at The Maples entirely."

"You wish."

"Yeah, okay. I know when I'm not wanted."

Gerry took her tea and stepped into the living room. She glanced at the mantelpiece and did a double-take. Instead of Bob's slim tuxedo elegance, Buddy's massive, grey-striped physique was on display.

"Oh, Buddy," she warned, stepping closer, but not *too* close. "You're taking an awful risk. If Bob catches you—" She left the consequences unvoiced. A group of elderly cats dozed on the sofa below the sacrilege.

She took another step towards the cat but its tail puffed and it hunched. She hastily backed away. "Okay, okay. I'm going." She walked back to the studio, remembering what Jean from the Cat Rescue and Adoption Society had said about feral cats—that some of them never became friendly or trusting; in fact, they often just ran away.

As she returned to work, Gerry muttered, "But so far, so good." Buddy was healthy, now neutered, and because the cat flap was operational, could come and go as he pleased, which meant he and Bob could avoid each other. She just worried that the battle for supremacy, when it came, might be bloody.

After lunch, while Prudence settled Dot to sleep, Gerry prepared a pot of tea to go with the currant scones Dot and Prudence had made. Dot had eaten part of one, but found it necessary to pick out the currants, which she'd dropped one by one onto the floor. It was amusing to watch the cats chew a currant, make the feline equivalent of a sour face, then walk away, disgusted. All except Monkey, of course, who ate one of the tiny fruits before Gerry finally swept them up.

"Never a dull moment," she commented to Prudence.

"Mm." Prudence poured herself a tea.

"What? You sound pensive."

"Well, Bertie and I have been thinking; how did the rug thieves know there were valuable rugs in the residence? I mean, it wouldn't be worth stealing cheap used ones; they'd get almost nothing from whichever dealer they took them to. Bertie said the rug dealer at the flea market who bought the Persian one paid the seller five hundred dollars. And it's worth way more than that."

"How much more?"

"Add a couple of zeroes."

Gerry added and her eyes widened. "Really? For a rug?"

Prudence nodded. "It's worn in places or it would be worth a lot more. Anyway, it seems to me—to us—that someone may have cased the residence before the robbery. We don't know how many other rugs may have been taken."

"Presumably, the manager of the residence knows, don't you think?"

"Not unless they inventory the odds and ends of furniture that come and go with their clients."

"Hm. I see. It's not nice to think of Mme Ménard living where there may be a questionable employee."

Prudence nodded, her expression grim. "Exactly. Not that she has anything left to lose after the fire." A house fire a few years earlier had destroyed almost all of Mme Ménard's possessions.

Now Gerry sounded thoughtful when she said, "You know, it doesn't have to have been a regular employee that spotted the rugs. There must be service people that go there—health care workers, cleaners, people making deliveries, even just plain old visitors, like you and Bertie."

Prudence nodded. "I know. It's a dead end. How would you ever narrow them down?"

Gerry shook her head. "I don't know, Prue. I just don't know." She brightened. "How's Lili? Still Bertie's true love?"

Prudence smiled. "Still. They go into his den when he doesn't want to watch TV with me and pore over antiques catalogues together."

Bertie had taken over Prudence's second bedroom as—and here his voice would drop at least an octave when he described it—"his man-cave." He'd installed a large desk, an easy chair, and various *objets d'art* that would have looked out of place in the rest of Prudence's modestly furnished mid-century bungalow.

"Cute," Gerry said distractedly.

Prudence stood up. "I can see you want to get back to work. I'll tidy up the kitchen. I'm here till teatime today, so enjoy yourself. While you can."

Gerry, her head full of rugs, Rebecca and Ian Murchison, and cats, always cats, wandered down the hallway from living to dining room and into the foyer. She stopped.

The heavy inside front door was ajar and someone, it must have been Prudence, had slid up the glass on the screen door so the foyer could air. Crouched on the sill, her head tracking from right to left and back, was Monkey.

As Gerry watched, the cat rose and pounced on a point midway along the sill and began digging energetically.

"Oh my God!" Gerry said, and, in turn, pounced on Monkey, lifting her up. "Monkey, why are you trying to take our house apart? First the bathroom, now the foyer!" She held the cat out at arms' length. "Why? Why?"

"What's all the drama?" Prudence said as she stepped into the room, wiping her hands on a dishcloth. "Quiet, or you'll wake the child."

Gerry hissed. "This *creature* was digging at the front door sill. At this rate, we'll have the walls and roof crashing down on us in no time!"

Prudence looked at Gerry. "Why are you so upset?" She bent and examined the sill. "A few splinters of wood removed. It's already quite worn from normal traffic. All it needs is a bit of paint."

Gerry calmed down and dropped Monkey. The cat began to groom. Prudence closed the inside door. "There: problem solved.

Cats have been being cats in this house for many years now, and it's still standing."

Gerry went into her studio and quietly closed the door.

Prudence and Monkey looked at each other. "Better lay off for a while," one grimly advised the other.

The other finished grooming and trotted back to the front door. She sat, looking down, cocked her head and listened.

The babble of children's voices mixed with that of several women trying to have conversations.

As usual, when she and Dot were around their peers, Gerry felt relaxed—as if, with all the other mothers nearby, she and Dot were extra-safe. The chaos of the kids contrasted sharply with the atmosphere of Christine's house. It was a modern bungalow with a flat roof, minimal interior walls, and Danish-modern-inspired décor. There was teak. There was an Eames chair. Surrounded by trees, the interior was dark, so a few large globes were switched on to cast their soft light.

"And I'd just had enough, you know?" Gerry was saying to Cyndi. "Do you ever—lose it?"

Cyndi snorted with laughter. "Only every day, Gerry! Pretty much."

Hilary called from across the room. "It's finding 'it' again—that's the trick. And you have to, when you're dealing with little kids." She gave Noah a squeeze and released him back into the melee. He found Dot and gave her a hug in turn. Dot, focused on eating part of an oatmeal cookie, looked startled. Noah moved on. Dot ate her snack.

"It wasn't the kid. It was a cat," replied Gerry, offering Dot a yellow sippy cup. Dot ignored her mother's outstretched hand. "The pica-cat, Monkey, was at it again, digging bits of wood off the front door sill."

Hilary laughed. "It's saying 'Let me out! Let me out!'"

Gerry shook her head. "No, that's not it. They have a cat flap, open from spring through fall. I don't know—it's having twenty non-human personalities to deal with, I guess. As well as the human ones."

"Twenty!" said Heather. "I thought you were down to nineteen. Natural attrition, you said, would slowly bring down the cat population at The Maples."

Hilary laughed. "Those sound more like your words, Heather."

Heather had first taken a degree in sociology, then in psychology. And she must have missed the playgroup when Gerry talked about her latest cat, Buddy. Come to think of it, Gerry reflected, Heather had been missing a lot of playgroups recently. And she looked tired. Must be working more.

Cyndi interjected. "She adopted another one. One from the homeless man who died in the woods."

"He growls at the other cats and at us, and it's only a matter of time before he and my cat Bob mix it up. But I thought, as he was used to being with other cats—Ian had six—that he'd adjust." Gerry concluded, lamely: "I just didn't think it would take weeks instead of days."

"Give it time," Heather counselled. "Are you still going into the city once a week?"

"Yes. But my three months are almost up. The exhibit opens next week."

"Well, you must be very proud, being part of such an undertaking," Heather said encouragingly.

"Yee-es. I guess." Gerry declined to say more, but she appreciated Heather's praise. Why shouldn't she feel proud of her conservation work? Why didn't she?

"Did you know that the Scandinavian goddess Freya, the goddess of lovers, rides in a chariot pulled by cats?"

"I'm speechless," said Gerry, hardly awake after sleeping in and barely making it to the train into Montreal. She sipped coffee from her travel mug and shuddered gratefully.

"I knew you would be," Bertie replied. "She's also the goddess of fertility, beauty, sex, war, death, gold and magic."

"So, like, uh, everything?"

"Exactly. And the cats represent the wild world of nature and the nurturing of the mother."

"Okaaaaay. And you're telling me this because—?"

"Oh. I just thought, if you were looking for a name for your new cat, you might like either Bygul or Trjegul."

"Biggle or Triggle?"

"Close enough."

"He *has* a name. I call him Buddy. But Biggle is tempting."

"Freya's cats are thought to be either blue—"

"Blue!"

"Or grey-striped. Prue told me, er, Buddy is a grey tabby, so I did some research and—"

Gerry turned to look at her friend. "Wait. Is that how you named Lili? From some research?"

"Well, not exactly. I mean, I already knew the song 'Lili Marleen' was about a poor girl whose soldier boyfriend gets killed and she's very lonely, so I thought—"

"Aw, you thought of Ian dying and Lili missing him and her throwing herself at you because you're tall and thin like Ian was."

"Oh." Bertie paused. "I never thought of that. I just thought she was tired and afraid and hungry."

"Yeah, all that, too. Bertie, what do you think happened out there? To Ian, I mean. When I found Buddy, I saw that the tent was all slashed on one side. Do you think Ian's killer did that?"

"Whoa, whoa, whoa. A: We do not know he was killed—on purpose. B: He may have cut his own tent for some reason—

like the zipper getting jammed. Or maybe he picked it from the garbage and it was already damaged. Thus, his need for tarps to cover it with." He corrected himself: "With which to cover it."

"Mm. You're still checking the cage, right?"

"Faithfully, Ma'am. Maybe we should just buy one from CRAS?"

"No, no, they don't mind. Jean's glad we caught two of the six. In another couple of weeks, it'll be warmer and we'll stop. Are you seeing Marion today?"

"No. She has an appointment. You want to go for lunch?"

"Okay."

"I know just the place," he said.

Just after noon they met outside the museum. They walked west for about five minutes then Bertie stopped.

"I don't believe it!" said Gerry.'

Café Katz said the handwritten sign in the window. And on another piece of cardboard taped to the inside of the door's window was printed: *People with cat allergies enter at their own risk.*

"I saw it last week." Bertie held the door for her. "It just opened. I couldn't resist."

There was a vestibule and then another door—to keep the cats safe inside. "Oh my God!" Gerry said excitedly. "They're mostly all kittens!"

Tiny rug-covered ramps led to little square dens in which curious faces appeared. Other cats were under tables, on the front window's low sill, or just on the floor. A white fluffy kitten tottered by in front of them.

A young woman welcomed them. "All our cats are for adoption. That's why most of them are young. Just the right age to make someone very happy." She beamed hopefully at the couple. Gerry didn't have the heart to tell her. She wondered if Bertie was tempted. And what Prudence would say if he succumbed to the kittens' charms!

"Just lunch for me today," she said, "but I'd love to visit with these guys."

"Of course. I'll bring you a menu."

"Cat hair in your salad?" Bertie snickered quietly. "Or maybe just in the kit–chen?"

"Shush. Let's just enjoy these babies. That we don't have to look after. Hello, beautiful," she cooed at a diminutive black and white shorthair who paused by her foot.

Back at work, she felt quite refreshed from her feline encounters and ready to sign off on the Emperor Napoleon's frame. It was her last day.

"Of course, you'll be coming to the vernissage?" queried Susan One.

"Of course," replied Gerry.

"And you'll have made your decision by then?"

"I think so," Gerry said cautiously. "There are a few more factors to consider."

21

They'd been too busy to attend church on Easter Sunday—plus, Gerry figured a less well-attended service might be easier with Dot, in case she had a meltdown. What with their Easter egg hunt, they'd been sitting down to breakfast when they'd heard the bell ringing from St. Anne's. But the following Sunday, Gerry dressed Dot in a nice little salmon-pink corduroy dress with embroidery on the chest and a pair of white tights, then headed out. Doug pleaded chores as an excuse not to go.

It was not the first time Dot had attended. They'd taken her to the children's service and pageant Christmas Eve, but she hadn't yet been a year old, and, after taking in the scene, still zipped in her snowsuit in the cold church, she'd fallen asleep before the Three Wise Men arrived at the stable, tripping over their robes and blushing below cardboard crowns.

Today was different. Spotting Doug's aunts Jane and Bette sitting not far from the entranceway, Gerry slid in next to them.

Jane, the elder sister, leaned close and whispered excitedly, "Did you see the doors?"

Gerry, settling Dot decorously between them (she hoped), asked, "Doors?"

Bette, seated furthest along the pew, leaned forward so she could see Gerry past Jane. "The church doors. The outside one is broken and the inside one too, the lock, anyway."

Gerry looked back at the entrance. "I didn't see anything. Was there a robbery?"

She looked around the church. All seemed as usual. Both sisters nodded, their faces lit up with interest. The organ, having filled the quiet with gentle improvisation, launched into the stately introduction of the processional hymn, prompting the congregation to rise.

By the end of the second hymn, Gerry knew that bringing Dot to the service had been a mistake.

For a time, Dot sat on Gerry's lap. Then she wriggled over to sit briefly on a delighted Jane's lap before sliding down to the floor. She watched the adults lower and raise the long wooden kneeler attached to the pew in front of them and tried to move it herself. Her strength unequal to the task, she waited until the kneeler was lowered, then sat on it, beaming up at her trying-to-pray relatives.

The old ladies beamed back. Gerry felt the beginnings of embarrassment and wondered if she could duck out early.

During the sermon, Dot got bored with the floor and stood on the seat next to Gerry, smiling at the people behind them. Gerry, half-turning to make sure Dot didn't wobble and fall, or try to climb over the back of the pew, saw faces mostly smiling back, but there were enough disapproving ones that she started to flush. She decided to make an exit.

Cannily, she gathered their coats and her purse before scooping Dot up and scooting for the now closed door. While dressing Dot in the vestibule, she looked at the heavy inside door.

Both doors had been ajar when they'd arrived, so she hadn't seen the damage. The inside one looked as if a sledge hammer had been taken to the lock.

They stepped outside, Dot unaware that she'd been pulled out of the service before time, happily crouched to look at something on the path. Gerry examined the outside door, made of considerably thinner wood than the inside one. It had probably only taken a shoulder to break its latch off its mounting.

Gerry, fearing for Dot's tights, directed her away from the dirt between the pathway's flagstones, which she was probing curiously, and onto the grass of the churchyard. Dot staggered among gravestones. Robins fluttered and darted among the old trees that surrounded the yard and the apple trees that bordered it on one side. Geese flew over toward the lake.

Faintly, along with all the bird calls, Gerry heard another hymn begin—the offertory. It wouldn't be long now before the service ended. She resolved to wait and deposit her offering after. Besides, she was curious to know what had been taken from the church.

Dot reached the back of the cemetery, where the memorial wall stood—a half-circle of stone topped with a cement cap, her grandparents' brass plaques set into its surface.

Gerry would have lifted Dot and showed her the plaques, tracing the names with her fingers, saying, "My mom, my dad—your gramma and grampa, Dot," but stopped, dismayed. The top of the wall was blank, only lighter squares of cement showed where the plaques had been.

"It was horrible," Gerry said, tearing up. "Plaques pried off old monuments too, not only the wall. Inside, they took the usual stuff: candlesticks, chalices. The minister had to rush to her other church, St. Martin's, to get what she needed, and then back to St. Anne's. And now the police have arrived."

"Anything metal," Doug said, adding succinctly, "Scrap." He brought them each a cup of coffee. They were sitting at the table while Dot played on the hearthrug. Bob was enthroned on the mantelpiece and from time to time, Dot would look up at him and meow.

"Scrap!" Gerry sounded indignant. "Scrap! Old plaques that have important family information on them? Scrap?"

"I'm sure the church has all that written down somewhere; there may even be rubbings of some of the monuments."

"You think so? So, we'll be able to replace it all?"

"Of course," he said soothingly.

"At least they didn't take the bell," she said bitterly.

"Probably ran out of time. That would have been worth more than all the plaques put together."

"Why, though? I mean, are people so desperate they have to rob churches?"

"I don't know, Ger." He sounded weary. "Some are. To some, it's just business."

"Some business," she said gloomily and sipped her coffee. "I asked about Sunday school. There's a twelve-year-old girl who sits in the vestry with the very young kids, like Dot. They just colour and stuff. It hardly seems worthwhile."

"Well," he said absently, looking out the window, "it could work as a break, eh? Just to sit in the church and think. Let Dot get used to being away from you."

"Away from *me*. What about you?"

"It's different with fathers. Kids aren't as attached as they are to their mothers. Don't you think?"

Gerry nodded. "I guess. Speaking of being away from Dot, we'll have to get a sitter for next Friday evening." He looked blank. "You know—the vernissage at the museum? You're my date, right?"

He smiled ruefully. "Oh, Gerry, I won't fit in. I'll go if you want me—"

"But you're an artist too," she protested. "Of course you'll fit in."

"I haven't been feeling very much like one lately. An artist who doesn't make art—isn't."

Knowing he didn't have a project he was currently working on, she said tentatively, "I don't want you to feel uncomfortable." And then, less certainly as he stayed silent, "I don't mind going alone. I can drive." As he said nothing further, she added, more firmly, "It'll be fine. I'll be fine."

He finished his coffee and stood. "Well, back to the Yacht Club. Sanding and varnishing one of the old wooden cabin cruisers. She's a beauty." He bent and kissed her. "Love you."

"Love you," Gerry said to his back, her eyes moistening.

Bob lazily flapped his tail and looked at his girl with half-closed eyes. Something, he thought, wasn't quite right. He surveyed the room. The enemy was not in sight at present. He allowed his eyes to shut.

Monday, the Markovs came to clean, and, as two weeks had passed, they stayed longer than usual. Their van was still parked at The Maples when Gerry and Dot returned from shopping and having a visit with Bea.

They took the side door into the kitchen and Gerry was surprised to see Natalya Markov on a stepladder, all the upper cupboard doors open. "What is it, Natalya?"

"Oh, dust. And spiders." She flicked a cloth and a clump of something wafted down. She was in her thirties, an attractive slender blonde. Not your stereotypical cleaning lady, Gerry always thought.

"Oh, yuck. Probably lots of cat hairs up there too. Thanks for thinking of it. Uh, I'll just get our lunch going. You carry on."

"I'm finished," Natalya announced, climbing down and collapsing the ladder with a loud snap. She smiled at Gerry and Dot. "I'll find Sergei. Time we went to our next client."

"The money's on the table," Gerry called.

"I already found it, thank you," Natalya called back.

By the time Gerry and Dot were at the table, eating, Natalya returned with Sergei, a short, strong-looking man. They exchanged goodbyes with Gerry and let themselves out. As usual, Gerry felt both lucky and guilty that she could afford to have her house cleaned. She asked Dot, who was mangling a banana, "Who's a lucky girl, Dot? Who's a lucky girl?"

"Would you, or you and Bertie, like to come to the vernissage at the museum Friday night? Doug doesn't want to."

Wondering why not, Prudence replied, "I'll ask him. What time is it? It might mean leaving Ginger to close up the café by herself."

"Seven to nine. I could drive us all in if you like."

"That would be nice. And young miss here—will stay home with Daddy?" She shovelled some more porridge into Dot's mouth.

"That's the plan," Gerry said cheerfully, then left them. As she walked to the studio, her smile slipped. She stared blankly at her desk. Work always helped—when she was upset. And she was upset.

She thought about Doug, how he spent his days looking after other people's possessions, their houses, boats, gardens. How he maintained the curling rink, worked serving at the Legion. How he did work outside at her house: cut the grass, cleaned out the gutters, pruned trees and shrubs. And inside the house: he'd replaced the downstairs' bathroom caulking and talked about repairing the front door sill with wood putty and then repainting it. And he still felt responsible for the house his sons were renting from Mary; would drop in and perform odd tasks there. No wonder he didn't feel like an artist anymore. When did he have the time?

"Vroom, vroom," Bertie said sarcastically as Gerry's Mini inched up the highway ramp.

"That's why we left two hours ahead of time," said Prudence. "So we don't have to worry about being late." She looked across at Gerry at the wheel, who she thought was looking a bit down lately. "I like what you're wearing," she said.

"Oh, thanks, Prue. I thought I'd go for arty, you know?"

To Gerry, "arty" meant wearing all black—turtleneck, skirt, tights, and shoes—which perfectly set off the multicoloured, embroidered vintage Turkish man's vest she'd found among Maggie's old clothes.

"Funky," said Bertie, approvingly. "Is that still even a word anymore?"

Gerry laughed and felt a little less tense. They were halfway up the ramp. "Of course. Men are lucky; they have their uniforms, their suits. Women have to assemble outfits to fit every occasion."

Prudence, dressed nicely in a royal blue blazer and skirt with a plain white silk blouse, which wouldn't have looked out of place in a boardroom or at church, didn't comment. She hoped her clothes would enable her to blend in, her ultimate goal at every social event.

"Not all men, you know," said Bertie. "Some would consider wearing what you're wearing, Gerry. All black with a snazzy vest."

Gerry smiled at him in the rear-view mirror. "Think you could carry it off, Bertie?"

"Yes. Why not? Is that a dare? Are we going to exchange outfits before we arrive? Because me in a skirt—I'm not sure anyone's ready for that. What do you think, Prue?"

"I think we're just killing time and talking nonsense because we're bored stuck in this traffic." She changed the subject. "I got a quote to replace my parents' plaques on the memorial wall. Five hundred each. I think I'll just get one with both their names on. I'm not just being cheap; I think they'd like that."

"I agree, dear," said Bertie, "though I didn't know them."

Prudence continued: "Anyway, it's five hundred dollars and they're not even made out of bronze anymore, though bronze is available. The church is recommending acrylic as thieves won't be interested in that."

"Huh," said Gerry. "That's interesting. I haven't heard from the church yet. Acrylic, eh?"

"It's a plastic world," Bertie commented. "Hey, we're nearly at the top!"

They were indeed; another ten minutes saw them briefly join the highway before they queued again to get off it. Traffic trickled toward downtown. Once they were threading their way through residential streets, their speed increased.

"Funny," said Gerry. "We covered four kilometres in one hour on the highway and now we're doing the speed limit on the actual city streets."

"Never mind," said Prudence, "we're almost there."

They parked inside—spiralling down, down, down—then made their way by foot back to the surface, emerging quite close to the museum.

Bertie said, "Ah, my old stomping grounds." His antiques shop was not far.

Prudence looked amused. "Stomp away, dear." He laughed and took her arm.

Gerry, trailing behind them, felt sad that Doug wasn't there to be arm in arm with. Someone called her. She turned and smiled. "Yvonne! You made it!"

Yvonne smiled and replied, "Well, it's not often I'm asked to a do at the museum. Thank you, by the way." Yvonne was dressed all in olive green with a cream sheepskin vest. Her pants were baggy with many pockets.

"You're welcome, I, uh, had an extra ticket. I love your vest."

"Thanks. It's Wanda's favourite though it's *faux*. She's happy when I throw it on the sofa and she can nest on it. I like your vest too. What are we going to see exactly?"

"It's all about Napoleon. And what artists were doing during his reign. Lots of battlefields and posing on horses. Not relevant to today at all."

"I don't know," Yvonne replied. "Autocracy is still with us. Militarism, too. Though the empire builders of our time have learned to hide themselves in their corporations. 'Twas ever thus."

Any pleasure Gerry might have been feeling for the evening was rapidly seeping away. She wondered why Yvonne had agreed to come. A thought occurred. "Yvonne, you're not going to, uh…"

"Poetry-bomb some stately dowager? Or some snotty director? Nah. What would be the point? I'm just here for the free food." She laughed.

They caught up to Prudence and Bertie at the museum entrance; introductions were made, and they joined the throng.

They soon found Marion, all dolled up and chatting with her fellow museum director, Francine. They were introduced to another very important person—Dr. Legasse—the man Gerry recalled Marion once accusing Francine of flirting with. Gerry didn't dare meet Bertie's or Prudence's eyes, as Dr. Legasse, was, like her, attired entirely in black for the occasion—with the exception of a Turkish vest.

Gerry slipped away from the group to find her two Sues and meet their spouses—who, she noted with increasing bitterness, had actually shown up.

She piled a plate with cheeses, pâtés, crackers and bread—and a few grapes, just so she seemed less of a pig—and went to stand near "her" painting.

The oval frame glowed, each flower and bee, each scroll and bead distinct. The eagle atop it, with his feathered legs (his funny baggy pants, Gerry thought), gazed nobly to Gerry's left.

The emperor, himself, in his gilded crown of laurel leaves, his royal ermine and regalia, gazed directly into her eyes, not expressing any particular emotion; he just looked like a regular guy. She lifted her wineglass and toasted him. "Nice knowing you," she said.

PART 5
PEETS

The ghost of Gerald Coneybear was worried. He watched the man move from room to room of his daughter's house. He watched her chatting with him. Could she not see he was a wrong one? Sense the cold evil coming from him? How could she allow him in her home? Near her daughter, his granddaughter?

This made the other problems seem trivial. Gerry would be whatever kind of artist she wanted. Prudence had obviously moved on from her disastrous marriage, didn't need his belated explanations of his relationship with her former husband Alex. His interventions had made little or no difference. Would make little difference. But now, with this other situation unfolding, he couldn't just stand by and do nothing, wait for disaster.

For disaster was coming—all the spirits of the house could feel it. They gathered in groups, their wisps mingling, communicating their disquiet without words. As, similarly, spirits all over Lovering were agitated, signalling to their loved ones as best as they could. Rearranging small objects, trying to be noticed, suggesting necessary changes.

He moved to the living room where his wife and sister sat in rocking chairs, each with the essence of a spectral cat on their lap; Deborah, the white one; Maggie, the calico. The calico opened its mouth in a silent hiss.

He stood between them, his back to the ash-filled hearth. They looked up at him with worried, insubstantial faces. He raised his arms and raged.

Ian didn't know exactly what to expect when he saw who had cut a hole in his tent, but it wasn't what he got.

To be fair, the first blow—the one that caught him by surprise and sent him tumbling backward onto his bed—came from the stranger. And the second blow as well. But that the two men he knew would allow this to happen, even, if half-heartedly, join in, was a revelation. He'd never known that they held him so cheap.

The words that they spoke were no surprise. He tried to reply, to reassure them that he had no intention of telling what he'd seen, that he was as guilty as they. But the growing pain in his chest prevented anything from coming out of his mouth. He didn't feel the third or the fourth blow.

The chest pain intensified, the hitting stopped, and the last physical sensation he felt was the sudden cold air on his feet.

22

Gerry sat on the sofa idly sketching. Cats were arranged around the room, including Bob on the mantel. Doug was supervising Dot's breakfast at the table. Gerry put the sketch pad down on the coffee table and picked up her bowl of granola-topped fruit and yogurt.

"You *might* have enjoyed it," she said to Doug. "But then again, after the first half hour, I had had enough. Bertie sure knows how to work a room, though; I think he already knew a lot of those people, clients maybe. And Marion had a good time."

"How is she?"

"She looked pretty well; all dressed up. She was using a mobility scooter. It seems more manoeuvrable than a wheelchair. What did you guys get up to?" She put the half-eaten yogurt down on the sketch pad and went to top up her coffee.

"We watched a movie. Then Dot went to sleep and I tried to watch TV but I fell asleep too."

She sat back down. "I know; I came home to a silent house."

Buddy entered the room and leapt from the floor to the back of the sofa. Gerry swivelled around to look at him. "Oh, hello, Buddy," she said a bit nervously. "Come to be with the family?" A baring of fangs and a growl was her reward. Bob opened his eyes and sat up. "Now, boys—" Gerry was beginning to say, when Buddy moved.

He jumped from the back of the sofa down onto the coffee table. Gerry clutched her coffee as Bob jumped down from the mantel to the table, landing on the part of her sketch pad that was hanging over the table's edge. Bob, losing his balance as the sketch pad tipped, fell sideways. The bowl of yogurt launched. Buddy sneered.

Gerry got most of the yogurt in her lap. Dot laughed. Doug went to get a rag. Buddy and some of the other cats dispersed, no doubt in part due to Gerry's loud expostulations: on cat ownership in particular. Winston, Franklin and Joseph, living up to their reputations as the greediest members of the pride, moved in, snacking off Gerry's jeans and sweatshirt, and the sofa and floor. Bob, having received some of the splatter, groomed.

Doug shooed the three boys away and began wiping up the now speechless Gerry, commenting, "Well, it's another glamorous morning at The Maples."

Gerry again found her voice. "At least," she said, taking a swig, "the coffee didn't spill. Okay, I'm going to get changed, and then Dot and I will go see Prudence."

"You just saw her last night. Why are you bothering her on her busiest day?"

"*Because* she phoned while you were outside." They both knew he'd been smoking but neither mentioned it. "She has something to tell me."

"Okay. Well, for a change, I have no work today, so I'll tackle some chores around here until you get back."

"Great. There's lots of laundry, as usual." She plucked at her soiled shirt. "And I'm about to add to the pile."

It *was* the busiest day of the week at Maggie's Café. The whole crew—Prudence, Bertie, Ginger, as well as another waitress working in the back of the room—was on deck. Every table was taken, and a small group of clients patiently waited at the front.

Gerry and Dot made their way to the cash. Bertie recoiled in mock surprise. "Dot! Come to help out your Uncle Bertie?"

"Meow," was Dot's cogent reply.

"More like add to the confusion," said Gerry. "Prue called."

"Yes. She has something *interesting* to impart." He waggled his eyebrows up and down.

Dot pointed and laughed. "Birdie!"

"My God! She said my name! She'll be orating by the summer. Ah, here's my wife."

Prudence sailed over with a tray of dirty dishes. "Table for four opening up over there, Bertie. I'm just going upstairs with Gerry for a sec."

They left Bertie courteously ushering a group of four *almost* elderly ladies through. "As a front-of-house man, there's no one like Bertie," Gerry cheerfully remarked, as she followed Prue up to the bakery.

"Apparently, he's irresistible to women of a certain age," Prudence said with a smile. "Or so he tells me. Coffee?"

"I'm good. What couldn't wait?"

Prudence poured herself a mug and sat. She handed Dot a sugar cookie. "This is a bribe, Dot, so you sit still for five minutes."

"Good luck with that," said Gerry. Of course, Dot proceeded to prove her wrong and nibbled at her treat during the conversation, gravely watching the women.

"I couldn't tell you over the phone; I was downstairs using Bertie's portable one and didn't want to be overheard." She took a sip of coffee. "Did you notice the new waitress?"

"Not really. I saw someone working, so, yes?"

"Rebecca Murchison."

"Oo. That *is* interesting. But I thought she moved away."

"Away but not far away—just the next village. Twenty-minute drive."

"And?"

"We're desperate for staff so I thought I'd take a chance. She admitted she's an alcoholic but said she goes to AA."

"Should you be telling me that?" Gerry asked, a bit taken aback at Prudence's sharing. "I mean, I knew she had a drinking problem; one of my friends told me."

"That's what I thought. But never mind that. On her resumé, she listed cleaning house, and when I pressed her for details, she said she worked for the same agency as your cleaners, the Markovs. And then she told me she and they cleaned the public areas at the seniors' residence as well as some of its individual clients' apartments."

"Okaaay. So they've all cleaned there. Didn't we agree that there must be dozens of service people visiting the residence?"

Prudence looked nonplussed. "For a change, you're telling *me* not to jump to conclusions?"

"That's right. We now know three people that went or still go to the residence on a regular basis. So what?"

"Don't you find it odd that Natalya Markov never mentioned it?"

"No. Why should she? We don't chat like you and I do, did, I mean do."

Prudence continued. "Never mentioned it even after the rugs were stolen?"

Gerry nodded her head and said, grudgingly, "Well, when you put it like that—"

"Ask her," Prudence urged, "and see what kind of reaction you get."

"Well, maybe. Anyway, I'm sure you have to get back to work and we have to buy something to take to Cathy's tonight. She's testing out her Asian cuisine on us and it's a mystery as to which one it will be."

Prudence smiled. "Sounds like fun. We'll be sitting with our feet up watching PBS with a cup of cocoa and a cheese sandwich."

"That sounds like fun too," Gerry called as she went down the stairs. After a pause while Bertie showed Dot pictures of cats at the cat café on his cellphone, they went to the grocery store. Gerry bought a pot of tulips for Cathy and a few packages of sesame crisp candy to keep in the car. On the way home, she crunched through a package.

Once home, Gerry handed Dot over to Doug. She pulled off her beret and caught Doug staring at her perplexedly. "What? What is it?"

He leaned over to peer closely at her head then relaxed. "Oh, phew. For a second there, I thought you had fleas. Reddish-blond fleas. To match your hair. Been eating sesame seeds?"

Gerry bent over, brushed her hands through her hair and watched the specks fly. "How on earth—?" She laughed. "I put my hat on the seat next to me and the package on top of it. Exit Gerry, wearing yogurt; enter Gerry wearing sesame seeds."

He smiled and kissed her. "Yummy mummy. Hey, I repaired the front door sill. Guess what I found?"

"That sounds ominous. Will I be happy about it?"

"Um, no. But it's interesting. Come and see." He led the way to the foyer and opened the door. The sill was smooth again and freshly painted.

"Looks great, hon. Thanks for doing that."

"No problem. It was ants."

"Ants?"

"A zillion of them. I lifted the sill, scooped out as many as I could and put some ant traps in before I re-laid it."

The light dawned for Gerry. "The cat! Why she was scratching! Wow, do you think that's why she was ripping out the bathroom caulking?"

He shrugged. "Who knows? Could be ants. Could be mice in the walls. Neat, eh?"

"She's a canny one," Gerry concluded thoughtfully.

Around five, they walked over to Cathy's, meeting Andrew and Markie, who were just coming out their front door.

"How was Arizona?" Doug asked Markie. "See a lot of your old friends?" They strolled on ahead, chatting.

Gerry, walking slowly holding Dot's hand, greeted her cousin. "Nice tan, Andrew. Good vacation? Lucky you going south twice in one winter."

Andrew kissed her then, bending from his great height, tried to kiss Dot, who backed away. "Oh," he said disappointedly, "she's forgotten me."

"It's temporary," Gerry reassured him.

"Peets!" Dot said, pointing at Andrew's shoes.

"Peets?" he queried.

"Oh, it's just something Bertie showed us on his phone today, a cat thing. Paws plus feet equal peets."

"I'm thinking of getting one."

"A cat?"

"No! A cellphone!"

"Oh. I can see how one might be good in an emergency…"

"Exactly. And for business. I think they're going to be huge."

Gerry shrugged. "If you say so. Any hints from Cathy about what's on tonight's menu?"

"She wouldn't say. But we know it'll be good, right?"

"Right."

Dinner turned out to be a full Indian feast. There were papadums with the dahl, pakoras and samosas as starters, and then lamb and chicken curries with fragrant basmati rice and naan. As well as vegetable side dishes. With this, Cathy, Andrew and Markie drank beer. Gerry, who didn't like beer, had some white wine. Doug drank ginger ale.

Throughout, Prince Charles was in attendance, slime dripping from the sides of his mouth. Gerry had packed a bland supper for Dot but the naan proved popular with her daughter

THE CAT LAUGHS

and, inevitably, as Dot pulled the soft bread to pieces, a telltale gulping sound indicated Prince Charles received his share. It didn't matter; there was plenty, and feeding Charles was all part of the fun.

Andrew and Markie described their vacation; all the art galleries they'd been to, the concerts and plays they'd attended. And Gerry described her three months' apprenticeship working on Napoleon's frame and how she'd been offered a job.

"And are you considering it?" asked Andrew. "I mean, you can't be a cartoonist and a trainee art conservator at the same time."

"No, you can't," she replied, sounding somewhat rueful. "So that's why I've decided—"

"Ta da!" Cathy appeared with a tray of assorted colourful squares and balls. "All homemade! And masala chai coming."

"Oo," Gerry said, totally distracted by the sweets. "One of each, please!"

Andrew was not distracted. "So? Are you going to change jobs?"

She looked at Doug. He cocked his head quizzically. "Let's just say, I'm still considering it. There's another project I'm trying to get going. And if that pans out—enough said. Let's eat!"

"And it's called 'The Cat Diaries'—or just 'Cat Diaries', I haven't decided yet. I've been setting aside so many ideas and now I need to start the drawings. But I don't want to leave Dot or Lovering every day so I've decided to turn down the museum's offer. I hope I'm doing the right thing."

The words came out all in a rush and Doug, carrying a sleepy Dot home from Cathy's, said, "Whoa, whoa. Is this another book or a strip?"

"A strip. I want to end *Mug*. I mean, the papers can always do reruns of him, but I need to change it up, do something new. And

I think most people like cats, the crazy things they do, and some people just *love* them."

"Have you talked to Denise?" Denise was Gerry's agent/manager/cheering section.

Gerry took a deep breath then let it out. "No. Not yet. I want to have a few finished strips to show her first."

"That makes sense." They walked a few steps in silence. "So, no more trips to Montreal?"

"No. Except for special events. Days out. Happy?"

"Very. I was dreading becoming a full-time, well, part-time carer for you-know-who. I know it hasn't been easy for you, but you know, she'll be off to kindergarten in less than four years, and before that there are local preschools she can attend, just half-days, but it's something."

"I know; some of my mom-friends' older kids are in preschool. I think I'll wait until she's two, maybe three; don't want to rush it."

"No. Look at the boys—all grown up. And it seems so recently they were little guys tearing around the house."

"Don't make me cry; it's been such a nice day."

"All right. We'll be happy instead."

23

Dear Diary,
 Finished painting the walls. Now doing the trim.

 The visuals: a cat smears a wall with a 'WET PAINT' sign on it by rubbing against it, walks through a paint tray, kicks the roller, which marks the floor, and then stretches its length up a door frame, leaving paw prints on same.

Dear Diary,
 I don't know what all the fuss is. Bathroom caulking is ridiculously easy to remove. And quite delicious.

 The visuals: pretty obvious, involving one very pointy extended claw, and then using mouth to tear off a long strip.

Dear Diary,
 While defending my territory, I discovered a fun new sport—spring boarding off a metal tray loaded with coffee cups.

 The visuals: the Bob/Buddy/yogurt "incident" reworked.

Dear Diary,
   Repotted a few plants. We quite enjoy gardening!

   Visuals: the famous incident involving two of the cats—Winnie and Frank, she thought—perched on top of the kitchen cabinets back when Gerry had been foolish enough to keep a few green plants up there. The aftermath: dirt and smashed plant pots and plants all over the kitchen while cats look down with smug satisfaction.

She was trying a new format: one large upright rectangle divided into four or three or two, depending on the narrative. And using different cats as models for each little story.

Now that it was May, something inside her had shifted, for the better. Or maybe it was because she'd made her work decision. It was properly spring outside; the days were longer, the snow was gone, and flowers were emerging. Along with insects, though the mosquitoes hadn't quite yet made an appearance.

And Prudence had taken advantage of this to bring Dot outside before lunch. Gerry could hear them through her now wonderfully open window.

She was beginning another entry headed: Day of Infamy!—which involved a *lot* of cat puke, and which, she worried, might turn off her more sensitive readers—when the phone rang. Muttering, "This one's more of a short story than a vignette; actually, it's an epic," she picked up and was surprised to hear Yvonne Punt's voice.

"Hello, Gerry. Is this a bad time?"

"No. Not at all. What's up?"

"Well, um, actually, I'm at the train station, and, er, I didn't realize there wouldn't be a taxi stand."

"Which station?" asked a baffled Gerry, thinking of the one in downtown Montreal.

"Well, Lovering, of course. Didn't Blaise tell you?"

"Oh, tell me what?"

"That I'd be coming out to see him today and maybe we could all have tea? After he and I discuss my manuscript?"

"Nope. All news to me. No worries. I'll come and get you. Won't be long."

Shouting her plan to Prudence, Gerry drove to Lovering station, to return fifteen minutes later with Yvonne. Gerry parked and walked Yvonne into the backyard to meet Prue and Dot who were preparing the vegetable patch for seeding.

"Just cut through there," Gerry said, indicating the path to Blaise's, "and knock on the sliding glass door at the back. Or walk around to the front if you prefer. I'll come over for tea in a couple of hours. Okay?"

A bemused Yvonne departed, saying, as she took in the houses, gardens and lake, "It's another world." Gerry assumed she was comparing Lovering to Park Avenue and couldn't have agreed more. She went back to work.

When she, Prue and Dot reunited for lunch, she could see the morning's activities had worn Dot out. Her daughter yawned twice while they ate and went to her nap without protest. Gerry and Prudence settled down for a good chat.

"So?" asked Prudence. "Did you ask Natalya her take on the rug theft?"

"Sort of," Gerry replied. "I said, I have a friend living there who needs a cleaner and asked if Natalya already cleans there for others. She said yes but she doesn't have time for a new client."

"And?"

"So, then I mentioned that my 'friend' was a bit nervous about security in the building after the robbery, and what did Natalya think?"

"And?"

"And that's when she broke eye contact and said she better get back to work."

"Huh. Suspicious."

"Yeah, that's what I thought." They sat for a moment in contemplation. Gerry spoke first: "Okay. Let's say Natalya and Sergei were involved. That doesn't mean Rebecca was."

"No. She didn't seem uneasy when we talked about her work experience."

"I've just remembered: her husband drives a pickup. *He* could be the thief."

Prudence grimaced. "Gerry, don't you think a pickup truck is a bit obvious for transporting stolen goods?"

"Not if it's done in the dead of night. But you're right—it's risky. A van would be better—the Markovs have a van."

The women looked at each other. "I don't see how we could possibly prove any of them were involved," Prudence said flatly.

"No," mused Gerry. "And none of it may be true. But I definitely feel a bit sick about keeping the Markovs on as my cleaners."

"Hm, yes, that is a problem." They thought about all the antiques contained in The Maples.

"They *have* been coming for more than six months," Gerry said. "If they were going to steal my goods, wouldn't they have done it by now?"

"Maybe they've been making an inventory of what's worth taking."

"For six months? Wait a minute! Natalya was poking around in the top kitchen cabinets a few weeks ago. Removing dust and spiders, she said."

Prudence sniffed. "About time too—you don't want stuff floating down into your food when you're cooking. But never mind all your possessions—don't forget, someone beat up Ian Murchison till he had a heart attack."

"But what did Ian's death have to do with a robbery? If it did. Was he part of a ring of thieves?"

Prudence sighed. "It's a puzzle. And I've got to go. Take care, eh?"

"You too. And thanks, Prue."

Dot napped a long time. Gerry got more done on her Cat Diaries concept. When Dot awoke, they went next door to Blaise's, letting themselves in at the back. Graymalkin came running to meet them. "It's only us, Gray," Gerry said soothingly.

Dot crouched and attempted to grab one of the cat's paws. "Peets!" she said triumphantly even as Gray's eyes narrowed and Gerry scooped her child to safety.

In the living room, they found a quiet scene: Blaise asleep with Ariel on his lap; Yvonne slowly turning the page of a book. Gerry held a finger to her lips but it was too late, for Dot roused the sleeper by letting out a firm "meow" by way of greeting, and pointing at Ariel.

Blaise woke. "Ah, Gerry. And my other friend from next door, Deborah Joy." He turned to Yvonne. "Also known as Dot. Is it teatime already?"

"Don't get up," Gerry said. "I'll get the kettle on."

"There are cookies on the counter," Blaise called.

During tea, they chatted about poetry. Blaise had finished editing Yvonne's manuscript and she was ready to submit it for publication. Unbeknownst to Gerry, they'd been working by telephone for months, poem by poem, and today's visit was to conclude the project by finally meeting face to face.

Dot stomped happily around the room, gingersnap in hand, every now and then stopping, pointing at someone's feet (or paws) and saying the word of the day: "Peets!"

Once Gerry had explained the word's etymology (something about the internet and cats, she said), the poets discussed it.

"Of course, as slang, the 's' at the end of a word already plural is acceptable," Yvonne said gravely.

"Yes," agreed Blaise. "It's colloquial. And don't leave out the 'cute' factor. Everyone loves a cute word." He smiled at Dot, wandering amidst his extensive potted plant collection by the front window. "Like Dot."

"Like Biggle?" interjected Gerry.

Blaise smiled again. "A perfect example."

Gerry explicated. "It's actually the name of one of Freya's cats. Bertie told me."

Of course, the poets didn't need to be told who Freya was, or even that she had cats. Blaise turned to Yvonne. "Have you met Gerry's cats yet?"

"I have not had the pleasure. Maybe before I go—"

"Oh, yes," said Gerry. "What time's your train? I'll drive you."

"Well, if it's not too much trouble. Thanks. I thought the 4:30? What time is it?"

Gerry rose. "Fourish. We should head out. Thank you for the tea, Blaise."

Blaise rose too, but shakily. "My pleasure, dear Gerry. And thank you for introducing me to Yvonne. It's been stimulating to be around another poet for a change."

"I'm the fortunate one," Yvonne said, awkwardly shifting from foot to foot. She gave Blaise a tentative hug then the three let themselves out the back door. Yvonne looked at the view again: Blaise's gazebo framed by mature trees and shrubs, the lake beyond. "I can't believe you get to live here." She sounded bewildered.

"We're very lucky," Gerry replied. "Oh, look, there's one of my cats."

That Thursday, it was Gerry's turn to host playgroup. She prepared the cheese and crackers, the grapes and strawberries, the Nanaimo bars. She made a pot of tea and one of coffee. And she waited for her friends to arrive, thinking about her phone call with her agent Denise.

Denise had been cautiously optimistic about Gerry launching a new "product," as she described the Cat Diaries. And, as usual, once Gerry had explained what she wanted, Denise had taken over the conversation. She agreed that *Mug the Bug* could probably go on with reprints, as long as Gerry produced some new content related to him from time to time. She promised to feel out the newspapers that currently ran Gerry's strips to get their reactions to less Mug and more cats. She inquired after Gerry's health and that of Dot and Doug, and then she rang off.

"Whew!" Gerry had said, and then she'd laughed; she seemed to always say *whew* after talking to high-energy Denise.

She remembered she'd forgotten to tell Denise that *The Candy King of Bubbly-Sauceton* was practically finished. "Rats. Oh well, next time."

She heard a car arrive in the front circular drive and peeked out a window. Cyndi and Sydney. Another car pulled in behind Cyndi's—Hilary with Noah. Gerry went to the front door. "Hello, ladies." A third car pulled in and the driveway was full. Christine and Jane stepped out. "Heather will have to park at the side," Gerry said. "If she comes. She's away a lot lately, isn't she."

Hilary said shortly, "She's got an appointment but said she'd try to come after that. Tell you more inside."

They settled in the living room. Gerry had brought an assortment of toys from the den and, after she'd erected a baby gate blocking the children from wandering off, she relaxed. "Now. Heather. What's up?"

Hilary took a deep breath through her nose then exhaled. "Her husband's found someone else. They've been going to counselling but he's adamant—he wants a divorce."

Cyndi swore softly. "Son of a—"

Christine's eyes became slits. "Anyone we know?"

Hilary shook her head. "He met her through work. At some trade fair or something."

Gerry didn't know what to say and blurted out, "But Heather's so *nice*!"

Cyndi snorted. "It's always the nice ones who get scre—left. Have they separated?"

Hilary nodded. "I'm helping with that. She won't be left financially the loser, if I can help it."

"I can't believe it," Gerry said, shaking her head. "Heather."

"Half of all marriages end in divorce," Christine said crisply. "This is my second marriage, you know."

"It's not quite that bad," Hilary interjected. "Around forty percent of first marriages end in divorce." She grinned at Christine. "So you and Heather make our little group's forty percent. Me, Gerry and Cyndi should be fine."

"Doug and I aren't married," Gerry said worriedly. "He's divorced. So I guess that makes him more stable? Less stable?"

Hilary shrugged. "Divorced, married, living together. The important thing is respect. And companionship. Do you laugh together? Do you build each other up rather than tear down? Those are the things that are important to me."

They heard someone knock at the side door, so Gerry got up, expecting Heather. But it was Edwina.

"Gerry, I just came to— oh, you've got company." They could hear the others chatting in the living room.

"No worries," said Gerry. "Want to join me and my mom friends for a coffee?" As Edwina hesitated on the doorstep, Gerry added by way of enticement, "You might get some ideas for one of your books."

Edwina considered this. "All right." She entered the kitchen. "But can you give Shadow his supper tonight and let him out after? I have an event in Montreal this evening and need to leave early to beat the traffic."

"Of course I can. Just leave the key there on the counter. That'll remind me. Good plan, leaving early, if it works. Traffic was horrible last week when I went in at that time—two hours! Everyone, this is my neighbour Edwina Murray, the author. She's going to observe all your mannerisms and put them in one of her books."

"Oh, cool," said Cyndi. "Can I be a femme fatale? I always wanted to be a seductress." She chortled.

Edwina regarded Cyndi's chunky vivacity. "Er…" she began.

Hilary held out her hand. "Hilary Southam, lawyer. You write mysteries, right? I can be your legal consultant."

"Well, actually," Edwina began again. "I have a copy of the criminal co—"

"Noah!" thundered Hilary. "Put Jane down!"

Edwina gave up trying to speak. She sat down and poured herself a coffee. "Oh goody—Nanaimo bars."

They discussed crime, divorce, theft, and murder. Edwina jokingly suggested she write about a mother's group, one of whose members is accused of murder. This brought an uneasy halt to the conversation as they all thought of their friend Monica, who had since moved away, and her harrowing experience.

"What?" Edwina asked. "You don't mean—?"

Hilary forced a laugh. "No. Of course not! But what do you think of the death of Ian Murchison?"

Edwina looked blank. "I don't think I—"

But before they could get into that, Heather and her son Peter arrived, and all everyone wanted to do was make sure she was okay. She looked tired.

"I told them," Hilary said.

"Oh, good." Heather turned to Edwina. "I don't believe we've met. Heather Kingsley. And this is Peter."

Edwina rose. "I should go."

"Not on my account," Heather said pleasantly.

"No, no. I've got some work to do. Gerry, Shadow usually eats between 5:30 and 6:00."

"All right. Enjoy your event."

"I won't. It's business. Has to be done."

They waited till they heard her close the side door, then Cyndi asked Heather, "So, how are you?"

Heather smiled wanly. "Bearing up. Getting used to the idea. Trying to explain to Sophie. Which reminds me, I have to pick her up from preschool in a little while." She sighed and looked at Peter. "He's too young to understand but I think Sophie does. A bit. Not that I do completely." She added a bit sadly, "The infidelity wasn't a deal-breaker for me."

There was a silence. "I know you prefer tea," Gerry said, getting up, "so I'll make some fresh." A thought occurred to her. "Do you use house cleaners?"

"No, we—I clean the house myself. It's not that big. Why?"

"Well, you did mention that some jewellery was missing, so I wondered…"

"Oh, I found the jewellery. All the pieces Stephen gave me, over the years." She seemed to choke up.

"Where was it?"

"In the bottom drawer of my bedroom bureau. Which is odd, as the rest is in the top drawer in a nice jewellery box my parents gave me."

"Sophie must have been fooling around," Hilary said.

"That must be it," Heather agreed. "But good idea, Gerry, to ask about cleaners."

"Yeah," Gerry said, then explained. "I've been thinking about all the little things most of us have had go missing, and how they might have something to do with the other robberies last winter. Just a dead end, I guess.

"Yes," Heather said wistfully. "Another dead end."

Gerry bunged a frozen pizza into the oven. "Come on, Dottie, let's go visit Mr. Shadow."

The dog was sitting in the hall when she unlocked Edwina's back door. He came slowly to greet them. I wonder if he's getting old, Gerry thought with a pang as he padded ahead of them into the kitchen. "Hello, sir. We've come to give you your supper." She let Dot empty the scoop three times into the bowl. They didn't have long to wait for him to finish; like most Labradors, he was a chowhound. Gerry got his leash. "Wanna go out, boy?"

He led them calmly around the yard, pausing to sniff the shrubbery and lift his leg. Gerry let Dot hold the leash close to his collar so she could feel like she was helping walk him. The dog agility equipment Edwina had purchased after her husband died—hoping it might help her and Shadow forget him and grow closer—was gone. Shadow had proved uninterested.

Instead, Edwina had invested in landscaping. The yard was a riot of early May flowering bulbs and perennials. "Well," Gerry said brightly, "I think we've dawdled out here long enough. Time to go back inside, boy."

After a biscuit and a long drink in the kitchen, Shadow walked into the conservatory. Dot followed him in while Gerry watched from the doorway. He jumped up into his favourite chair and curled up. Dot stroked his paws and crooned, "Peeeeeets."

24

It was another beautiful Saturday, and Doug and Gerry decided to take Dot for a walk in Lovering, finishing up at their favourite café. They parked at the IGA; that way, when the morning's pleasures were ended, they could get the groceries. As they walked, they met people they knew and people they didn't, some with kids, some with dogs. Dot had to greet all the dogs; her parents asking for permission first.

It was a long walk for her, and she seemed happy to settle into a chair at the café and gnaw on a croissant. Bertie took their order, but Rebecca Murchison brought it to them. "Hi, Doug," she said, surprising Gerry a little.

"Hi, Rebecca. Thanks." He reintroduced Gerry and introduced Dot.

"How do you know her?" Gerry asked after Rebecca left to serve another customer.

He looked embarrassed. "Uh, I don't know that I should say."

"You never said you knew Ian's sister, even after I told you I met her by his shack." Gerry began to panic, thinking of Heather's marital disaster. "All this time, whenever we've discussed him, you never said."

"It's kind of confidential." He leaned closer. "I see her at the meetings."

"Meetings?" asked a bewildered Gerry.

"At AA," he said, dropping his eyes to the table top and looking blank.

"I didn't know you still go to meetings. I thought—"

He laughed and she didn't like the tone of that laugh. "You thought I'm cured? That I don't want a drink every day? When I see you and our friends drinking? Why do you think I still smoke? It takes the edge off the craving."

Dot had stopped eating and was looking at her parents' faces.

Gerry blinked back tears. This was a Doug she didn't know. "I'm sorry. I—"

His face softened. He took her hand. "No. I'm sorry. I'm sorry that I'm a forty-three-year-old drunk with an assortment of odd jobs, three adult sons, and no home or money of my own. I'm sorry I'm a failure."

She jerked her hand away. "You're not a failure," she said fiercely. "You're a success. Three sons raised and they all seem like good guys, who love you. You can fix anything. You're kind." She stopped, then added, "And I love you. We both do."

"Love isn't enough, Gerry. I struggle every day."

She looked him in the eye. "I didn't know. I didn't. How could I? I didn't even know you were still going to meetings."

"I should have told you. But I was ashamed. Some people at the meetings have been going for twenty years. Or more."

"Well, good for them, is all I can say. If it helps."

Rebecca came over to ask if they needed anything. They didn't. Gerry watched her walk away with bleak eyes. "I saw her come out of the community centre a while back. Her husband had come to get her. He seemed angry, and she was staggering."

Doug nodded. "She said at a meeting that she'd had a relapse."

"A relapse?"

"It's a disease, Ger," he said wearily. "It flares—the craving. And she's been having troubles at home with her son, Robert."

She reached for his hand. Dot began to cry.

Whenever she was upset, Gerry took refuge in work. Over the next few days, she threw herself into developing the Cat Diaries. And she couldn't help thinking, maybe, if Doug could find more time to do *his* art, he'd be happier. And she was nervous about having the cleaners in her house, now she suspected them of—what? She wasn't sure. When they arrived that Monday, she pretended Dot was unwell as an excuse to stay home and watch them.

Sergei worked upstairs while Natalya toiled on the ground level. Apart from quick hellos and goodbyes, there was no chatting. They arrived at eight-thirty, worked quickly, at ten took a fifteen-minute break, which they spent sitting in their van, and departed promptly at noon. They were as they appeared to be—diligent workers.

After she fed Dot and settled her for her nap, Gerry wandered the house, assessing its contents as if she was a thief. She knew they would want stuff not easily traced, but, actually, most of the furniture, ornaments and silverware at The Maples was not unique. She could see it appearing at an auction or in an antique store or, as was more likely, at a flea market, without drawing attention.

If you were going to take furniture, you'd need a van at least the size of the Markovs'. In the dining room, she smiled at the thought of anyone trying to remove the heavy giant table.

"Good luck with that, eh, Harley?" She petted the cat, who was roosting on one of the dining room chairs. He stretched and kneaded the towel that protected the chair's upholstery. His brother Kitty-Cat was slumbering on the next chair over. She gave him a pat as well. So the Persian rug underneath the table was probably also safe; too hard to access. Unless the thief had a penchant for rugs.

She wandered into the den and thought that the new TV was probably worth more than any of those dining room chairs. Monkey was curled up on the red leather sofa and opened an eye as Gerry sat down. *So, seriously, what would I take? The TV, some* china figurines, the silverware. Maybe a few end tables. Not worth the bother, really.

But, she reasoned, what if that's your business? What if you go out every night, steadily. *Then* you'd make money as you'd be dealing in bulk. And didn't Doug say stealing scrap metal, which was what had been taken from the church, *was* a business?

"Holy crap!" The cat jerked and uncoiled. "Oh, sorry, Monks. Not you. For once." No, she thought, it's *organized* crime. In the true sense of the word. *Well* organized. Not like what Ian had done, taking what he needed.

She looked closely at Monkey's head. "Monkey, I just noticed—you have a giant black M on your forehead. 'M' for Monkey. Menace. Mischief." She stroked the beast and it purred. Result. There hadn't been Monkey vomit for a while. Gerry crossed her fingers.

She drifted into the studio and frowned at her desktop. A Mug. She should draw a Mug. At least two new *Mug the Bug* strips a week, Denise had said. All right then. But first, she just wanted to finish the drawings for the Cat Diary entry about the bathroom caulking…

"Maaaa! Maaaa! Ma! Ma! Ma!"

"Coming, Dot. Mama's coming." Gerry ran upstairs. "What is it lovey? A bad dream?" She picked up a tearful Dot and cuddled her. "Let's get ourselves a drink and then we'll look at your library books. And then we'll go to the library and get some more."

Tuesday, Prudence arrived and made snickerdoodles—big round sugar cookies coated in cinnamon sugar and probably Gerry's favourite cookie of all time—with Dot while Gerry feverishly worked on Cat Diaries and *Mug the Bug*s. Wednesday, Gerry and Dot went to a local plant nursery to buy seeds, came home and sowed carrots and peas. Thursday was playgroup at Hilary's. And on Friday Gerry took the train into Montreal. But this time, Dot came with her. Bertie read them their horoscopes from his paper, and was a great help, lifting Dot's stroller on and off the train, and pushing her all the way to the museum.

"I'll leave you here," he said. "Enjoy your first visit to the museum, Dot."

Gerry took Dot first to Conservation where Sue Two fussed over her while Sue One made coffee. "Oh," gushed Sue Two, "I can see why you've decided to stay home; she's adorable."

The adorable one grinned, burped and dropped her sippy cup for the umpteenth time. Gerry picked it up. "Yeah, everybody keeps telling me 'They grow up so fast,' that I thought I'd try to focus on her a bit more. I have the rest of my life to be an artist. And I'm developing a new strip." And she was off, telling them about the Cat Diaries.

When the Sues' break was over, Gerry pushed Dot around the museum, finishing in the kids' art room, where Dot could get out of the stroller, and crayon on big sheets of paper laid out on the floor. A few other parents and children were already there.

When she realized that she was supposed to leave her masterpiece of multi-coloured squiggles, Dot protested—loudly. A somewhat flustered Gerry tore away that portion of the paper and put it and Dot back in the stroller. After surrendering her employee pass at the door (regretfully—how often did one get to wander around the private areas of Montreal's largest fine arts museum?), they strolled over to Marion's.

As the elevator ascended, Dot's eyes widened in awe. Gerry tried to remember if she'd felt fear during her own first elevator rides but couldn't. Anyway, Dot seemed fine, as long as she got to press the buttons and see them light up. In fact, she became fretful when it was time to get out.

Marion greeted them sitting in her wheelchair. "This is what passes for exercise these days," she said as she slowly wheeled down her apartment's long hall into its living room.

Gerry released Dot, who went directly to Marion to examine the chair. She squatted next to one of the big wheels and ran her hand around the spokes. "Well, young ladies, tell me all your news."

So Gerry described their gardening, library visits, playgroup, how Prudence was baking with Dot, and how she, Gerry, had decided not to take the internship at the museum. As she chatted, she watched Marion.

Her friend seemed thinner and frailer, but as alert as ever, though she fumbled for the right word sometimes. A timer dinged in the kitchen and Marion seemed relieved when Gerry said she would dish out their lunch. She slowly wheeled into the dining room, Dot stumping along behind. "Just TV dinners, I'm afraid," said Marion. "And low-salt, low-fat, low-flavour ones at that."

"That's fine," said Gerry. "I can always add salt. And Dot is used to bland food. You should taste baby food; it's—" Gerry had been going to say disgusting, but paused.

"I probably will be soon," Marion said grimly. "I'm down to my last ten teeth." Then she smiled. "But it's good to see you. Now, let's eat."

They munched on their hamburger patties swimming in gooey gravy, mashed potatoes and peas. There was a tiny blueberry muffin for dessert. Gerry made tea and Marion talked about the past—about the lunches she and her husband had enjoyed at local delis and restaurants back when he'd had his own law practice and she'd been his clerk. About elegant suppers at little bistros or grand hotel dining rooms. About greasy spoon diner breakfasts. About their various vacations over the years: to Paris, Rome, the Mediterranean hot spots of the 1950s and '60s, where the beautiful people gathered. Going up north to chalets in winter and out to Lovering in summer where her family had had a cottage.

Gerry broke the flow by asking, "Will you be coming to Lovering this summer? To stay at Cathy's?"

Marion looked away into the distance and murmured vaguely, "Oh, I don't know. I don't know. I get so tired."

And Gerry, seeing her friend—usually so feisty and up for adventure, now brought low—felt as though something precious had been lost. They left soon thereafter.

Dot jabbed at the elevator buttons again and screamed as Gerry settled her into the stroller in the building's foyer. The child was tired, yet everything around her was too stimulating to ignore. As Gerry trudged toward the train station, she noticed Dot's head begin to droop to one side. Once on the train, Dot stirred briefly before falling back asleep in Gerry's arms.

Saturday was a family day. Gerry and Doug had been careful with each other since his revelation about his struggle. Now, if he was going or had been to a meeting, he told her. And when she saw him slip out of the house for a cigarette or smelled it on his clothing, she didn't tease or comment, as she might have done before.

They went up to the woods in the morning, when Dot was freshest, and took turns carrying her when she flagged. Doug put her up on his shoulders with her legs around his neck, and Gerry smiled at them, feeling life was good.

They walked all the way to the sugar shack, the forest floor carpeted with white trilliums. Gerry and Doug kept a close eye on Dot to make sure she didn't pick any. They sat on a fallen tree and ate lunch—Gerry's classic ham and cheese with mustard and mayo, while Dot had just cheese. They all drank from juice boxes, laughing when Doug stuck two of the tiny straws to his head like antennae, waggling them at Dot and then at Gerry. She took them from him and stuck the short ends in her mouth, letting them dangle like fangs. They trooped home, singing nonsense songs.

On Mother's Day, Doug and Dot brought Gerry breakfast in bed. She had to stay there quite a long while after she awoke, waiting for them to get organized, but it was worth it. They sat on the bed and ate.

There was buttered toast. There was bacon. And coffee. And a bouquet of red roses. Cats, drawn by the smell of bacon, began to gather. The boys jumped on the bed as a group. Dot hissed at them. They jumped off. Then Jay, looking her cutest, crept forward and stretched, putting her paws on the edge of the bed. Dot leaned forward and tried to kiss her. Jay ducked away and sat back down on the floor.

"Good job defending breakfast, Dot," Gerry said encouragingly.

Dot wiped greasy fingers on the coverlet. Doug wiped her fingers with a napkin. "Well, Mother-of-the-Year, what are you going to do today?"

"Maybe, a big, fat lot of nothing. How does that sound?"

"Let's hear it for nothing!" he said. "Hip, hip, hooray! Come on, Dot, say it. Hip, hip, hooray! Hip, hip, hooray!"

Dot managed some manic laughter and hand-clapping before falling sideways on the bed. Gerry went to take a long bath. The rest of the day passed harmlessly enough, playing in the yard and garden, watching TV. And then Monday rolled around again.

25

On Sunday night, the cats seemed restless, unable to settle. As Gerry and Doug watched murder mysteries on TV, one cat after another wandered into the den, surveyed the humans stretched out on the couch, then left with an air of disapproval, as if silently shaking their heads.

"What?" Gerry finally said in exasperation to Bob, who stood staring gravely. Usually, when she sat, he liked to sit on her. Instead, he turned and padded away. She got up and followed. He led her into the living room, paused by the fireplace, and then leapt onto the mantel—revealing nothing.

"What?" she said softly, scratching his forehead. "Are you warning me to be vigilant, Bob? Are you on guard?"

He purred and closed his eyes. "That's a yes, I think. I'm worried about tomorrow too. But we'll figure it out."

Mother and Monkey were sitting on the room's sofa, looking toward the kitchen door. Gerry said, "The kitchen, eh? All right, I'll keep an eye on it."

Back in the den, Doug was snoring. Gerry curled up next to him and watched the rest of the show. She announced to the cats in the room—the big ones, Harley and Kitty-Cat—"I want to know who done it."

They blinked inscrutably as if to say, *Oh, we know. We know who done it.*

Doug left early the next morning; he was going to help the Hudsons repair some loose stone steps at the library. "Good pay, too," he said, kissing her and Dot goodbye. "Masonry is hard work. I'll enjoy it though. Beautiful day."

Gerry hadn't shared with Doug any of the suspicions she and Prudence had about the Markovs, or about Rebecca and her husband. What would have been the point? They had only guesses and conjectures. And yet—

She pushed some more porridge at Dot, who batted her hand away. The child seemed fretful. Gerry noticed she had a runny nose. How ironic: she'd lied about Dot being ill the previous week in order to stay home and watch the Markovs, and now she was. "Caught a little cold, sweetie?" she asked tenderly.

Dot sniffed and Gerry wiped her nose. "All right, we'll take it easy today, if you're not feeling well." She lifted Dot out of her chair. A tap at the side door and a glance at the clock confirmed that the Markovs had arrived.

Gerry let them in and watched as they changed their shoes in the side porch. That makes sense, she thought, indoor shoes for indoor work. "Dot's still sick so we'll be home again this morning."

Sergei nodded and moved ahead into the house carrying a vacuum cleaner.

Natalya held one of Dot's hands and said, "Oh, too bad."

"Do you have any kids, Natalya?"

Natalya shook her head. "I want, but Sergei says later, later. He says we need a lot of money. But I'm thirty-seven so not much time left, I think."

"One of my friends had at least one of her kids over forty," Gerry said, thinking of Christine. "And they're all healthy."

"Yes. It is possible but I would like to know my children for a long time. You are lucky. Having Dot so young. You have another one?"

Feeling this was getting a bit personal, but after all, she'd started it, Gerry said, "Uh, we haven't decided. Still lots of time, I think."

Natalya nodded. Then abruptly, she said, "Time to work," and went to get The Maples' vacuum cleaner out of the downstairs closet.

Gerry stepped out of her way and took Dot into her studio. Vaguely, she wondered where all the cats had gotten to. As she'd walked through the house, she hadn't seen any. Of course! The vacuum cleaners. One upstairs and one down—a cat's worst nightmare. I wonder where they hide? Or if they all just go outside.

A listless Dot dozed on the room's green velvet sofa. Gerry worked at her desk. If only it could be this peaceful all the time, she mused. Not that I want Dot to be sick. She felt her daughter's forehead. It was a little warm. Maybe she should take her temperature. When the Markovs have gone, she decided. The thermometer was upstairs and she didn't want to go up there when Sergei was working. She didn't like feeling uneasy in her own house.

She went into the kitchen and made herself a cup of tea, getting a juice box for Dot. Only Monkey was visible, loitering around the kitchen door that led to the side porch. "Okay, Munks? Hungry?" But the cat ignored the tub of kibble on the kitchen floor.

Gerry returned to the studio, hearing the drone of the vacuum cleaners. Natalya was in the den; Sergei sounded like he was right overhead in Gerry's bedroom. She closed the door of the studio, felt Dot's flushed face and went back to work.

Around ten, she heard Dot stir and gave her the juice. "How are you, pet? Better? You still feel a little hot."

The juice seemed to revive Dot and she slipped off the sofa and began to explore the studio. Now that Dot was awake in this most precious room, with its delicate bamboo wallpaper and numerous *objets d'art* and old books, Gerry couldn't concentrate.

"No, Dottie, don't touch that. No, love, you can't climb the bookcase. I know—" She got her sketch pad and some pencils. "Let's go into the den and watch TV. Puppets, lots of puppets."

"Puhpuh," Dot said joyfully, and careered ahead of Gerry toward the den. The silence in the house suggested the Markovs were outside on their break, likely in their van.

They spent a happy hour with the puppets then went in search of a snack. In the hall, Natalya passed them with a smile on her way to clean the studio. Gerry could hear the sounds of water running as Sergei cleaned the upstairs bathroom. Monkey was still in the kitchen.

"Are there mice, Monkey?" Gerry opened the lower cabinet doors and listened. "I don't hear anything." Monkey's lip curled. *Well, you wouldn't, would you?* she might have been thinking. The cat stared at the kitchen door that led to the side porch.

"Oh, all right! I give up! Just don't start destroying our house again. What is it?"

Gerry opened the door, and Monkey padded onto the porch, settling beside the boot tray. Dot followed the cat, sat down on the floor, and began playing with the footwear.

"No, don't touch that, Dot. Dirty. Dirty. And you." She addressed the cat. "No more chewing on people's shoes."

She bent to pick Dot up, then paused and looked closely at Sergei's boots.

Like at least half of Lovering's men, he wore the ubiquitous golden leather workboots. They looked to be in good shape. Except—the tongue of the left one was frayed at the top, as if it had been gnawed by something. Like a cat.

Gerry quickly flipped the tongue down. There, in indelible marker, so he could find them quickly from piles of similar ones at the curling rink, Doug had written "D.S."

"Okay," Gerry said faintly. "Okay, everybody. Let's get our snack and go back to the den."

Monkey accompanied them. Once in the den, Gerry closed the door, feeling shaky. There was no lock on the door, but still… She turned the TV back on but reduced the volume. Dot ate crackers while Gerry watched the clock. One hour till the Markovs leave. Fifty minutes. Forty-five. At thirty-five minutes to go, someone knocked at the door and Gerry jumped.

"Gerry, any more bathroom cleanser? Sergei finish."

Gerry replied and found her voice raspy in her throat. "Yes. There's a new one under the kitchen sink."

"Okay. Thank you."

Ten more minutes went by. A quarter to twelve. Ten to twelve. With five minutes to go, Natalya was again at the door. "We finish, Gerry. You leave the money somewhere?"

Gerry swore under her breath. Usually, she left the cash on the table in the living room. Where was her purse? Probably in the kitchen hanging off a doorknob where it usually was. She swore again, thinking fast.

"I'm coming," she called. "Dot, just stay here, okay? Mommy has to do something."

Dot, entranced by a game show's contestants dressed in costumes, a show she usually didn't get to watch, didn't notice Gerry let herself out of the den and close the door behind her. Monkey came along.

When Gerry reached the kitchen, she saw the Markovs on the side porch, changing their shoes. Don't look. Don't look at their feet, she warned herself. But Dot's word—peets—popped into her head, and an absurd urge to laugh bubbled up. Don't look at their peets. What stopped her was the chilling thought that she might be just five feet away from the person who had killed Ian Murchison—and had been cold-blooded enough to steal and wear his boots.

She took a deep breath and forced herself to look up as she handed Natalya the money. "Thank you." She made herself smile.

They mumbled their thanks and goodbyes before getting into their van. Gerry stood at the sink, gazing out the window. Sergei lit a cigarette while Natalya, in the passenger seat, smiled and waved as Sergei backed the van up. Gerry sagged. She hoped Natalya wasn't involved but wasn't sure that was possible.

She thought about what she was going to say, then phoned the police.

"He'll deny everything, of course," Prudence said. She held a tissue to Dot's nose. "Blow, Dot, blow."

Dot blew.

"Of course," Gerry said. "He could say he bought the boots somewhere second-hand. But hopefully, if the police search his home, they'll find other stolen goods."

"I imagine they were skeptical?"

"Yeah. I had to explain twice—about Doug giving his boots to Ian."

Prudence said slowly, "The police will know whether Ian was found with his boots on or not."

Gerry whistled. "Yes! That's going to be critical. Good for you, Prue. But I don't know how Sergei knew Ian, knew where he lived. And why beat him up?"

"Well, that's where Rebecca's husband comes into it, don't you think? Could he have been Sergei's accomplice?"

"Gosh, Prue, I've just remembered that time I saw Rebecca coming out of the community centre, a white van pulled up next to her husband's pickup and the two drivers had a talk. I didn't see the van's driver though, so that's no good." She sighed. "And Sergei could just say that Rebecca or her husband gave him Ian's boots after he was dead. We won't know for ages, I suppose. Doug has to go today and identify his boots. Maybe he'll find out more."

"Are you going to work today?"

"I suppose. But I'm exhausted. I couldn't sleep last night, kept imagining an angry Sergei arriving at the house if the police told him who ratted him out."

"Well, I brought some Plasticine for Dot to make 'cookies' with. You're welcome to join us."

Gerry grinned. "Good luck keeping it out of her mouth. No, I think I'll go outside, see if any seeds are up."

"You can plant beans now. We should be safe from frost."

"Thank you, oh farmer's daughter. I will plant beans."

Half an hour later, after fending off cats who thought the freshly turned soil was perfect for digging, Gerry straightened up and rubbed her back. The peas had sprouted, but the carrots hadn't yet. She knew they could be slow to germinate. She turned her gaze toward the lake.

Peace, tranquility. She very much hoped her suppositions about Sergei and about Rebecca's husband, Rick, were false. So many lives were about to be ruined if they were true. Natalya's hopes for a family. Rebecca's already fragile sobriety. And if Sergei knew about Ian through Rick, the reason for the attack still eluded her.

Doug came home for lunch. He'd identified his boots and learned nothing new. He and Gerry admired Dot's "cookies" and pretended to taste them.

"No," Dot said firmly, removing a garish pink and yellow concoction from Doug's hand.

"Actually," Gerry said, "Dot and Monkey are the heroines. If they hadn't drawn my attention to Sergei's boots, I'd never have noticed the chewed bit. Or thought to check for your initials."

"Let's get you down, Dot," Prudence said. "And then I'll head out. I need to check if I still have my new waitress."

It was two weeks later that the following appeared under police news in the *Lovering Herald*.

A criminal ring has been apprehended in connection with multiple thefts across the area, including incidents at the Lovering seniors' residence and St. Anne's church. Those arrested include Sergei Markov, 41, Richard Graham, 46, and Robert Graham, 21. Authorities have also reopened their investigation into the death of Ian Murchison, which is now being treated as suspicious.

According to investigators, the Grahams were drawn into the scheme through Markov, an émigré working as a professional cleaner with a long but quiet criminal background. Sources suggest Richard Graham met Markov through a home renovation job, where Markov, under the guise of hiring help for one of his cleaning clients, offered off-the-books cash jobs. Over time, financial pressures and a growing trust between the men reportedly gave way to deeper involvement in Markov's illegal activities. Robert Graham, Richard's son, is believed to have joined at his father's urging, assisting with surveillance and transport during several thefts. What began as occasional small-time collaboration escalated into an organized pattern of break-ins and property theft that has now spanned months.

Gerald Coneybear raised his arms not in rage but this time in victory. "We did it!" he said to the two women sitting in their rocking chairs by the hearth. "Well, these two did it actually. My extraordinary granddaughter and her cat. Say 'Grampa,' Dot."

Dot zoomed a toy car around and around the rag rug while Monkey's head followed her actions. Dot looked up at Gerald and clearly said, "Gampa." Her parents, relaxing at the table after dinner, didn't notice.

"You hear?" said Gerald. "She's bloody marvellous. Can still see me at, what?—eighteen months?"

"Perhaps," said his wife Deborah softly, "she's going to be a sensitive."

On the mantelpiece, two cats lay stretched out, tails touching—one a dark grey tabby, the other a black-and-white tuxedo. From time to time, one of the tails would twitch.

Through the front wall of the house, a tall thin form slowly moved. It went up to the grey tiger and leaned its wispy head in close. "Hello, Growler. Found yourself a good home?"

The cat blinked at its former owner. Ian hovered uneasily near the other three ghosts. "Is it all right if I—?"

"I suppose…" Gerald began ungraciously when Deborah interjected.

"Welcome," she said quietly.

"Of course," Maggie said with more vigour and glared at her brother. "Whose house is it anyway?"

Monkey stared up at the two male cats, her eyes malicious slits. If they don't see each other, she supposed, they don't have to fight. They can just tail thrash it out.

Her lips stretched and lifted. Her lower jaw dropped, just a little. And the cat, almost, laughed.

ABOUT THE BOOK

The poems by the fictional Yvonne Punt first appeared under my name in the magazine *The Nashwaak Review* 50–51 and in the anthology *Portrait of Greenwood*, the Greenwood Centre for Living History, Hudson, Quebec, 2009. (Greenwood is the house on which The Maples is based.)

You can read about the restoration of the portrait of Napoleon in ceremonial robes on the Montreal Museum of Fine Arts' Conservation Department website, from which I shamelessly borrowed the techniques Gerry learns.

I'd like to mention my friend Jan Jorgensen, who was recovering from an illness when I wrote her what I hoped was an entertaining letter about my cats' diary entries, and which led to developing the idea included in this book.

And thanks must go to my daughter Yasmine, paralegal, and her partner Michael, lawyer, for their assistance with the criminal code regarding a definition of murder. If I've misinterpreted it—or any other facts in the book—the error is entirely mine.

ABOUT THE AUTHOR

Born in Montreal and raised in Hudson, Quebec, Louise Carson studied music in Montreal and Toronto, played jazz piano and sang in the chorus of the Canadian Opera Company. Carson has published eighteen books: *Rope: A Tale Told in Prose and Verse*, set in eighteenth-century Scotland; *Mermaid Road*, a lyrical novella; *A Clearing*, her first collection of poetry; *Executor*, a mystery set in China and Toronto; her trilogy (to which *Rope* is the prequel) *The Chronicles of Deasil Widdy: In Which, Measured,* and *Third Circle*; *Dog Poems*, her second collection of poetry; *The Truck Driver Treated for Shock*, a collection of haiku; and *The Last Unsuitable Man*, a psychological mystery. And, of course, there are the eight (so far) Maples Mysteries: *The Cat Among Us, The Cat Vanishes, The Cat Between, The Cat Possessed, A Clutter of Cats, The Cat Looks Back, The Cat Crosses a Line* and now *The Cat Laughs*.

Her poems appear in literary magazines, chapbooks and anthologies, including *The Best Canadian Poetry 2013, 2021* and *2024*. She's been shortlisted in *FreeFall* magazine's annual contest three times and won a Manitoba Magazine Award. In 2019 her novel *In Which* was shortlisted for a Quebec Writers' Federation prize and for a ReLit Award. She has presented her work in many public forums in Montreal, Ottawa, Toronto, Saskatoon, Kingston, and New York City.

With two cats, she lives in St-Lazare, Quebec, where she writes, shovels snow, or gardens, depending.

Eco-Audit
Printing this book using Rolland Enviro100 Book
instead of virgin fibres paper saved the following resources:

Trees	Energy	Water	Air Emissions
4	7 GJ	2,000 L	241 kg